The Battle For Waylon

The Battle For Waylon

BOOK ONE IN
THE GOLDEN ARROW CHRONICLES

Steffen Seitz

Copyright © 2009 by Steffen Seitz.

ISBN:	Hardcover	978-1-4415-4686-9
	Softcover	978-1-4415-4685-2

All rights reserved. No part of this book may be reproduced or transmitted in any form or by any means, electronic or mechanical, including photocopying, recording, or by any information storage and retrieval system, without permission in writing from the copyright owner.

This is a work of fiction. Names, characters, places and incidents either are the product of the author's imagination or are used fictitiously, and any resemblance to any actual persons, living or dead, events, or locales is entirely coincidental.

This book was printed in the United States of America.

To order additional copies of this book, contact:
Xlibris Corporation
1-888-795-4274
www.Xlibris.com
Orders@Xlibris.com
64465

Golden Arrow

Assassin—Egon
Knight—Richard
Bowman—Lord Ive
Berserker—Ragnhild
Messenger—Deacon
Tracker—Theron
Rider—Xurxo
Healer—Alicia
Magician/Sorcerer—Myrddin
Hammer/Mace/Pike man—Maccabee
Whipmaster—Skinner
Spearman—Gary
Double-bladed swordsman—Hildebrand

"If we don't end war, war will end us."

—HG Wells

Prologue

Joab pulled his wool coat tighter against his body, shivering in the cold winter air. His leather helmet sat oddly on his head and he tightly held his cheap wooden shield and expensive sword. At least, he sourly thought, expensive for a peasant. For the cursed nobles it would be considered garbage. These pompous, arrogant nobles were now seated behind him, dressed in shining armor and wielding deadly lances, mounted upon warhorses that cost more than all of his belongings.

Joab shook his head, clearing it of these traitorous thoughts. He had chosen to be here—to stand in the front line and fight against the evil Morr invasion. He sacrificed this, the harsh march and meager rations—and possibly his life—, for his family, and it was not a decision he regretted.

The Sid force, Joab estimated it to be just below two thousand men, stood atop a small rise. The frosted ground was thawing in the sunshine, yet small clouds of vapor drifted upwards from the waiting soldiers. They had been deployed into six divisions—three infantry, three cavalry. The flanks were led by a division of cavalry, with the peasant infantry happily waiting behind them, content to hopefully remain unused for the duration of the battle. Joab was not so lucky. He was positioned in the fourth line, directly in the center of the division. The King himself led the center division, and had arranged them to a more defensive stance, placing the cavalry behind the infantry. The King was with the cavalry, his wife and their youngest child hiding with at the camp only a quarter mile from the army. His oldest son, though hardly old as he was only fourteen years of age, led the right flank.

Suddenly the opposing force came into view. A large troop of cavalry led the march, the rest of the army seeming to be dragged along chaotically. All of them wore red battledresses, the peasants clothed in red-dyed cloaks and coats. From Joab's point of view it seemed as if it were only part of the army advancing steadily towards them, the rest far behind and struggling to catch up.

Suddenly a loud roar rose from the Sid. The cavalrymen raised their spears and lances, bellowing at the top of their lungs. Even Joab pounded his fists into the air and added his voice to the cheer as adrenaline coursed through his body.

By now the Morr knights had all come into view, and Joab's suspicion was confirmed, showing that it was just a third of the coming force. The Morr knights raised a battle cry of their own and spurred on their horses, thundering towards the Sid right flank.

Still calling their blood chilling cries, their Sid counterparts dug in their spurs and shot forward. The knights from both sides leaned forward, their couched lances held tightly against their bodies and their legs pushing strongly against the stirrups. Joab held his breath as the two forces smashed into each other.

A loud clash resounded through the open plain, Joab turning his eyes away, as the knights collided with each other. The loud sounds of battle echoed across the countryside, the grating sounds of metal sliding across metal and hacking into flesh seeming to travel outwards in waves, paralyzing the other soldiers in fear. The momentum of the charge carried on, the knights that were not killed or unseated in the initial clash ripping through the opposite force and swinging around to charge again.

Joab would have watched longer and cheered with the rest of the army if the next force hadn't charged onto the battlefield. This division, advancing hurriedly towards the center ignored the heavy fighting taking place on the right and drove right towards the center—at Joab and his fellow peasant infantry.

The Sid peasants huddled together, hiding behind their shields and raising their swords to meet the oncoming tidal wave of Morr knights. Joab's heart pounded wildly within his chest and sweat ran over his fingers, the young peasant quickly wiping his hands on his cloak one last time, waiting for what would happen next.

Although disorganized and chaotic, the sheer energy of the cavalry charge pushed back the whole division, instantly slaying the peasants who had been placed in the first two lines.

Joab was swept from his feet, the air being knocked out of him from the raw power of the hit issued by the knights. As Joab gasped for breath a Morr officer, his visor lifted for better vision, thundered past him, swinging his sword downwards in a long undercut attack. The blade past just inches from Joab's chest and the peasant soldier's eyes widened in fear. He could have been killed. Joab forced himself onto his feet and stuck out his shield as another knight shot past. The Morr swung a hard blow at his shield, shattering the wooden buckler and seeming to destroy his arm as well. Before the knight could get far enough though, Joab spun around and slashed his sword across the man's back, the knight falling from his horse.

Joab, his eyes blazing with anger, fear, and a savage thirst for Morr blood ran to the dismounted man and lifted his helmet from his head, exposing his contorted face. Then Joab thrust his sword forward and cut off the man's head.

As the head fell to the frosted ground Joab staggered backward. He had killed a human being. He had taken the life of a young man. Disgusted with himself, yet aware that he was caught in the middle of a bloodbath he did the only thing that his shocked mind could tell him to do—run.

Joab fled to the right, where the peasants were now streaming towards the center to help. The first five lines of the Sid center had been completely demolished by the cavalry attack, the furious warhorses having run over the peasants and trampled the poor soldiers. The area was littered with dead and dying people, moans gently drifting into the cold air, the billowing vapors eerily reminding Joab of souls escaping from the tormented bodies. Near him other peasants were rejoining the fight or fleeing in fear of the Morr. Joab glanced behind him quickly and saw that the left flank was now locked in a cavalry fight while the reluctant infantry held back to act as a reserve.

Joab hurdled over dead bodies, slipping in the blood and retching upon himself as he remembered the horrible sight of the decapitated head. A Morr infantryman, detached from the main force of foot soldiers, charged at him and Joab dove to the side, picking up a chipped sword as he rolled to his feet. He was now clear of the fighting, to the right of the Sid army.

The man ran at Joab, shrieking a bloodcurdling scream, and launched into a whirlwind of attacks, spinning from one to the next. Joab backed away, pressing into the side of the soldiers as more Morrs hit the flank of the army and the Sid infantry rushed to meet them. The man hit a two-handed attack at Joab, the young peasant barely managing to get his sword positioned for the parry. The blow jarred his arm, seeming to vibrate through his body and he dropped the sword. Now Joab possessed two lifeless arms. He threw himself at his adversary, tackling the confused man and butting his head into his chest.

Joab popped up, fear evident in every feature of his face. Quickly he spun around. A large group of Morr knights, all wielding swords, their broken lances lying upon the ground, surrounded a single man—the prince. The prince's silver crown that circled his helmet had been broken, and his long silver cape lay in shreds on the ground, yet he fought on bravely, his arm a blur as it defended the rain of blows that were being poured down on him.

Joab hesitated, torn between loyalty and life. Suddenly one of the knights crashed their sword upon that of the prince, the latter's arm shaking with the enormous impact. Another knight, wearing an open visor, took the opportunity and lunged forward, throwing his whole body from his horse and devoting all of his momentum to the blow, smashing his pommel into the Prince's helmet.

The heir's helmet dented inward and the teen slouched in his saddle, sliding sideways. The man screamed his victory, his piercing gray eyes momentarily locking on Joab, who hurriedly turned away. Then the Morr ripped the prince from his saddle and spun his steed around, galloping away from the scene of the battle with his hostage. A wave of bile spewed from Joab's mouth, disgusted with his traitorousness.

Then Joab was running for his life once more.

Joab sprinted as fast as he could, away from the battle, the images, the disgust, and the awful knowledge of his disloyalty. He turned his head as he ran, gasping in fear. Behind him the troop that had just subdued the prince was now thundering after him. The young peasant's legs pounded upon the ground, carrying him forward faster than they had ever before—yet it was not fast enough.

The knights were steadily gaining, and Joab was confused as to why they bothered to hunt down a single peasant. As Joab turned his head back, grunting in exasperation to outrun the horsemen, he realized why. The camp, containing all the baggage, which included a lot of valuables, the tents and pavilions, and the royal family, were just a hundred yards from where Joab sprinted.

Roaring in pain and anger, Joab gave his final effort, pushing every ounce of energy and submitting his whole will to running as fast as he could. The camp neared with painstaking slowness, yet the crushing sound of hooves did not gain as quickly anymore.

Finally Joab was there. He broke into the confines of the site and ran to the stables, in hopes of finding a horse with which to escape. Suddenly an image floated through his mind: his family, his younger brother, aspiring and intelligent, celebrated for his amazing gift of archery, his wife, gentle, kind, and loving, and his son, still within her womb.

As a wave of compassion and love seized him, he turned and removed a sword from the rack of weapons beside the stables, selecting a decent shield as well. The love that coursed through his body seemed to give energy to his arms and a fierce desire to do good and avenge the evil he had committed just moments ago upon the battlefield. Joab roared his battle cry, screaming the name of his beloved wife. Then he charged toward the King's pavilion and the royal family.

The knights thundered into the camp and sprang from the horses, the leader, a tall officer, barking orders at the other horsemen. The Morrs spread out as if the raid were planned, running towards the stables, armory, and the pavilions of the nobility. The leader and four of his aides dismounted and drew their swords, slowly advancing towards Joab and the King's pavilion.

Joab fought back the wave of cold fear that threatened to engulf his body. He breathed in deeply and exhaled a large cloud of vapor, the love for his family chasing away any fear that existed anymore within him. As the men advanced slowly, Joab backed towards the pavilion.

Suddenly shrieks and cries echoed through the camp as those left behind were stolen from their tents and slain mercilessly. Behind him a cry cut through the air as the Queen realized what had happened.

Now the group of Morrs advanced, running at Joab, twirling their swords in the air as they prepared to kill the solitary defender of this camp. The leader reached Joab first, thrusting his sword forward. Joab had never received training as a warrior, yet a sudden rage gripped his body and he slapped the sword aside, jumping into a series of offensive attacks he never knew he could actually do. The leader was taken off guard and in moments he lay on the ground, bleeding from multiple wounds. Then the next knight advanced, yet as the group crowded around Joab, their skill and training won over him and soon Joab fell to icy ground, a fatal gash gushing blood from his chest.

As the dark waters of death crashed over Joab, the young peasant struggled to remain alive. The Morr reemerged from the tent, the Queen held tightly in their arms. The young boy, ten years of age, ran from the pavilion shrieking in fear. As a knight chased after him Joab turned and grabbed hold of the Morr's leg. The man fell to the ground and cursed loudly. He spat at Joab and shoved his dagger at him, embedding it in his shoulder. An icy lance of pain drove through his body like lightening, and the agony darkened his mind and the peacefulness of death crowded closer than before.

In his last living moments, Joab heard the Morr depart with the Queen. Then the ground shook as a wave of Sid cavalrymen rushed through the camp, bellowing the name of their captive leader, the prince. No nobleman stooped down to help Joab, nor did they acknowledge him at all as they murdered the Morr looters and proclaimed their victory.

Joab breathed in deeply for the last time in his life, calling to mind the comforting image of his family one last time. Then, slowly, he eased into a world of peace.

Chapter 1

Leif silently yawned and stretched, slipping out of his bed and quietly dressing himself. Beside his cot lay his mom, sleeping peacefully. Leif smiled and grabbed the cheap hunting bow he used, silently disappearing out the door.

It was a beautiful day: the sky was a sea of blue, dotted with little cotton clouds that were slowly drifting to the east. It had rained the day before and little puddles had formed in the ditches at the side of the road. It was a perfect day to hunt.

The boy, Leif, ran down the muddy road, eager to get started. The knight at the gatehouse nodded towards Leif and he nodded back, grudgingly.

He didn't like the knight, or any nobles for that matter. They had stolen his father. Leif hadn't been born yet, and all he knew was what his mother had told him. His father had been forced to serve Siddian, Leif's country, and had died in the process, leaving his mother and an unborn child—Leif.

Leif was torn from his thoughts as he reached fork in the road that marked his stop. About a mile into the forest was a serene pond, a favorite place for the deer to stop and drink after a rainy day like yesterday. He left the road, walking to his forest and thinking of his father's story.

His Dad had been murdered at the front line. Leif wasn't sure if he should have blamed the nobles or the Morrs. He held a grudge against both. The letter telling of his death had come a month late, when all the nobles were sober again, done celebrating their victory. It was written in messy handwriting and had ink smudges all over it. Apparently the scribe had written a lot of these letters. His mother had burned it.

Leif sighed, leaving his thoughts behind to concentrate upon what was most important now. This hunt would decide what they would eat for the next month. Leif ducked behind a tree, about 25 yards from the pond, where three deer were drinking peacefully. Leif drew an arrow, fitted it to the string, and looked at the deer. They were totally unaware of him, and were still gently lapping at the pond. Leif needed a better position, so he moved a little to the right. Suddenly, a twig snapped beneath his foot, and the deer looked up at him. Two of them pelted away, deeper into the forest, but the third stood still, looking in his direction. Leif didn't move.

Slowly, the deer started trotting towards the street, just fast enough for Leif to sneak behind it without making a sound. Once the deer got to the street, he stopped. Leif dove behind a tree and drew his arrow backward, at half-draw. Then he waited.

The deer looked left, and then walked onto the deserted road. There he found a clump of grass, and started eating it. Leif drew back his arrow to full-draw, leveled his bow, and . . .

A giant battle horse came thundering down the road, with a man sitting on top of it. The man's golden cape was billowing in the breeze, and a quiver of arrows was slung across his back.

The deer saw the man, and sprinted toward the forest, several meters away on the other side.

Leif had barely enough time to turn his bow, in order not to shoot the stranger, and the arrow whistled past the man's head, about a foot and half wide of his nose.

In surprise, the man fell from his horse, which thundered on for another short distance before realizing that its master was on the ground.

Leif hurried onto the road and drew another arrow, all in one fluid motion. This he fit to the bowstring, and swiftly pulled it back. Then, just as the deer was entering the woods, he let it fly, and it hit the animal on the back of the neck. The deer toppled forward, and lay twitching in the grass. Five seconds later, the deer lay unmoving with three more arrows in its body.

Leif looked away. He hated killing. He knew it was necessary and essential for survival, but that didn't mean he enjoyed it.

Quickly Leif pushed these regretful thoughts out of his head. Dropping his bow, he hurried over to the fallen man and apologized.

"Not your fault, young man. It was I who messed up your shot, not you me." The man said, and smiled at Leif.

The man's black hair were lying on his head in complete disarray, and Leif couldn't help but notice the beautiful black-wood arrows in the man's quiver, and the expertly curved dragon bow slung over his back.

The man saw Leif's eyes, and understood the longing he saw there. "Nice shot you had there, young man." He complimented, "I'll take you and your game home if you want."

Leif considered the offer. He didn't know the man, but he did sound trustworthy, and Leif was very tired. Finally Leif smiled politely and accepted. A couple of minutes later, the two were seated on top of the horse, with the deer slung over Leif's shoulders, and trotting towards Keldon.

Once they arrived at the gates, the guards there saluted the man, and let him through.

Leif was puzzled by this, because the man looked more like a standard archer than a person of great wealth or status. He surely wasn't a nobleman, was he? All of the ones he knew (which weren't very many) were rich, arrogant men who wouldn't think twice about a young peasant-boy. Leif smirked; most of them would have probably ordered him whipped for attempted murder!

Leif pushed the thoughts out of his head, deciding that there was no way this man was a noble. The two continued through town, the man eyeing the hovels skeptically. He asked Leif where he lived and the young boy directed him to his small, one-room hovel.

"Could I speak to your father, young man?" The stranger asked, and Leif coldly replied, "My father passed away before I was born."

The man looked stunned with an honest look of concern on his face and said, "Oh, I'm sorry, could I speak to your mother then?"

Leif nodded and hurried into the house. He told his Mother that a man was waiting outside for her, and she hurried out to meet him, taking care to praise her son on his beautiful prize.

Leif smiled and prepared the deer, gently cutting the meat into slices. He would have to sell half of it so they could pay their taxes. They would keep the rest for food, giving the Duke's kitchens the tenderloin and sirloin, as the law demanded when killing King's deer. Those were his jobs: money and food. His mother, being a widowed woman, hardly found a job. No one wanted to employ her so she simply opened her own business, repairing clothes and patching worn cloaks. Even this didn't get them very much money, so survival was a constant struggle.

It took Leif at least half an hour to prepare the deer for sale, and when he finished his mother entered the hovel accompanied by the stranger.

"He wants a word with you, Leif", she said, motioning to the man.

Leif walked to the man, who offered his hand and Leif shook it. "I don't think you told me your name." he said, and Leif smiled, "Sorry, it's Leif."

The man nodded and said, "I'm Lord Ive."

Leif's jaw dropped and he mumbled an apology for his bad conduct earlier on. The man was a Lord! The news rocked Leif like an earthquake, shaking the very ideals he had based so much hatred upon. Leif shook his head quietly; apparently there were exceptions to Leif's earlier theory, for the man did seem nice enough.

"I have an offer for you," Lord Ive continued, "Tomorrow there will be tryouts in the castle, to become the apprentice bowman of the Golden Arrow. If you want, you can come as my personal guest."

Leif's jaw dropped even lower, if that was possible. "The Golden Arrow? I thought they were just a legend."

Lord Ive shook his head. "They're real all right," he said.

The Golden Arrow was a group of elite soldiers who were the first line of defense, and the first line of attack. They acted as the intelligence service of the King, and were his eyes and ears during battles. The legendary group consisted of the twelve best soldiers in the kingdom, and each estate supplied one. Arash, the estate in which Leif lived, had always supplied the bowman, and each one of the other estates supplied another person. Leif had heard of battles in which the Golden Arrow had played key parts and won major victories, but he had thought them to be legends and fairy tales spun around the miraculous victories.

Leif quickly accepted the offer, and got the deer ready to sell. Then he marched into the market place and was able to earn himself a couple of silver pieces. These he took back home, where his mother had already prepared a thick broth with the meat.

———

Leif woke up early the next day, and got his bow and arrows. He grabbed his quiver, and emptied it of its hunting arrows. The hunting arrows were simply wooden sticks, with some feathers at the end, and the front was sharpened to a point, which was hardened in a fire. Quickly he ran to the little shelf in the corner and grabbed his twelve beauties. They were twelve bronze arrows, which he had bought with the money he had earned by doing extra chores.

Leif called goodbye to his mother, and ate a small slice of bread. Then he walked outside and waited for Lord Ive to come, as he had promised.

A few minutes later, Lord Ive rode into sight, and Leif walked to him.

"Here, I got these for you," he said, handing Leif a leather quiver filled with willow arrows and a black-wood bow.

Leif stared at the present. "No—I can't accept these. They're—that's too much, and besides. That would give me an unfair advantage."

Lord Ive looked at Leif and shook his head. "Take them," he said, and added, "Trust me, this will not be an unfair advantage."

Leif looked at Lord Ive and shook his head, confused.

"The boys you will be up against will just about all be rich and sons of barons. These boys will have the best and most expensive bows. And, the fee to enter the tryouts is 20 gold pieces, and that's a lot. Don't tell your mother that." He added.

Leif was amazed. 20 gold pieces! That was a lot of money. His treasured bronze arrows were half a silver piece each and this nobleman, who, according to Leif's previous definition should be a pompous fool, was offering to pay forty times that amount!

Minutes later the two trotted into the castle, and Leif took in the sight with wide eyes.

The massive keep was decorated for the event with brilliant red and gold banners hanging from its edges. A giant space had been cleared to host the competition, and Duke Alexander was sitting in a golden tent near the center of this. Archers were walking all over the place, and Leif stared at them in amazement.

Lord Ive had been right; all of the young men wore rich and expensive clothes. They ranged from twelve years old to eighteen. All of them carried beautiful bows, some carrying dragon bows others carrying magic elf bows, while yet others even carried Cursed bows. The arrows in their quivers were also very diverse. Almost all of them had black-wood shafts, but the heads of the arrows were different: dragon arrowheads, steel arrowheads, and some even White arrowheads.

Leif shook his head in amazement. White arrowheads cost about 10 gold pieces each. That was the price of a fair horse!

Lord Ive left Leif to stare in wonder at the different people gathered, while he walked over to the registration tent, and wrote in Leif's name. Then he paid and returned to Leif's side.

"Okay," Lord Ive began. Leif's head turned toward him, "Yes?"

"You've been registered. The first task will begin in a couple of minutes, so get ready. There will be three tasks in all that determine who is to be the apprentice. Good luck," he said, giving Leif the "thumbs up" sign. Then he headed towards the Duke's tent—apparently he was a judge.

The first task was simple: discs were thrown into the air, and the contestant would try and hit them. They were graded on how long it took them to get ready, their accuracy, the amount hit, and how many arrows per disc.

The amount of discs increased until four discs were being thrown at the same time and the contestant had to hit them all before they fell to the ground.

Leif was towards the middle of the group of boys, and when his turn came, he clutched his new bow nervously and nocked an arrow onto the string. Then he waited.

He had already decided his tactic beforehand. None of the boys had been able to hit all four so far, so Leif knew that if he could accomplish that he could win. His strategy was simple: speed before accuracy. It was a slight risk, but risks were necessary and he was willing to take them.

The first disc was thrown into the air, and before it had begun its downward arc, it was lying on the ground, shattered. A few people whistled, and Leif smiled.

The crowd hushed as the next disc was thrown, and hit equally as quick. The third and fourth discs were thrown together, and Leif hit the first one before it had gotten to its highest point. Then Leif reached backward into his quiver, fitted another arrow onto the string, and pulled backward into a full draw, all in one fluid motion. Leif released the bowstring, yet frowned as the arrow completely missed its target. Leif breathed in deeply—he had to stay calm.

The discs continued flying, yet Leif missed again and again. His fingers grew sweaty and he began to perspire with fierce concentration and nervousness. As Leif tore back his bowstring yet again, his sweaty fingers slipped and the string shot forward prematurely, several archers snickering behind him as the arrow dug itself into the ground ten feet from where Leif stood. Finally it was the last round.

The four discs were thrown into the air. Leif was ready. He hit the first one a second after it left the hand of the thrower. Leif hurriedly pulled another arrow from his quiver and fitted it to the bowstring. He sacrificed aiming for getting off a quicker shot and paid the price. His arrow skidded across the ground as the final two plates reached their highest point in their arc. A split second later Leif had another arrow nocked and ready. This time he quickly aimed and released. The young peasant boy didn't take the time to watch his shot, instead smiling as he heard the satisfactory burst as the plate broke. Rushing to hit the last plate, Leif blindly grabbed for his final arrow, fumbling for it and dropping the shaft as tried to fit it to the bowstring. The final plate exploded into a thousand pieces as it hit the ground and Leif sighed. Apparently the better strategy would have been accuracy before speed.

The second task was easier than the first, but more competitive. A target was set up 50 yards from where the archer stood, and the bowman had one minute to loose as many arrows into the target. The objective was to get as many points as possible, with the center circle being worth ten points, the next ring five, and the outermost ring one.

Leif had the standard 24 arrows in his quiver, like most of the other boys. Leif knew that he wouldn't be able to loose all of the 24 arrows within a one-minute time limit, and so he wondered if he should go for speed or for accuracy. He decided to change his tactic; after all, the other one hadn't worked at all. He would shoot as accurate as possible rather than as fast as possible.

This thought brought back a memory of advice Lord Ive had whispered to Leif before the tryouts, "Remember, quality over quantity."

Leif nodded repeating the sentence under his breath.

Once again, Leif was in the middle, and he patiently waited as the other contestants shot. Most of these boys ignored the obvious lesson that Leif had been taught in the first task and decided to get off a quicker shot rather than sacrificing a couple precious seconds to aim. They too paid the awful price, yet the average was still fairly high—the majority achieving great scores between eighty-five and a hundred.

When Leif's turn finally came, he walked up to the line, and did what most of the other archers before him had done too; he took ten of his arrows and stuck them head first into soft ground, so he could get them quicker. Then he nocked an arrow onto his string.

When the whistle blew, his start signal, he drew back to a full draw, and sent the first arrow flying at the target: bull's-eye. This time Leif only spent speed on nocking the arrow, but devoted a couple precious seconds aiming. The second and third arrow followed the first, embedding themselves in the center circle. A couple whistles and scattered cheers were heard as Leif was able to keep up the amazing record. Finally the whistle sounded, alerting Leif to the fact that he only had five seconds left. Leif quickly loosed his last arrow, this also joining the eleven other arrows in the center circle.

Finally two whistles sounded and a judge wrote down Leif's score as the young archer went to collect his arrows. He saw he had shot half of his quiver (12 arrows) and was pleased. He had spent an average of five seconds an arrow and managed an amazing feat: all twelve arrows were in the center circle! As Leif gently removed the arrows, pulling them out as close to the arrowhead as possible to avoid bending and breaking them, he slowly did the math. As Leif plucked the final arrow out of the soft target he nearly dropped it in astonishment. He had gotten an astounding 120 points! That was a new record!

Pride coursed through his body and he lifted his head with dignity, glancing at the judges. They were smiling and Leif thought bitterly, *See, a poor peasant can do the same thing as you arrogant aristocrats!* This sour thought immediately vanished as he saw Lord Ive who smiled genuinely and winked as Leif walked over to a tree to rest.

The third task was the hardest of them all. All of the people who had bad scores were called out and had to leave. Thankfully, Leif wasn't among them. Then the Duke explained the third task.

"For the third task, we will let loose a wild boar at you. You must kill the boar, and you will be evaluated on the following subjects: time, speed, amount of arrows used, and efficiency. Knights will be waiting at the edge of the area in which you must fight the boar. If need be, they will come to the rescue, but otherwise you will be left alone. The reason we had to let many of you go, was because this task is very dangerous. Injury is definitely possible, so we want to protect you. Any who want to leave voluntarily may do so. Finally, those who are not allowed to continue are welcome to watch. Good luck." The Duke sat down again, and Lord Ive nodded at Leif, and he immediately understood the reason for his new black-wood arrows.

The remaining boys, now about twenty, got into line to begin the fight. A fence was built around the clearing, and knights and shining steel armor entered the fence, standing every 10 yards or so along the fence.

Leif ran quickly to Lord Ive who was frantically motioning to him.

"Take this," he said, handing Leif a beautiful hunting knife.

Leif shook his head, "No, I can't accept this. You've spent more than enough money on me already." he said.

Lord Ive, "Don't worry; you might be able to repay me soon."

Leif stared at Lord Ive confusedly, wondering what this strange sentence meant, yet all he got in return was a grin.

Then Lord Ive jogged back to the judging tent: the final task had begun.

The first boy walked onto the field, with an arrow already set on the string. The young man nervously wiped his hands on his leather chaps that he had changed into at the announcing of the task and breathed in deeply several times, attempting to calm himself. Leif felt nervous too—not just because he knew that he would be in the same position in a couple minutes, but because of the horrible tales of wild boars he had heard about. Peasants went into the woods to find a runaway hog and came upon a boar. The animal killed all of them, the rest of the village finding their gored bodies heaped upon a pile there a day later.

On the other side, the boar was let onto the field. Leif shuddered as he beheld the horrible sight of the ugly beast. The whole crowd hushed to a deadly silence as it lowered its head. Then it charged.

Its small legs carried the boar as fast as it could, shooting at the boy like an avalanche as it rumbled over the ground at its helpless victim. The young man took one last breath and drew his bowstring to a full draw. The first arrow the boy sent pierced the boar on the side, and immediately it veered off course, grunting and snorting. Now it was alert and mad—not good. The boy had already set another arrow on the string and took another shot. This one went wide, and the boar charged again, the nervous boy scrambling out of the way.

The young man, maybe 15 or 16 got out of the way just in time. The boar's right tusk tore the pants of the boy's right leg, and blood began oozing from it, painting the summer grass in an ugly red.

The boy quickly rolled away from the boar, fitting another dragon arrow onto his bowstring as he did so. Leif silently cheered the boy on, willing for him to end the boar's sad life quickly. The next shot the contestant let fly pierced the boar's cheek, and it wailed in pain.

The boy quickly loosed another shot, but not before the boar had began its final charge. The wild boar had now abandoned all caution, knowing that death was inevitable. It charged on a straight course at the young man, its eyes aflame with a savage thirst for human blood. The crowd's collective intake of breath seemed to spur the boy into his final action and he raised his bow, loosing his last arrow point blank.

The arrow sped toward the boar and slammed into its head, hitting it right between the eyes. The boar died right there, but its momentum carried it on. It plowed into the boy, who went down with a shout. Blood poured onto the field, but no one knew whose it was: the boar or the boy's. The whole crowd, Leif included, jumped up and began yelling at the top of their lungs: cheering for the young man, yelling at the knights, and hurling insults at the dead boar. The knights reacted quickly, dropping their shields and sprinting towards the boy, cutting away at the boar, while one dropped his steel broadsword and picked up the bloody heap of a person. He carried him to the hospital tent where a healer would care for him.

Leif swallowed, suddenly unsure of what to do.

The line of boys kept getting shorter, and only twice did the knights have to intervene, hacking away at the boar and rescuing the poor victim.

Finally it was Leif's turn. He stuck his new hunting knife in his belt and nocked an arrow onto the string. Then he stepped into the enclosure, his heart hammering in his chest. Then Leif sent up a silent prayer for strength, and suddenly a wave of peace washed over him, calming him as his hands grew dry and his mind focused.

A knight let in the next boar, and Leif took in its features instantly.

It had a jagged scar, which cut across its face, and its snout was a blotchy black with little white dots and black whiskers. Its tusks were huge, and curled out of its mouth. The ugly beast was a rusty bronze color, and matted with thick dirty hairs. Its whole body heaved as it breathed, its eyes blazing with fury and the boar shook his head defiantly at the knight one last time. Then it turned its large body towards its next victim—Leif. It snorted and charged.

Leif swallowed hard, his eyes zeroing in on the animal's most vulnerable areas: the opening behind the shoulder blades, the area just behind its head that held the exposed spinal cord, and its horrible face. The hideous creature ran as fast as its stubby legs could take him, shooting at Leif with such intensity and fury that a worm of fear worked its way into Leif's mind. His face reset with grim determination, Leif waited until the boar was in point blank range. Finally, when it was about five yards away, Leif pulled the string back into full draw and released the arrow at the boar's charging face.

Without seeing the result of the shot, he dove to the right, out of the boar's charging path. Then Leif risked a quick glance over his shoulder to see the result of his shot. The arrow had pierced the boar's left eye, and blood was gushing from the wound. The red liquid dripped onto the grass and it wailed in pain and frustration, whipping its head around to spot its opponent. Drops of blood raining from its contorted face, the boar charged once again.

By the time the boar had begun its second drive, Leif had managed to put some distance between him and the beast, and get a second arrow on the string. He turned, and saw the boar sprinting at him. Leif's eyes narrowed as he drew back the bowstring slowly. Then he released the string, his mouth twitching with the hint of a smile as he heard the soothing twang of the bowstring and the crunching sound as it penetrated into the animal's chest.

The boar roared in fury, pitching forward unto the grass. A puddle of blood formed around the beast yet a supernatural strength seemed to pull it back onto its feet and the boar charged for the last time.

Leif's face stretched into a mask of concentration as he gripped his bow, tightly, aware that this would be his final shot. He took a final deep breath and aimed carefully. Then he released the arrow.

It plowed into the animal's right shoulder, and the front right leg snapped in two. Leif admired his shot, pride keeping him rooted to the spot. The dying boar slammed into him, Leif's pride disappearing into a tidal wave of agony.

The two tusks cut into his thighs, and he cried in anger and hurt, adding to the noise of the boar's wails. Lances of excruciating pain drove through Leif's body and tears exploded from his eyes as the boar's thick blood splashed onto his face. Warm blood gushed from his wound, and his hand flew to his belt, pulling out the hunting knife. He thrust it blindly forward; an insane rage gripping him as he repeatedly stabbed the poor creature. The boar gave one last shuddering breath and lay still. It was dead.

Leif howled in pain, yet a savage smile spread across his face as he realized his victory. The boar's blood leaked onto his clothes and clung to his skin, his own mixing with it and creating a horrible puddle upon the ground.

Strong hands lifted the boar off Leif, and pulled him to his feet. Remarkably, he could walk without as much as a limp. The remains of the poor animal were carried away, the boar's face still contorted into its final horrible expression.

As Leif stared at the beast, a wave of regret washed over him. The animal had never asked for this. It didn't want to die. What had it done wrong? Just because it was born as a vicious beast, whose instinct was to kill, it had been sentenced to death. Leif lowered his eyes, ashamed at what he had done. One of the soldiers prodded him on, pointing to the hospital, and Leif moved toward it, the pain of walking pushing his other thoughts and emotions away.

He hobbled to the healer's tent, and opened the flap. Then he walked inside and collapsed on one of the cots.

A few seconds later, a woman hurried over to him and forced open his mouth. She poured a hot, bubbly, red liquid down his throat, and immediately his legs became numb. Then the woman cut off the pants in the area of his two wounds, and covered them with a wet, leafy substance, which soaked into the skin.

Fifteen minutes later, the woman came back and removed the substance. The skin in that area had magically healed. Although Leif couldn't feel his legs, he somehow knew that if he could, they would be fine.

The Healer came back a few seconds later with a green potion which she forced down his throat.

This potion was the opposite of the first potion, and was bitter and thick. Leif was tempted to spit the potion back at the lady, but he refrained from doing so and was rewarded: the pain in his legs had ceased to exist—Leif's earlier theory had been correct.

The woman smiled at him, and only then did Leif actually get a good look at her.

She had inviting blue eyes, which were filled with wisdom, but also with understanding. Her dirty blonde hair hung just past her shoulders, and it seemed to shimmer and glow as the sunlight reflected off the blonde highlights, dazzling Leif. She smiled at him, revealing her immaculately white teeth. Leif involuntarily smiled back and slowly got up.

The woman made no move to stop him, so Leif slipped off the cot—a group of knights immediately lowering another contestant onto it. The boy was a mess. Half his face was torn in two and blood seemed to ooze from every part of his battered body. The boy moaned, and immediately the woman that had healed Leif's wound attended to him. Leif left the tent.

In the sun, he saw that the third task had just finished, and that the knights were cleaning up the remains of the last boar, while another knight was helping the boy who had fought it walk towards the healing tent.

Leif looked up at the judge's tent, where the judges were all discussing the scores, and seemed to be coming to a decision.

The judges waited until the healing tent cleared while the Duke and Lord Ive silently conversed. As the crowd waited in nervous anticipation, the knights cleared away the fence and the mob rushed forward onto the open space, the nobles even standing in the puddles of blood that littered the field.

Finally, the last boy hobbled out on crutches, and the crowd, which had been conversing quietly hushed immediately. The Duke slowly stood, savoring the moment of suspense, as his eyes scanned the crowd.

"First, I would like to thank all of you for participating, and for trying your best." He said, smiling kindly at the crowd.

"Next, I would like to announce the prizes for the different places." The crowd seemed to lean forward, the silence pressing against the Duke as he unfolded a crinkled piece of parchment.

"Third place gets 100 gold pieces. Second place gets 250 gold pieces, and finally, first place gets 400 gold pieces and a chance at becoming the bowman apprentice of the Golden Arrow!"

The crowd cheered, and the Duke let them carry on for a little while before raising his hand to silence them, obviously enjoying the attention and excitement directed toward him.

"Third place goes to . . ." the crowd hushed in anticipation. "Tyler, son of Baron Ludwig!"

The crowd cheered, and a sixteen-year-old boy was pushed forward. The boy sported a long gash down his leg, and was limping slightly. His quiver of dragon arrows was half empty, and his black-wood bow was slung over his shoulder, unstrung.

The Duke stood up again and shouted, "Second Place goes to . . ." again the crowd was quiet, leaning forward slightly as they waited. The Duke smiled as he read the name from a piece of parchment, "Philip, son of Earl Holger!"

The crowd cheered again, louder this time, and a bedraggled young man hobbled forward. Leif recognized this boy as the first contestant against the boar, and saw that all of his white arrows were still in his quiver. His Cursed bow was in his hand and was unstrung. The boy walked to the front, shook hands with each of the judges, and took his 250 gold piece award from the Duke, an enormous smile upon his face as the crowd continued applauding.

The Duke let the cheering go on longer this time, and when he stood, it died down very slowly.

"Now, for the final prize," the Duke said, his eyes sweeping across the gathered crowd. "The winner of this prize gets 400 gold pieces and an apprenticeship to the bowman of the Golden Arrow. This lucky young man is . . ."

The crowd had gone deathly quiet, waiting for the Duke to announce the final name. The Duke seemed to eye each nervous contestant separately, adding to the suspense. Finally he looked at his paper and shouted, "Leif!"

Leif fell from the stool he was sitting on and stumbled forward. He was too surprised to speak, and accidentally walked to the wrong side of the line to shake hands. The crowd laughed good naturedly, and Leif joined in, his mind still numb from the realization.

Leif shook hands with all of the judges, and when he got to the Duke, he was handed a giant sack of money. Leif's eyes widened at the feeling. He had never held half this much in his whole life! Still stunned, he smiled at the Duke.

"Congratulations," the man said, his eyes twinkling.

Finally, he got to the last man in line: Lord Ive.

"Looks like I've got myself an apprentice," he said, his eyes dancing mysteriously, and his face spread with the hint of a smile.

Leif's jaw dropped. "You—you're my—you're my new mentor?" he asked incredulously, his former surprise being doubled by this discovery.

Lord Ive nodded and smiled, "Don't worry; I won't be easy on you."

Chapter 2

Leif woke up with a smile upon his face, the faint taste of goose meat still playing across his tongue. He slipped out of bed and into his clothes, carefully strapping his quiver to his back. Then he tiptoed over to his Mom, who lay peacefully in her bed, exhausted from the long day before, and kissed her gently on the cheek. After quietly closing the door, he tore a chunk of bread from a loaf upon their rickety table and left the house.

Leif's biological clock was working well. The faint outline of the sun's rays highlighted the horizon, telling Leif that it was just before sunup. He walked down the streets of Keldon, gently massaging his sore arms, and, with an evident grin upon his face, remembering the night before.

When Leif entered the hovel with the prize money and had dusted off his shoes, he vividly recalled his astonishment. His mother had draped a red tablecloth, something Leif had never seen, over the table and right in the middle sat the most astonishing thing of all. Fresh from the oven and still steaming, the goose caused Leif's mouth to water by just looking at it. His mother stood beside the table, dressed nicely and with a warm smile.

"Congratulations Leif," she said, hugging him as he placed the heavy sack of money onto the countertop. "I saw the whole thing. You were brilliant!" She said—genuine awe obvious in her voice.

Leif was speechless. He had had no idea that she was watching the whole time. "The goose?" he asked.

She smiled once again, her whole face lighting up like a warm candle, "I got it right after the third task and cooked it at home. The nice nobleman came by and told me you'd won just a minute ago. I knew you were going to anyways. What, with that amazing show you delivered in the second task—you should have seen the other boys! Most of them nearly dropped their bows!"

Leif laughed and sat down, his mother giving him a large piece of meat.

"After I saw you get hurt in the final event I nearly died in horror. Those cold-hearted knights wouldn't even let me onto the field!" She cried indignantly. "And they didn't let me see you in the hospital tent either!"

Leif gently placed a steaming chunk of meat into his mouth. His eyes opened in wonder as an explosion of flavors danced through his mouth. The gentle meat seemed to dissolve as Leif chewed, the delicious aroma of the goose swimming through the hovel and the delicious meat providing the best dinner of Leif's life.

Leif shook his head, pulling himself back to reality as he watched the start of a new day. Storeowners began setting up their wares; apprentices hurried to their masters' houses, merchants weaved through the streets on carriages and horses, others setting out to run errands. Leif chuckled. *For me everything is different now,* he thought, *yet the world is as it was before.* Sighing in strange contentment, he trudged on.

Finally Leif came upon the gatehouse. Lord Ive was already waiting, no doubt having come from a guestroom in the castle. He held a small yew bow and a blackwood bow was slung over his shoulder. Leif hurried forward, eager to talk to his master again and examine the yew bow that most likely now belonged to him.

"Hop on," Lord Ive ordered once Leif had gotten to the gatehouse. Leif pulled himself onto the horse on which Lord Ive sat and held onto him as the two trotted down the road. After five minutes of riding they turned left onto a small road, cutting through the forest, and finally, a minute later, stopped in front of an old house. The house, or shack rather, was obviously one room and stood beside the country road. A large field spread out from the hut, ending on each side with the forest. Closest to Leif was a shooting range to practice archery. Further back was a small pavilion, housing a variety of weights and other instruments designed to increase fitness. An odd obstacle course was also present, running down most of the right side of the property.

Leif slipped down from the stallion and Lord Ive dismounted, removing the horse's bridle and saddle, as well as the bit, and let the beautiful steed run free over the field.

"Now let's get down to business," Lord Ive said, handing Leif the yew bow and a package of blackwood arrows. Before Leif could say thank you, Lord Ive continued.

"You will run here in the morning, and arrive before the sun has left the horizon. I will be here as well and for the first week we will drill your basics. First comes the obstacle course which you will complete daily. If you don't finish it fast enough you'll do it again. And again, and again—until you finish it when I deem it to be appropriate. Then we will move on to the shooting range and following that will be my favorite part—lunch. After lunch I'll decide the rest of the training, which will mostly consist of weightlifting and fitness. Okay?"

Leif nodded. "When's dinner?"

Lord Ive laughed. "Don't worry. We'll be done before sunset so you can spend the evening at home."

Leif smiled and put down the yew bow, resting it against the side of the shack. "Do I start now?" he asked, motioning to the obstacle course.

Lord Ive nodded. "You're going to need that bow though," he said, "And I'd try it out first."

Leif pulled back on the drawstring once and remarked, "I think I'll be okay."

Leif walked over to the course and breathed in deeply a couple times. It seemed quite long, and muddy too. From where Leif stood he saw several targets, some high up, some to the sides, but all only reachable through an arrow.

Finally Leif lifted the leather flap concealing the entrance to the course and ran forward—right into a wooden beam. "Oof!" Leif let out a gust of air and his hands flew to his head. "That'll leave a nasty bump," he muttered and crawled forward, picking up his bow.

The first sector was fairly simple. It consisted of many wooden beams bolted across the path to wooden walls, one on each side. The ground was extremely muddy and covered in deep puddles. Leif ran through the area, crawling below beams, hurdling others, and diving through certain difficult sections. Once Leif got to the end he cautiously lifted the flap and, careful not to bump into any odd beams or bars, continued the course.

Five yards ahead of him stood a strange door, connected by a hinge to a target high up on the wall. Leif ignored the target and ran toward the door, falling in the process and covering himself in mud. Leif picked himself up again, only to slide into a deep puddle and drop his bow. Grunting in frustration he dove back into the puddle, which was more or less a water-filled pit, and groped around for the bow in the murky water. Leif's hand connected with a strange, pointy object and he clambered out of the pit. His heart hammering, due to both fear and exhaustion, he stuck his hand in again, feeling the object once more. "Oh!" Leif laughed, pulling on the piece. The object slid out of the mud and Leif recognized his bow—the string had snapped.

Hurriedly Leif restrung the bow and cautiously ran to the door. There was no handle and nothing else to grab. Frustrated now more than ever, he dug a quick hole and put his hand underneath, pulling as hard as he could. The door didn't budge. Leif stood up, searching for some kind of lever, and finding none, he swiftly gave the door a strong kick. A dagger of pain drove through his foot and Leif yelped in surprise and hurt, dropping the bow once more and staggering backwards—into the water pit. Leif resurfaced a moment later and spit out a mouthful of water, pulling himself out and picking up his bow again. "Fine!" he spat, nocking an arrow. Leif's eyes narrowed in concentration as he pulled the bowstring backwards to a full draw. Suddenly the string snapped, the upper part of the string flitting upwards and slashing across Leif's face.

Leif screamed in pain as warm blood trickled down his cheek. In the background he heard faint laughter and Leif spat on the ground, enraged both at Lord Ive and the hellish obstacle course before him. Forcing himself to be calm, Leif restrung the bow and was dismayed to see he had just one bowstring left. Calmly, and making sure to notice the limit of the bow, Leif drew back to a half draw and released his arrow, making sure to aim extra high so the weak bow would hit the target. The arrow darted forward, clanging against the target, and falling to the ground.

Leif shook his head in disbelief, "You have got to be kidding me!" he said, nocking another arrow and raising his head to aim. Suddenly his eyebrows drew together as he noticed that something was different.

"The door's open!" he cried, charging through the door.

As Leif continued through the obstacle course, climbing over a wall and crossing odd terrains loaded with pits and hidden traps, he realized that each target was made of metal and opened the next door. Minutes later he reached the final section.

Leif crawled through the door and into the last sector, scanning the area in front of him. As in the first two sections, two walls were to the side of the area, making sure that Leif did not take some odd roundabout way. Beside him was a platform, and as Leif stared ahead, he yelped in surprise and fear and clambered onto the small stage. Before him was a large pool over which a taut rope had been strung. But that was not what had caused Leif's outburst. The pool was filled with crocodiles.

Leif looked behind him, opening his mouth to cry out in dismay as the door fell shut, when a crocodile sauntered onto the land, Leif's shout dying within his mouth as his throat clenched together in fear. Leif wiped his sweaty palms on his pants and reached upward, grabbing on to the rope. The crocodile moved towards him, as if encouraging Leif to get away before it was too late.

Leif breathed in deeply and said a quick prayer. Then he began to move down the rope. The second Leif left the platform the crocodile jumped onto it, its jaws opened wide to display its many teeth. Leif's eyes widened in fear and his heart hammered faster than before as he placed one hand in front of the other, slowly advancing down the rope. The crocodiles below him continued swimming around, oblivious to their meal as it moved steadily forward over the pool.

Leif made sure never to look down, instead focusing all of his energy—and fear—into getting out of the obstacle course alive. As Leif continued onwards his arms began to ache and his heart hammered faster. The exhaustion from before worked its way into his arms and it took every ounce of Leif's strength not to let go. Finally, after having painstakingly inched all the way, Leif plopped onto the platform on the other side and got out the bow. Making sure not to look at the hungry crocodiles, Leif drew back to a three-quarters draw. Suddenly the string broke, the excess pressure having snapped it in half again. Thankfully the cord whizzed past his head, though Leif swallowed in fear as one of the crocodiles left the water, creeping upwards onto the land beside him. Leif quickly removed his last bowstring from his pocket and fitted it to the bow, always keeping one eye on the creature now five meters from him. Leif was surprised the crocodile couldn't hear his heart thundering within his chest or smell the fear radiating from him. Finally the bow was strung again and Leif fitted an arrow to it, pulling it back to half draw and making sure to listen to the drawstring. As he heard the string protest the pressure he released, the arrow leaving the string slower than any other he had ever seen before. Without watching the result, Leif moved forward towards the door, his whole body quaking in fear as the crocodile pulled itself onto the platform. The second he heard the familiar clang and the door opened, he shot forward and sprinted into the sunlight, not stopping until he heard the door shut again. Finally he collapsed onto the ground, his whole body shaking in exhaustion.

Lord Ive walked over. "How was the bow?" he asked.

Leif faced him, anger evident in every part of his face, "Do you want to kill me?" he asked, the words coming out so forceful and harsh that Lord Ive flinched.

"No," Lord Ive curtly replied. "The crocodiles won't hurt you, trust me. And," a smile flickered over his face, "What did you think of that bow? Was it a little too tough?"

Leif snorted disrespectfully. "How can I trust you if you fill the course with crocodiles?!"

"Because they're illusions created through advanced magic by the Golden Arrow's magician."

Leif shook his head in disbelief. Finally he regained his composure and stood up; shaking off the final tendrils of fear that still clung to his body. He remembered Lord Ive's question. "The bow was weak," he said, "and you really had me fooled."

"I know," Lord Ive answered. "I saw the whole thing from a small window. You were too scared to notice. I was very impressed though." Lord Ive's tone changed. "As for the bow," he said, "I told you to test it." Lord Ive pointedly looked at Leif whose face darkened in embarrassment as he mumbled an apology.

Lord Ive smiled, "I won't waste my words, Leif," he said. "Next time just listen, okay?" Lord Ive smiled as Leif nodded.

"Now, as for the bow . . . I might have a solution for that." Lord Ive revealed a fine blackwood bow that had been hiding behind his back and tossed it to Leif. Leif stood up and took the weapon, the handle fitting perfectly into his hand. The bow was beautiful, the black grains sliding perfectly in either direction from his hand. The bowstring was twined to perfection and attached the standard way, its loop having been pulled over the top of the bow and squeezed through the small crack there. Leif pulled it back to a full draw and slowly easing it back into place. "Beautiful," he whispered.

"Blackwood bow, fletched by the Master Fletcher in Keldon, waterproof bowstring, thirty-five pound draw weight, and your new bow," Lord Ive recited. "Try it out."

Leif nocked an arrow onto the bow and pulled the string backwards easily, sliding his hand along his jawbone until the bow reached a full draw. Then he aimed at a nearby tree, and released. The bowstring's twang sounded like music to Leif's ears and the string gracefully moved back to its position, the arrow that Leif had shot countering its sound as it thudded into the tree positioned fifty yards from where they stood. Leif smiled.

"Great!" Lord Ive said. "Now get that arrow and do the course again. You were three minutes too slow."

Leif pulled back on his beautiful drawstring and released, the arrow shooting towards the target. Leif didn't see the outcome; just hear the familiar thud, for his hands were already fitting the next arrow to the string. A couple seconds later this arrow followed the first and Leif smiled as he saw that his first had hit the center circle. Leif continued, the pattern releasing arrow after arrow into the center circle, his arms a whirlwind of movements as they took an arrow from the quiver, fitted it to the bowstring, drew back, and released, all in one fluid motion, the hands flitting back to the quiver to repeat it. Finally his quiver was empty and Leif looked up. Lord Ive moved from the shadow of the hut and walked to the target, which was fifty yards from where Leif stood.

"Twenty in the center, two in the second ring, and two in the outer ring," he said, "Average of about six seconds per arrow."

Leif whistled in astonishment of his own feat. "Wow!" he said. "I'm really good!"

Lord Ive raised his eyebrows as he walked over to Leif. "Hold this," he instructed, handing Leif his arrows and an expensive watch. "Hit that large golden button on top when I say start and hit it again when I'm done." He pointed to a round button on top of the circular clock.

Lord Ive got out his bow and strung it quickly, putting his right hand to the quiver. "Start!" he yelled, pulling an arrow and fitting it to the string. He immediately drew and released the arrow, the missile thudding right in the center of the target. Leif's eyes didn't have time to focus on Lord Ive again before the next arrow was on its way, thudding beside the first in the bull's eye. Lord Ive continued; his right arm a blurred windmill as it pulled an arrow from the quiver, set it, pulled back quickly, and released. Leif's eyes wandered to the target as arrow after arrow thudded into the soft center ring, creating a dense forest of shafts. The clock clicked as the hand crossed the one and continued onwards towards sixty. Leif looked up again and saw Lord Ive release his final arrows into the center circle. Finally the last one shot from his bow and struck the target, splitting the shaft of another. Leif pressed the large button and looked at the watch. The hand stood at the twenty marking. "One minute and twenty seconds," Leif breathed, awe at his master's amazing feat clearly evident in his voice.

Leif repeated the time louder to Lord Ive, who hadn't even broken a sweat. After some quick calculation Lord Ive said, "About three seconds an arrow, all bull's eyes." Lord Ive shot Leif a belittling look. "Pride is never necessary. Everything can be achieved as long as you have a humble heart," he said.

Leif stared at the ground, red-faced in shame. "I'm sorry," he said.

Lord Ive smiled. "It's okay, no one's perfect. I think it's time we took a rest anyway."

Lord Ive headed toward the shack and Leif followed.

Leif had never been in the hut before, but Lord Ive had gone in several times; to get food, a snack, or some provisions.

The hut had a stove in one corner, with cupboards along the wall that were filled with random ingredients and cooking utensils. On the other side a shelf ran along the wall, filled with herbs, potions, bows, strings, and arrows. Opposite that was a wardrobe with some cloaks and some armor, and was also filled with archery necessities. The final side consisted of the door, and a small shelf that held a display of knives. The middle of the room was occupied with rickety table, which was standing on an old, worn red rug.

"Have a seat." Lord Ive said, nodding towards the table.

Leif sat down, and Lord Ive put a warm cup of tea in front of him, with some bread. Leif nibbled at the bread, still taking in his surroundings.

"Okay," Lord Ive began. "I'm going to give you some background information on the Golden Arrow, since the Meeting is in about two-and-a-half months."

Leif was confused. For the past month they had simply trained, never discussed strategy, the Golden Arrow, or anything related to fighting. They had just spent the whole time honing Leif's archery skills and improving his fitness level.

"What's the Meeting?" Leif asked, a strange feeling telling him it wouldn't be his last question today.

Lord Ive held up his hand. "I'll explain, but I'm going to start at the very beginning and work my way through all your questions. When I'm done you can ask anything you want."

Lord Ive frowned. "That's probably not a good idea is it? We'll be late for the Meeting if I let you ask *anything*. Oh well, here goes:"

Lord Ive started, "The Golden Arrow was formed in the very beginning of Siddian's history when King Sedgwick the Great banded the different tribes together to form the first Alliance. Back then, the leaders of the different tribes were simply the best warriors, and each tribe was special in its own way. The Brants were great knights, while the Securese were great with two-handed battle-axes; we from the state of Arash were skilled in archery, so on. Anyways, Sedgwick was able to band the different estates together to resist the attack from the south. The different leaders of the different tribes got together, and formed the Golden Arrow. The Golden Arrow governed the nations then, voting on decisions. The invaders from the south were defeated by Sid's first army which was led by the Golden Arrow. Instead of disbanding afterwards, the group decided to form a new nation with the Golden Arrow as its government. This worked perfectly at first, until Sedgwick's great-grandson, Seth, became the leader of this council. Seth was a very power hungry leader and attempted to kill the other Golden Arrow members and become the sole ruler of Siddian. His dark plan was uncovered though and he was slain by the Golden

Arrow, yet these horrible events had left their mark—so the new Golden Arrow met and decided to install an honest and trustworthy leader. To do this they voted amongst themselves, and got their first king. If the king was dishonest and bad, the other members had the power and duty to dethrone him, and even to *kill* him."

Lord Ive looked at Leif, yet the apprentice was still confused.

Lord Ive continued, "Over the years, the Golden Arrow evolved. For a while it was known as the "Guardians of Freedom" and they constantly checked that the King did not become a horrible leader. This didn't work though, for the King was never able to do anything without having a Golden Arrow member bar his way. So the troop evolved and became a force of elite warriors that fought under the King and served only him. That is what it is today. It is an elite military force made of the twelve best soldiers in the Kingdom. Each state in the Kingdom is responsible for one soldier, which fights in that state's traditional manner. For example, as I said earlier, we, the state of Arash, were extremely skilled in archery which is why Arash is now responsible for supplying the bowman to the Golden Arrow. Brant gives the knight, Securis the berserker, so on . . ."

"The King of Siddian is voted from the Golden Arrow, but when the new king leaves the Golden Arrow he is no longer part of it. He has no more say in their action except that now he commands them as he does the rest of the military. He cannot dictate their strategy or anything else, only their objective. The Meeting is an event in which the different members of the Golden Arrow get together to discuss different issues. Sometimes the Meeting involves holding council with the King. The current leader of the Golden Arrow is Captain Richard, the knight from Brant."

Leif's expression had cleared now, but he still had a lot of questions to ask. Lord Ive however was prepared, and held up his hand. "Wait," he said. "Now that you know a brief history of the Golden Arrow, I'm going to explain a couple other things. For example, because the King comes from the Golden Arrow, his heir must spend time as one of its members. This is to ensure that Siddian's ruler always has military background and knowledge. If he were to die during his time of service, and the King does not have another heir, than a new lineage would be started. Thankfully this has never happened." Lord Ive breathed in deeply and set a determined face as if he was about to face an entire army on his own. "Now," he said, his voice sounding bravely before this army. "Ask your questions."

Leif laughed and said the first question that came to mind, one that had been nagging him since Lord Ive had invited him to compete in the tryouts. "Lord Ive, why am I allowed to be part of the Golden Arrow? Isn't it illegal to become a military officer as a peasant?"

Lord Ive nodded. "Technically speaking, yes. But the Golden Arrow is special. The bowman, Rider, berserker, and Tracker are allowed to be peasants. That is because these must have a special gift or talent. The Rider and berserker must possess both a gift with which they are born and a talent. The Rider must possess the gift of inner peace through which to soothe animals and the talent of being able to effectively work with them. The berserker, who is called a berserker because he has the ability to enter a frenzied rage on the battlefield, also known as going berserk, must possess this gift to enter this rage and be able to kill multitudes of warriors and survive the most horrific injuries until this rage passes. The same exception has been made for the tracker and bowman because peasants who have grown up hunting or tracking in the forests are best equipped for these positions whereas many pompous, fat nobles will not even touch a 'peasant weapon' like a bow or expend the effort of learning and following tracks. Only the best may join the Golden Arrow."

Leif smiled at the indirect praise he had been offered, yet his face also held an expression of surprise for how Lord Ive had spoken of his fellow nobles.

Lord Ive noticed the expression, and after a short, but fierce, internal debate, he said, "I was also born a peasant," he said, his glassy eyes paying tribute to the memory. "The nobility used us. They treated us like dirt. That is partly why I joined the Golden Arrow: to reform the nobility and introduce equality that hasn't existed since the beginning of Siddian."

Leif leaned forward; intrigued by this glimpse of his life that Lord Ive had shown Leif.

Lord Ive shook his head. "I'd rather not speak about my past," he said. "Any other questions?"

Leif thought for a second, remembering his tea and quickly taking a sip, discovering it to be now cold.

"Is there any . . . protocol I should be aware of in the presence of the King or other nobles?"

Lord Ive laughed. "Just be respectful like your mother no doubt taught you to be. Come on!" Lord Ive said. "We're warriors, not feeble ladies who spend hours drinking tea and eating powdered crackers!"

Leif laughed, pointedly looking at his teacup. Lord Ive joined in the laugher. "Fine!" he cried in mock surrender. "I'm a feeble lady!"

Once the laughing had ceased and a more serious atmosphere settled Leif asked another question. "Are there any other apprentices or am I the only one?" Leif asked.

Lord Ive shrugged. "That's one of the things we'll find out at the Meeting. We introduce and test the new apprentices," he answered. Seeing Leif's puzzled expression, he added, "I am preparing you for the test.

This is the time period in which you prepare. Then you must complete the test, and you are judged according to how well you do. You either become my official apprentice or you leave. If I think you're too young and skilled to leave, then I can keep you as my apprentice for the next test two years later." Lord Ive looked at Leif and said, "Yes, we have a Meeting every two years, and let me tell you. I will not keep you as my apprentice for another two years. You either make it or you don't."

Lord Ive saw Leif's next question coming, but he let him say it anyways. "What do I do during the test?" he asked.

Lord Ive smiled; it was a classic apprentice question. Now came the classic mentor answer, "You pass."

Leif smiled, "No really, what do I have to do?"

"You have to pass, that's what." Lord Ive repeated.

"Okay. What do I have to do to pass?" Leif said again.

"Surprise!" Lord Ive said, and got up. The talk was over.

A week later Leif felt that he had just about mastered his ground skills. He had cut a whole second from his shooting, also shaving off a minute from his obstacle course time. His body was a living monument to his tireless work. His arms were twice the size they had been before he began training—back when he had simply been some scrawny peasant boy. His fitness seemed to have peaked and his archery skills had been honed to nigh perfection. Basically, Leif felt he was fitter than ever before.

Finally Leif decided to tell his master this.

Leif approached Lord Ive slowly. "Um, Lord Ive?" he said tentatively, unsure how to say what was on his mind without sounding prideful.

"I feel like I've learned a lot," he began. "I know there is still a lot to learn, but I think that I have reached my—" Leif hesitated, "peak in archery skill. Is there anything else I need to learn?"

Lord Ive smiled at Leif, recognizing his difficulty with phrasing the question and accepting it. "Yes," he said. "But most of your training will occur after the Meeting. Right now I am preparing you to pass the Test so that you can become my apprentice and then learn everything you need to know. But there is one other thing you must be able to do in order to pass the Test."

Leif nodded, eager to know more. "What?" he asked.

Lord Ive smiled, "How to ride a horse."

Leif's shoulder's sagged. He hadn't expected that, although now that he thought about it, it seemed obvious. *I can't ride a horse!* Leif thought. *Now I'll never become his apprentice.*

Lord Ive realized Leif's dejected state and nudged him. "Cheer up," he said. "It's really easy and lots of fun."

Lord Ive walked over to the shack where his mount grazed. She was a large white mare, and Lord Ive smiled as he saddled her. "Her name is Rosamond," he said, affectionately petting her. Then he mounted, pulling Leif up to sit behind him. Making sure that Leif was holding on properly, Lord Ive tapped her sides and the two shot off down the road.

Once they reached the castle courtyard Lord Ive led Leif to the stable, tucked in a corner. The stable boy in charge there saluted the bowman, and asked politely, "What do you need, sir?"

Lord Ive waved him off. "We'll be okay," he said, "Just got to find this young man a friend." Then Lord marched into the stable, Leif tagging along behind him.

A narrow walkway led between the stalls, giant warhorses breathing down onto Leif. Leif stayed close to his master, oddly afraid of these large beasts, yet also in awe. A surge of pride coursed through him as he imagined himself atop such a steed, flying through the wind.

Finally they got to the end of the path, where a large black horse sat, defiantly staring at Leif. "Let's try this one," Lord Ive said, sliding open the stall's heavy iron door and saddling the beast.

Outside they entered an enclosure, existing specifically for equestrian purposes. The ground was covered in fine brown powder and the area circled by a large brown fence.

"Get on up," Lord Ive said.

Leif breathed in deeply and tried to clamber onto the stallion, sliding right back down. Lord Ive laughed. "Put your left foot in the stirrup," he instructed. Leif lifted his foot as high as possible, jamming it into the stirrup. "Now hop onto him."

Finally Leif sat upon the giant warhorse, yet somehow it didn't feel right—he didn't feel . . . connected. Suddenly the stallion charged forward, madly galloping towards the fence. It abruptly changed direction, thundering now towards Lord Ive. Leif screamed in fear as he pulled on the reins with all his strength, holding on for dear life. Lord Ive dove out of the way just in time, rolling into standing position, yelling at Leif to jump off. Leif couldn't. The crazed charger continued pounding towards the opposite fence, when suddenly it stopped. Leif shot from the saddle like an arrow, arcing through the air over the stallion, and thudding into the ground. Leif rolled over and moaned loudly, a throbbing headache pounding through his head. Lord Ive walked over, "I think we should find you a different horse."

Leif nodded weakly and picked himself up, holding his head as his vision spun. Then he staggered after Lord Ive into the stable.

Once Leif felt better the two decided to continue searching. Lord Ive led Leif to the back again, passing all of the giant warhorses, which Leif feared more now than before.

"How about him?" Lord Ive said, pointing at a brown horse, sitting peacefully in its stall, chewing hay. Leif smiled, already fond of the horse, although he hadn't even seen it earlier, as the other steed's presence had cast him into shadow.

"He's perfect for you," Lord Ive said, inspecting the horse. "By the time he is large enough to be a full-fledge warhorse, you will know him well enough and be experienced enough to properly handle him."

Leif nodded, "He *is* perfect."

Leif looked down at the horse's nameplate which read Philip. "Hello Philip," Leif said, leading him from his stall. The gentle stallion peacefully followed Leif, allowing himself to be led to the enclosure where Leif saddled him, Lord Ive teaching Leif how to do this. "It you want to be successful with him then you better get to know him. That starts with being able to put on his saddle properly."

Half an hour later Leif mounted Philip, easily sliding into the saddle. Leif breathed out in wonder. Atop Philip the world seemed different. Earlier he had felt afraid and insecure, never taking in the awesome feeling. Leif smiled, the awesome sensation of freedom pounding in unison with his heart, as an unbreakable bond formed between him and Philip.

For the next hour Lord Ive trained the two, attaching a long rope to Philip's bridle and letting him go in circles around Lord Ive. As they did this, Lord Ive corrected Leif's form and explained how to properly ride Philip. Lord Ive continued to teaching Leif for the rest of the day, stopping only for lunch and brief breaks. Finally, at the end of the day, Leif was able to properly sit upon, and stay upon, Philip, whether the stallion was walking, trotting, or even galloping.

Once training was done, Leif slid from Philip's back, massaging his sore legs. Lord Ive smiled, patting Philip on the neck and praising both him and Leif. "You're doing great!" Lord Ive said. "Now we only have to teach you how to shoot accurately as you ride him at a full gallop—alone."

Leif moaned, thinking of all the sore days to come. Then he unsaddled Philip and put away the equipment. A couple minutes later he led Philip to the nearby fountain and proceeded to pour buckets of water over him, washing the gentle stallion as Philip neighed in pleasure. Finally Leif led

Philip back to his stall, generously pouring oats into his trough as he ignored the loud protests from the adjoining cell.

Then Leif hobbled after Lord Ive, groaning as he mounted Rosamond behind him, holding on to Lord Ive's midsection as they trotted to Leif's hovel.

Leif and Philip bonded greatly over the following weeks, Leif learning everything about his horse. Finally, after two painful weeks, the two went on an excursion with Lord Ive and Rosamond, traveling through the forest. Leif whooped loudly as they shot through the woods, the trees blurring in his vision, the wind whipping through his hair, Leif and Philip becoming one as they thundered onward. Lord Ive smiled at his apprentice, urging his horse forward. Leif countered, pushing Philip as well. The two horses surged forward, galloping down the path. Philip slowly gained on Rosamond, yet the experienced horse didn't back down, the race continuing until they shot out onto the highway. Leif and Lord Ive slowed their mounts down, patting their neck as the exhausted horses' heads hung low, their tongues lolling from their mouths.

Lord Ive looked at Leif, a large grin plastered on his face. "I think you're ready for the Test," he said.

Leif continued to train diligently, continuing to improve his relationship with Philip. Leif spent the first half of his day riding him, both to acquire new equestrian skills and to condition Philip. The other half he spent with Lord Ive, simply keeping his excellent fitness level. After another week Leif was able to shoot from Philip's back, guiding the charger with his knees and sticking the reins in his mouth. After another week Leif had almost perfected this, loosing arrows at a gallop from fifty yards.

Finally, five weeks after having met and forged a deep friendship with Philip, Lord Ive sat down again to talk with Leif in the cabin.

"I feel as if I have taught you everything you need to know to complete the Test." He began, "So, do you have any questions for the Meeting, or anything at all concerning the Golden Arrow?" He asked.

"Yes," Leif promptly replied. "I was wondering if you could tell me about the current Golden Arrow. That way I won't feel like a complete outsider."

Lord Ive nodded. "Okay. Well, our leader is Captain Richard. He is a strong man and does his job very well. He is the knight of the Golden Arrow. Next would be Theron. He is the tracker. That means he is specially trained in following people and groups. He is very good friends with Deacon, the messenger, and they often work together in their missions.

Xurxo, our Rider is very important to the whole group, but especially to those two. He provides us with transportation and likes to surprise us by always arriving on a different animal. His job is to fight with beasts. Then comes Myrddin. He is an old man man, rumored to be 212 years old! He is our magician/sorcerer and takes care of anything related to magic or spell casting."

Lord Ive paused briefly to collect his thoughts, and then continued on, "Alicia is our healer. She takes care of us and is the only woman." As Lord Ive spoke of her, his eyes twinkled.

Lord Ive started again, "Next we have Hildebrand, the double-bladed swordsman of the Golden Arrow. He is an amazing fighter and a great man. His best friend, Maccabee, is the hammer/mace/pike man. Skinner is our whipmaster. He is extremely skilled in fighting with whips and is a necessity to the Golden Arrow's success. He can be kind of shady and likes to keep to himself though. And finally comes Egon. He is the assassin, but a very funny, outgoing man. I bet you'll love him." Lord Ive added—a faint smile playing across his face as Leif realized that he and Lord Ive must be best friends.

Leif nodded, still making mental notes about each of the warriors as Lord Ive led the way into the hut.

Finally Leif decided to ask an important question, one that his mother wanted an answer to as well as him. "When is the Meeting?" he asked.

"Actually," Lord Ive said. "It is three days from today. So, if you don't have any more questions, I would like to give you some things necessary for the Test."

Lord Ive got up, walking to the wardrobe that stood in the corner as Leif watched in anticipation, already nervous of what would occur in just three days.

"If we ever want you to become a bowman apprentice, then we better get you looking like one," Lord Ive said as he threw open the wardrobe doors, revealing a shiny red combat suit.

Leif gasped at the beautiful sight. The combat suit consisted of a long shimmering, red dragonhide robe, a coif of the same substance, and a belt to hold the robe in place at his waist.

"Don't just sit there," Lord Ive said. "Try it on!"

Leif smiled, removing the suit from its hanger and slipping into it. The lightweight dragonhide material reflected the rays of sunshine penetrating through the small window, a spectrum of red colors playing across the walls.

The robe hung just past his knees, split down the middle to allow him to ride. The coif sat comfortably on his head, the material hanging to his shoulders to protect him his neck and cheeks.

Lord Ive smiled, "Looks nice," he commented, opening the other side of the wardrobe to reveal the same suit, only larger. "It's mine," he said, motioning to the larger suit.

Then Lord Ive took a small square piece of dragonhide cloth, unsheathing his hunting knife as he did so. Lord Ive handed Leif the knife and, holding opposite sides of the cloth, pulling it taut, he smiled and said, "Try and rip it."

Leif gently stabbed at the material yet it didn't even scratch the surface. "Come on!" Lord Ive said. "Attack it like a man!"

Leif smiled and stabbed downwards hard, expecting to puncture the cloth or at least rip it from Lord Ive's grasp, yet the knife, slipped from Leif's hand as he met the durable dragonhide. Lord Ive laughed, putting the cloth back to where he had found it.

"Am I allowed to wear this for the Test?" Leif asked.

Lord Ive looked at Leif and said, "No, you *must* wear it for the Test."

Leif was surprised. This gave him quite an advantage over any wild beast. *Maybe there are no wild beasts, and I just have to shoot well to become an official apprentice. Maybe it isn't so hard.* Leif thought to himself.

Lord Ive seemed to be able to read Leif's mind. "And don't think this will give you any sort of advantage. The Test will be more than double as hard as the tryouts. And yes, I have seen more than enough people fail."

Chapter 3

He was holding a sleek, new bow made of a dark wood. In hands he held three perfectly fletched dragon arrows, their red rocks glinting in the moonlight. A red leathery armor was draped across his skinny frame, his only defense against the thousands of scarlet-clothed warriors steadily marching towards him.

The boy nocked an arrow and aimed high, hoping to hit someone in the crowd of soldiers. Beside him other archers did the same. A man yelled "fire!" and the young archer released the string, listening to the familiar thrum of his bow.

Behind him a battalion of infantry advanced, preparing to hit the enemy with a frontal attack. At their flanks several rows of cavalry anxiously awaited their turn to fight, readying themselves for a chance at glory. A man yelled a command and the troops advanced, streaming through the archers and charging at the enemy.

A great clash of metal was heard as the lines collided. Agonized screams echoed across the plain as first men hit the ground. The knights couldn't hold it any longer. Without waiting for the signal they spurred on their horses and thundered toward the enemy, a cloud of dust rising in their wake.

The archers had reloaded again and the moon was temporarily blocked from sight as a cloud of arrows arced toward the enemy. The cavalrymen now hit the flanks, driving their charge inward towards the baggage. The enemy held their ground though, beating back the attack and the knights turned, galloping in a wide circle to gain momentum for their next charge. The infantry in the front had stopped advancing, momentarily halted by their furious adversaries.

Behind him the youth heard a voice. It was comforting and slightly familiar. It was the voice of his leader. He was sure of it. The boy had never seen the man, but he knew it had to be him. He turned, seeing the man for the first time.

The knight had on gold-trimmed dragon armor and wielded a long two-handed broadsword. His long hair was fluttering in the breeze. Behind him stood the castle, a huge fortress of stone, loaded down with defenses.

The leader took a step towards the boy, saying something. His voice sounded comforting, even if the youth couldn't understand what he was saying. Suddenly the knight's voice changed, growing cold and menacing. As the man's tone changed, so did his figure, the armor morphing into scales and the face into that of a serpent. The graceful hair grew into long horns and before the frightened boy could react, the man pulled a blade from his coiled serpentine body and stabbed him in the back, the ice-cold dagger digging into his skin and seeming to freeze his very soul . . .

Leif woke up with a start, wiping the sweat from his brow. Dim sunlight filtered through the small window in the hovel. He controlled his breathing, got up, and tiptoed to the corner where his clothes lay. He quickly slipped into them, wondering about his dream.

Who had stabbed him? Was it just a nightmare, nothing to be worried about? He wasn't sure, it had seemed so real, so—possible. He shook his head and walked outside, kissing his mom goodbye as she had woken up to see him off.

It was still early, the sun's rays barely edging over the horizon. Leif let out a breath of relief, Lord Ive had specifically told him to be at the shack just after sunrise. Leif looked back at his mom, standing in the doorway, a loving smile adorning her face. He closed his eyes, committing the picture to memory, smiling as the warm love his mom and him shared burned in his heart. Then he began his jog to the training place.

Today was the first time in his life where Leif would leave the immediate area of Keldon and see the outside world. He was slightly nervous of the coming Meeting, and even more so of the Test, but beneath the superlative emotions lay a deep curiosity.

As Leif jogged his mind wandered, thinking of what the Test could possibly be and what the Meeting would be like. Leif nearly stumbled as he remembered that the King might be there. No one in his whole family had ever seen him, except perhaps his father. Leif sighed; he wasn't sure whether he should adore the King or hate him. It had been the King that had called Arash to defend Siddian's border, which led to his father's death, yet the King was the King, and he knew that he had to respect him.

Finally Leif arrived at the field that served as his training ground. Lord Ive was finishing packing, loading a small packhorse with provisions consisting mostly of arrows. When Leif arrived Philip neighed happily, attempting to tug free of his rope. Leif smiled, running the last few steps to his beloved friend and affectionately patting his neck.

For a second Leif considered telling Lord Ive about his dream, yet he finally decided not to. *It was a simple nightmare. Why bother him with something small like that. He'll only think that I'm a little child.* Leif thought, shrugging off the thought.

Finally Lord Ive finished. "You ready?" he asked.

Leif nodded and so they mounted their steeds. Behind him Leif noticed that the he had saddlebags slung over the back of the saddle. After a quick examination Leif saw that they were filled beautiful clothes, made of rich materials. Leif ran his hands over a shirt and his eyes widened in realization. "It's Silk," he breathed.

Lord Ive nodded. "I asked the castle's tailor if he could fix me a couple nice shirts for you."

Leif nodded his thanks, and the two touched their heels to their horses' sides, spurring them into a light walk. The packhorse followed them, attached to Rosamond by a short rope.

Lord Ive and Leif rode all day, resting briefly for lunch at a small inn. Later that evening they crossed the border into Securis, Leif grinning from ear to ear as he left the confines of Arash. Finally, when the sun touched the horizon, Lord Ive and Leif entered the town of Dechsburg.

The Lord of the town accepted Lord Ive happily, inviting him to a large dinner celebration where Lord Ive was the guest of honor. As jugglers, storytellers, and dancing bears entertained the guests, Leif snuck out to his room.

Here Leif changed into his dragonhide suit and grabbed his beautiful blackwood bow. This he strung quickly and, grabbing a sack of arrows, he ran outside to the archery range.

The range was empty, yet it included eighteen targets, two at twenty five yards, two at fifty, two at seventy-five, and so on. Leif chose to start at a hundred yards, getting used to the extra bulk of the suit, which was barely any. Within a couple of minutes Leif felt he had mastered the ability to shoot while wearing the combat suit, so he decided to try shooting at two hundred yards.

Leif concentrated extra hard, his eyebrows drawing together as he sighted the target. Shooting two hundred yards required large shoulder and chest muscles, which Leif had been acquiring for the last months. To lessen the burden Leif "leaned into the bow" as Lord Ive had taught him. Leif used his whole body to pull back the string. His shoulders drew outward, his chest protruded forward to pull it back yet more, and even his legs pushed in opposite directions to pull the cord back to his ear. Finally Leif aimed, not choosing to do so down the length of the arrow, which at this distance was impossible, but rather with his gut. Leif simply knew how to position the bow to shoot at this distance. It may have been practice or luck, or simply that Leif was born to do this, but Leif knew just how to hold the bow, and finally he released.

The arrow whispered as it left the string, shooting forward into the sky, traveling in a perfect arc. Leif didn't have to hear or see it thud into the center circle of the target. He already knew it had been a perfect shot. Smiling, Leif chose another arrow from the bag and repeated what he had done.

Leif woke early the next morning, an hour before sunrise. Yawning, he quickly dressed himself and then trudged downstairs to the Great Hall. Lord Ive was already there, talking to the Lord of Dechsburg, a large and cheery fellow. The empty plate that sat in front of Lord Ive showed Leif that he had already eaten. Leif received a plate of fruit, bread, and cheese, and he went to sit beside his master.

The Lord of Dechsburg was speaking. "—found out that Morrigan has forged an alliance with Ashtoreth, the cursed nation south of them. The devil-begotten Morrs are losing the little honor they have left."

Lord Ive nodded in agreement, and the Lord continued. "I also heard that the Dark Elves are pulling together and marching towards the Morr border. I'm guessing that they're the ones that made the alliance. The Morrs have seemed mighty suspicious lately anyways. They seem to be preparing for something. According to one of my sources their army is preparing for something, as is their navy. I simply hope they've given up on us."

Leif shoved a piece of bread along with a thick slice of cheese into his mouth, chewing happily as the many vivid flavors of fresh food rewarded his taste buds. Beside him Lord Ive was questioning the Lord once more.

"What about the Alliance?" he asked.

The Lord nodded, as if he were getting there. "That's the other thing. The King just met with the Council of Waylon and the leader of Arganon. They've signed the Old Pact once more: the Alliance is as strong as ever."

Lord Ive nodded again. "Seems like tensions are awfully high, huh?" he remarked.

Now it was the Lord's turn to nod sadly and ask questions. Leif ignored the two now, rather focusing on his breakfast, as the Lord caught up on the latest gossip of Arash.

Finally, once both the Leif's appetite and the Lord's knowledge had been satisfied, Lord Ive and Leif left. The Lord said goodbye to both, wishing them well, and then they left the town of Dechsburg, just as the sun crept over the horizon.

Once again Leif and Lord Ive rode at a walk, Lord Ive teaching and explaining various things to Leif as they clattered down a paved road. The two continued this way until the sun reached its highest point, and they left the road to eat beneath a large oak. The Lord of Dechsburg had given them plenty of food, so as the horses rested and ate, Lord Ive and Leif picnicked and stretched their cramped legs. An hour later they continued on their journey.

Leif was awed once more as they crossed the river Flumen on a massive stone bridge. Lord Ive was forced to pay a copper penny for their crossing, and so they the clattered across it. Leif watched with fascination as the water gently, but swiftly, flowed east. Leif had seen streams and even small rivers, but the Flumen was much greater. It spanned nearly seventy yards and was of a brown-greenish color that looked pleasantly natural. Once they had crossed Leif resumed his inspection of the countryside.

The two rode through countless villages and passed even more farms and fields. The area was simply dotted with these fields and farmers. Every now and then men passed them, usually farmers, but a highway patrol or group of armed men did occasionally thunder past.

Finally, when the sun was low in the sky, Lord Ive pointed ahead. Leif squinted to see what he was pointing at and recognized a large dot on the horizon.

"The capital," Lord Ive said. Leif stared in awe at the blurry dot: the largest and most important city of Siddian.

Suddenly Lord Ive pulled Rosamond to the side. Philip followed suit, Leif not even having to signal the turn with his reins. Lord Ive pointed at a large boulder that stood there, a smaller rock balancing atop it.

"That's our signal," he said, urging Rosamond into a canter to follow the faint dirt track that led past it. Leif followed him and the packhorse, trying desperately to commit the picture to memory.

Lord Ive kept a steady pace, trotting towards the Meeting place. After twenty minutes they came upon another landmark. This one was the opposite of the first. A small rock lay there, with a much larger one balancing precariously upon it. Now Lord Ive turned again, trotting in a slightly different direction. Here the path was not even visible, the only markers being bent pieces of grass that betrayed the fact that the whole Golden Arrow had ridden in this direction.

Half an hour later the two entered a forest. There was not path to follow here, Lord Ive seeming to follow a set of signs and hidden markers as they picked their way through the woods. The forest was not particularly dense, with the undergrowth not impeding their journey at all. Lord Ive had slowed to a light walk, as to allow the not-so-skillful packhorse to move along at the same pace as Rosamond and Philip.

Finally Leif heard voices. His heart hammering dramatically in his chest, Leif urged Philip forward, as Rosamond increased pace as well. Suddenly they burst into a clearing, pulling to a stop.

The clearing was large, but naturally so; it did not look as if a gardener had to come by regularly and hack away at the forest. The grass was pleasantly short, and small daisies grew in it, adding to the pleasance of the area. A line of tents stood on the opposite side of where Leif and Lord Ive stood. Leif quickly counted, smiling as he saw that there were thirteen large golden tents and two smaller silver ones.

"There's another apprentice," Lord Ive remarked, Leif smiling in answer.

Suddenly the tent flap of the central tent was lifted and a group of men walked out. Leif breathed in slowly, awed to be in the presence of such mighty warriors.

Then Lord Ive spurred Rosamond forward, and slowly she walked into the center of the clearing. Leif hurriedly followed, listening as Lord Ive called a greeting, the others echoing it. Leif managed a curt hello as well, smiling nervously at each of the men.

As the group acknowledged Leif's presence, Leif saw the other apprentice emerge from his tent. Leif managed a smile at him, and the boy waved back. The apprentice wore dull gray dragon armor, but no helmet. He had long, brown hair that reached to his shoulders and a commanding face. The boy seemed to be well-trained and Leif estimated him to be about fourteen.

As the apprentice disappeared back into his tent, Leif studied each of the warriors in earnest. He immediately spotted the sorcerer/magician, Myrddin, who was leaning on a long staff and had a braided white beard that reached his waist. He also spotted Lord Ive's best friend among the group, Egon the assassin. Captain Richard was also easily distinguishable. He was broad shouldered and held a giant broadsword. He too wore dragon armor, but his shone a brilliant white. Suddenly the armor seemed to shift as it turned red. Then it lightened into pink. Then orange. Then green. It seemed that the armor changed colors every few seconds.

That must come in handy when he is trying to distract his opponent while fighting, Leif mused.

Leif was able to match the names with Lord Ive's description and he gasped as he spotted the only woman, the healer of the Golden Arrow. Leif knew her name was Alicia, and he immediately recognized her; it was the woman that had attended to him at the tryouts! As Leif continued examining each warrior, pairing the short, stern spearman with the name Gary, and the muscled, hammer-wielding man with his rightful name,

Maccabee, he realized that Deacon, the messenger, and Xurxo, the Rider, were not there.

The quick evaluation took only a few seconds, in which the warriors warmly greeted Lord Ive and Leif, who simply smiled and nodded respectfully. Then Lord Ive said to the group, "This is my new apprentice, Leif. Leif won the tryouts in Keldon, and has shown he is worthy to be called a bowman apprentice of the Golden Arrow, but we have yet to test him."

Leif smiled, and dismounted, as Lord Ive had already done. Then he took the two horses to the shed, hurrying out of the spotlight.

In the musty shed, Leif saw more horses in separate stalls, and finally he found one with a sign that read: Rosamond. Leif led Rosamond into her stall, and poured some oats into her food trough. Then he led Philip to the back, where three stalls were labeled: Apprentice Horses, and unsaddled him. Leif led him into his stall and fed him as well. As Philip munched on his food, Leif busied himself by cleaning his friend.

While Leif was cleaning Philip, a shout echoed from outside, and Leif dropped his brush and sprinted outside.

He threw open the door of the shed and ran into the clearing where all of the warriors were gathered, including the other apprentice. Lord Ive was standing between Alicia and Egon, laughing quietly.

The whole congregation was looking up, into the sky, and Leif followed their gaze. His eyes narrowed as he saw that a large black speck was slowly descending towards them.

As the dot got closer and closer, it began to take shape. It had a large body, and a long neck, with a triangular head. Attached to its body were two giant wings, and beneath the body were two huge, muscular legs. Flying behind the massive body, was a long tail, which ended in a deadly spike. It was a dragon.

The dragon came closer and closer, and finally hit the ground, where Leif saw that the dragon was blue. Suddenly, its color shifted and it was white. Then red. Then orange.

As the massive being, which was about the size of ten warhorses, landed, two men jumped off the dragon.

The first was a large man, with blonde hair, and a billowing golden cape. The man was wearing a green dragon suit, and had a bejeweled dagger at his side. He was Deacon, the Golden Arrow's messenger.

The next person that hopped off had to first secure the reins he was holding, which he handed to Myrddin, who used magic to attach them to the ground. This man was wearing a fine, white fur vest and black dragon hide chaps. The man had a sword attached to his belt, and a joyous smile stretched from ear to ear, the aftermath of an exhilarating trip on a dragon. Leif instantly knew that this man was the final member of the Golden Arrow; he was the Rider, Xurxo.

Deacon checked to see that Xurxo had gotten off the beast before saying hurriedly, "We must adjourn the Meeting! We must fly immediately to the King who requests our assistance in pressing matters! I have no idea what it is about, just come; maybe we can finish the meeting later."

The gathered group looked at Deacon as if he had just come from a different planet.

"Adj—Adjourn the Mee—Meeting?" Maccabee sputtered.

"Yes! Now!" Deacon yelled, expecting everyone to follow him.

"One second," Captain Richard said, and pulled Deacon to the side to talk in private.

Leif couldn't hear anything besides the first sentence which was, "Are you mad?!"

Then the two talked in hushed voices until Sir Richard nodded and addressed the group, "Leave everything! Get only what you need for one to two days time! Leave the horses and the tents! GO!" the captain roared.

The camp sprung into action. Everyone grabbed what they needed, and ran back into the clearing, where four more dragons and their Riders had appeared, as if on cue.

Leif had been busy dumping Philip and Rosamond more food and getting his bow, so he hadn't seen the new beasts arrive, yet he didn't care. The dragons were kind of scary.

Finally all the necessary preparations for a possibly lengthy trip were made and the group boarded the dragons. Lord Ive chose a particularly large one, and Leif sat down behind him. The enormous axe man took the final seat. His name was Ragnhild, and he was a giant, towering into the air an impressive seven-and-a-half feet, with broad shoulders and a scarred, but muscled upper body. He had a long red beard and a messy mesh of hair that hung past his shoulders. For protection he wore magically enhanced leather armor and carried a massive double-bladed battleaxe. In short, he was a warrior to be reckoned with.

Minutes later, the thirteen members of the Golden Arrow were airborne, and on their way to the capital.

⟶

The group was standing in the Main Hall of the King's Castle moments later, and the King was briefing them on their mission. The cavernous hall was richly decorated with a banner representing each state and the King's own coat of arms hung behind his throne. The throne had red cushions on it and a long back which was plaited gold. The throne was elevated, sitting on a small stage. The King stood before the Golden Arrow, wearing a purple battledress and a long red cape. A golden sword had been drawn on the King's battledress and a decorated scabbard hung at his side. The King was not wearing his crown; instead, he had on a circlet which was also plaited in gold. His long brown hair flowed to his shoulders and his blue eyes seemed to sparkle as he talked.

"As you probably know, we just recently renewed the Alliance, and that Morrigan and Ashtoreth are getting ready for some mass invasion. Well, just three hours ago, a messenger from Waylon flew in, telling me that the Waylin Islands are under attack. An hour later, I received news that they surrendered Rhona. Now the Morrs are moving inward to the next island."

The Golden Arrow was for the most part nodding, and a scribe was sitting in a corner writing down word for word what the King was saying, his quill flitting across the page like a small sword.

The King spoke up again, Leif hardly daring to breathe in the presence of the land's most powerful man. "I want you guys to back up Waylon," he said, "Since that is part of the Alliance—Military Allegiance. Do this until I can muster enough troops to make a difference. I've gotten a team of dragons ready to fly you to the coast, and another team is waiting there to take you to Arran. Don't worry, all your necessities have already been packed, since I think I know what you guys need." The King smiled. "Good luck."

The Golden Arrow bowed as a group and backed out of the Hall.

Outside a group of dragons were waiting, and a very confused Leif mounted one, choosing to sit behind Lord Ive.

"What's going on?" He hissed into his mentor's ear.

"I'll tell you when we're airborne," Lord Ive told Leif, and the two got comfortable in the leather saddles.

Seconds later, the dragon on which they were sprung upward. Leif held on for dear life, as the dragon pumped its massive wings and they rose in the air.

After about five minutes, the dragon was gliding comfortably just below the clouds, and Leif was doing his best not to look down. Leif gulped, and tightened his seat belt.

"Okay. What is happening was what you asked, right?" Lord Ive shouted over the wind rushing past them.

Leif didn't want to open his mouth, so he just nodded.

"Back during the beginning of the kingdom, Siddian was very weak compared to other large nations like Morrigan. To stay safe, Siddian joined the Alliance, a large agreement between Siddian and two other nations. These two other nations, Arganon and Waylon, are located on the other side of the Sea. Waylon is the closest to Morrigan and owns a set of islands that is between Siddian, Waylon, and Morrigan, right in the middle of the Sea. Morrigan has wanted these islands for a long time because that way they would control the trade between Arganon, Waylon, and the mainland. Arganon is a very strong nation to the east of Waylon. The reason Arganon has never launched a campaign to conquer Waylon and then control the Sea is because it is a very honorable nation that stays true to its word and us. We would be forced to come to Waylon's aid and thus start a large and lengthy war that would ruin both of us and leave Morrigan to march right over us."

Leif nodded, attempting to cram countless years worth of history into his brain in a few seconds while flying several hundred meters above land.

"Waylon concentrates more on the economy than keeping their land safe, which will one day be their downfall, while Arganon is good in both. So, what we are doing is flying to Arran, which is one of Waylon's islands. These islands are called the Waylin islands, and Rhona is the closest one to Morrigan. The Morrs have already conquered this one, and now they are pushing on toward the next island: Arran. From there, I am guessing they will conquer the rest of the islands and then finally Waylon itself even. Our job is to stop the Morrs from accomplishing that." Lord Ive finished yelling the explanation, and Leif nodded his thank you, still not ready to open his mouth.

For the next two hours, the dragons continued at the same altitude and same speed, but suddenly they dropped, and Leif accidentally opened his mouth and retched. From here, they could see the Sea, and finally dragons slowed down even more, until finally gliding to a rest on a hilltop, about a hundred yards from a city.

The large city was about the size of Keldon, and for a minute, Leif felt a pang of homesickness. He was reminded of his mother, who he now dearly missed.

Lord Ive saw this and said, "I understand. When I left home for the first time, I had a bad case of homesickness myself. But don't worry, it'll subside soon."

Leif nodded again, and loosed his legs from the saddle. Then he jumped down and followed his mentor to another group of dragons, which were waiting near the beach. Leif looked at the beach and saw that there was a large harbor near the town, with lots of trade ships. He also saw all the war vessels, which were moored about two hundred yards from shore.

Leif walked over to the dragons and mounted a blue one, because Xurxo had boarded before him, and he trusted Xurxo. The dragon's blue color changed to a deep purple as Lord Ive clambered on after Leif, sitting between him and Xurxo.

Once mounted and tied on, the dragons took off over the sea. For some reason, now that the Sea was below him, Leif didn't find flying that bad, and the ride was definitely more peaceful, and had less rough spots. Xurxo seemed to be able read the air, because he would fly around invisible barriers, ensuring a smooth ride. Other Riders seemed to be less aware of these updrafts and areas of turbulence, often flying right through them. That had made the earlier ride quite uncomfortable.

"Lord Ive?" Leif asked his mentor.

"Yes?" he replied with an arched eyebrow.

"Why does our dragon hide armor not change colors, and why is it less heavy and hard, and why does dragon armor not do this?" Leif asked.

"Whoa! Lots of questions! Okay," Lord Ive said, considering where to start. "Dragons have no armor until they become adults, then they grow armor, which is at first gray, and then it slowly becomes white. After that it gets the ability to change colors. Our dragon hide armor comes from young dragons that haven't developed armor yet. Later, dragons can shift colors, and the really old and talented ones can even portray their emotions with the color of their armor. The reason that dragon hide armor is easier to get and cheaper is that babies and young dragons are easier to catch and kill than the fully grown, mature ones."

The dragon on which Leif and Lord Ive were riding vibrated with a deep growl.

Lord Ive laughed while Leif shuddered. He would hate to have a dragon as an enemy.

On a sudden impulse, Leif asked, "Did you ever know my father? He died in the invasion defense in the Year of the Dog."

Lord Ive's face suddenly clouded with emotion. His face seemed to age ten years in a few seconds, deep creases and old pain reclaiming lost territory upon it. A single tear slid down his cheek.

"I knew your father," he replied.

Leif leaned forward, eager to hear more, "Tell me about him," he begged.

Lord Ive opened his mouth to explain more fully when—suddenly, Captain Richard hollered, "We're under attack!"

In front of them, dragons were zooming at them, shooting forward at break-neck speed; the dragon's earlier growl hadn't been because of what Lord Ive had said, but because it had sensed enemies!

Chapter 4

The Golden Arrow had six dragons under their control, but about twelve were flying at them, flames shooting from the mouths of closer ones.

"Get out of here! I'll buy ya'll some time!!!" Leif heard Xurxo scream, as Xurxo maneuvered his dragon away from an oncoming enemy one.

Sir Richard repeated Xurxo's orders in his louder and more commanding voice.

The Golden Arrow Dragons slowly retreated, until they turned and fled amongst the enemy flames.

Xurxo, Leif, and Lord Ive stayed behind. Lord Ive yelled to Leif, "Get out our quivers and our bows!" His earlier pain was forgotten—now only survival mattered. Leif hastened to obey; searching the packed equipment behind him, while Xurxo expertly guided their dragon out of the paths of the enemy fire and their deadly tails. When he saw an opening, he took it, and within minutes, two enemy dragons had fled, one bleeding after having its armor cracked by Xurxo's dragon's tail, and the other one having its master burn to death on its back. Dragons continued shooting at Xurxo's dragon, flames gushing from their mouths, their spiked tails swinging in great arcs, and their masters attempting to slice through the wings with their own swords.

It was chaos. Dragons spun and whirled around each other, roaring at their enemies, yet unsure of who was who. Two beasts collided, the resounding clash causing Xurxo's dragon's head to whip around in agony as he watched the heads explode and the cries echo loudly.

Finally Leif spotted the pack with the archery equipment, but it was too far away.

Leif cursed under his breath and removed his legs from the saddle. He held onto a pack, and leaned forward, reaching for his bow. He grabbed the bow and his quiver. Then he pulled them towards himself and . . .

Xurxo swerved to avoid a fresh gush of flames that were directed at him, and Leif slipped. Xurxo swerved again, and Leif toppled over the edge. Leif screamed as he plummeted toward the Sea and toward certain death.

Lord Ive glanced backward for Leif and emitted a cry of agony. "LEIF!" He roared, and Xurxo looked behind him, letting loose a long string of curses.

Suddenly, a volley of arrows cut through the sky, and pierced the wings of Xurxo's dragon.

The dragon lurched, trying its hardest to stay in the air.

Another volley of arrows followed the first, and the dragon plummeted towards the Sea below. The enemy dragons pursued Xurxo's dragon, diving after them.

The dragons caught up with the injured dragon, which was trying to stay airborne.

The enemy Riders pulled out their two-handed swords and cut their restraining belts. Then they attempted to board the other beast, while Lord Ive punched and kicked and did anything he could.

Xurxo dropped the reins, unsheathed his sword, and cut his seat belt. Then he started hacking at any Rider who came too close.

Leif continued to fall, screaming in petrified fear.

Suddenly a dragon dove down towards him, and grabbed his back by his claws. The dragon slowed his dive by spreading his wings, and he did this just in time, because Leif was wrenched to a dead stop about a yard from the water.

The dragon holding Leif hovered above the water for a second, and then it flapped its wings and began to rise. As it did so, it flung Leif into the air, and dove beneath him.

Leif landed on the dragon's back and was grabbed by a set of strong hands.

Leif looked up and stared into the eyes of his leader: Captain Richard.

"Get on back. What happened to Xurxo and Lord Ive?" Sir Richard asked.

Leif clambered onto the last seat, and strapped his legs to the saddle. Then he secured himself by pulling a belt over his legs. As he did this, he realized that he was still holding his bow and his quiver. Most of his arrows had fallen out of the quiver, but he put on the quiver. Afterwards he set an arrow onto his bowstring, just because it made him feel better.

Still gasping for breath, Leif remembered Captain Richard's question.

"I fell off while the fight was going on, but it didn't look too good. Where are the others?" Leif asked, speaking the last part in a whisper, his heart heavy as he realized what may have happened.

Captain Richard's face became a mask of steel, but he didn't say anything.

"We scattered after the attack; more enemies came from the back, and we fought. They retreated now, but we are separated and lost," a voice said from in front of Richard.

Leif's eyebrows drew together in puzzlement and he bent to the side to see past Sir Richard's bulk.

There sat the other apprentice. The young boy's hair was slightly singed, and he was bleeding from his cheek. He had taken off his helmet, which had a major dent in it. The young man's sword, as well as Sir Richard's, still dripped with fresh blood, and Leif shuddered as he imagined what his fellow apprentice must have witnessed. Leif also noticed that the dragon's armor had some burned black spots on it, and Leif understood. It seemed that fire left marks on a dragon's armor, but didn't harm it other than this black scorch mark.

Leif took a deep breath, forcing himself to be come as his mind flooded with images of what could be happening to his master. Leif's sight grew blurry and he wiped away the tears, cursing himself for his childness.

"Proceed to checkpoint!" Richard barked at their Rider, who was wearing thick leather armor and also had a bloody sword at his side. The Rider nodded, and pulled at the dragon's harness. Then he produced a whip from his side and whipped the dragon around the neck.

The dragon roared, emitting a gush of flames, and rose rapidly.

Minutes later they were in the clouds and speeding towards a goal that Leif couldn't see, for it was dark out, and the moon wasn't full yet. Leif had hardened both his heart and his mind, permitting no thoughts of Lord Ive to enter. *He is fine*, he repeatedly told himself.

Exactly an hour later, the group landed on a hilltop about a hundred yards from a large circular castle. The group jumped off the dragon, and the Rider led the beast towards a giant stone building a couple yards away from the castle.

The group waited and minutes later another dragon landed, this one bearing Hildebrand and Maccabee. Then another one landed with Deacon and Theron, and one with Skinner, Egon, and Gary. Finally two landed together, the first one landing in a flaming red color, which turned to a mad blotchy purple. Alicia jumped off this one, and the second one held Ragnhild, who hastily jumped from the massive beast, and ran to a tree. There he vomited several times.

The congregated members of the Golden Arrow waited all night for Xurxo and Lord Ive, but they never came.

———⟫———

As the sun peeked over the horizon, Leif left his spot at the window.

The Golden Arrow was now lodged comfortably in the circular castle that Leif had seen the night they had arrived. Lord Ive and Xurxo still hadn't arrived, and the whole group, except for Skinner, had stayed together in the same room, keeping lookout for the two men.

Leif had begged Captain Richard to be allowed to get a dragon and search the sky, but Sir Richard had forbidden it.

"First and foremost, it's too dangerous, and if they're not captured they'll come. I'm sure the two are capable of taking care of themselves." Richard had said soothingly, although he didn't seem too sure of it.

Now Captain Richard was ordering them to bed.

"We're here to complete a mission, and we're not going to leave without having first finished it. I miss the two men as much as any of us, but as faithful servants of the King and of Siddian, we must complete our mission and stop the Morrs. If we stop the Morrs, we are also helping Lord Ive and Xurxo, who are probably now their captives."

Leif winced at the probable truth, yet Sir Richard, his face a mask of steel, continued. "Let's get some sleep, finish our mission as fast as possible, and then we can rescue our two comrades. Understood?" Sir Richard's voice had lost its commanding, bold tone, and had been replaced by a tired and worried tone. The man definitely needed sleep, and Leif couldn't help but be amazed at the man's steadiness under such stress. Even in times like these, he was following orders without question.

Leif couldn't sleep, and since they left at noon, he busied himself by getting arrows from the Lord of the Castle, and catching up on what was going on here.

Leif was able to get nearly a thousand dragon arrows, and five new bowstrings. Leif was glad not to have lost his beautiful bow, yet this happiness seemed incomparable to the utter sadness of the loss of Lord Ive.

I'm a soldier! Leif thought to himself as he walked down the stone hallway to the Lord of the Castle's room. *I must be strong in times like* these. *That is what Lord Ive would have done. That is what my father would have done.*

Finally Leif reached the Lord's room, the purple coat of arms on the door revealing to whom it belonged. Leif breathed in deeply and then exhaled, breathing out fear, worry, and sadness. Then he knocked on the oak door.

A servant opened the door, ushering Leif in. The servant disappeared behind a second door, reappearing moments later to allow Leif into this room. Leif entered slowly, remembering to bow as he came before the nobleman.

Leif was greeted with a deep, booming laugh. "Come here m'boy!" the Lord said, Leif straightening to see a large, cheery man beckoning Leif to take a seat in front of his messy desk.

"Paperwork," the man sighed. "Never was good at it, was I?" he said.

Leif, confused as whether to give an answer or not decided to ignore the question. "Sir," he began. "I just want to talk a moment."

The Lord nodded, and Leif proceeded. "I would like to know what's happening here. I understand that the Morrs have attacked the Waylin Islands, but," Leif searched for the right word, "Could you clarify this?"

The nobleman nodded, the cheeriness seeming to subside as he was pulled back to the harsh reality of what would happen to his fiefdom. "The Morrs," he began, spitting the word as if tasted bad in his mouth, "Took over Rhona a couple days ago, and now they're attacking us here, on the island of Arran. Once upon a time, Waylon was governed from this island. To make sure that it couldn't be conquered all in one sweep, three different fortresses were set up to keep the balance of power even. These are located in a direct triangle with almost perfectly straight routes between these important castles. The first one of these was conquered in a single night, about two days ago. This one was located by the sea, acting as a naval port, and it was attacked and conquered by the Morr navy. The other one, Drayton, was recently defeated, for this one served more as an Air Force headquarters, and so the Morrs won that battle using their fleet of dragons. Drayton is now their headquarters here in the Waylin Islands. So, the Morrs control the sea and the air, and the only thing stopping them from controlling the ground is the last point of the triangle. Kingstan was always favored as a military post for foot soldiers, not Riders and sailors, which is why we will most likely be leaving to reinforce it before the Morrs lay siege to this great castle."

Leif nodded as he realized the true desperation of the situation.

"Kingstan is the Waylin Island's last stand," the Lord ended.

Leif sighed; the Morrs' had control of the air and water, and needed to conquer a single castle to receive control of the land. If Kingstan was conquered, then all hope would be lost. They *had* to keep this famous stronghold safe and secure, or at least use its advantages to put a large dent into the Morr forces.

Once noon arrived Sir Richard's apprentice toured the castle, waking up all of the warriors. When he got to Leif's room he found the young man sitting on his bed, bow in his hands.

"Um—you need to wake up." The apprentice said.

Leif smiled. "I am," he said, and before the apprentice could leave, he added, "What's your name? You never told me."

"Cuthbert?" the boy replied promptly. "What's yours'?"

"Leif."

Cuthbert nodded and said, "Sir Richard wants you in the Main Hall, packed and ready in an hour."

Leif nodded with another smile at Cuthbert. "Sure," he said, and started packing.

Leif entered the hall exactly an hour later and saw that Captain Richard and Cuthbert were already there.

The Main Hall had a massive arched ceiling and a long rectangular table in the middle. Raised a little on the other end were a set of chairs and another table.

Richard was arguing with Theron about where to go, and Cuthbert was sitting on one of the packs.

Leif walked over to Cuthbert and sat down next to him.

Cuthbert acknowledged his presence with a slight nod and said, "Hey, I feel really bad for you and for your mentor. If you need any help, just ask."

Leif nodded his thank you, and minutes later the two were talking as if they were best friends that hadn't seen each other in years.

The two talked happily for over half-an-hour, until all the Golden Arrow members had assembled. Richard stood to address them, "Okay. Some knights have ridden ahead with our luggage, and are taking it to Kingstan. This is our last stronghold on Arran. The Lord of this castle has painfully decided to evacuate, and burn everything of use for the enemy. Knights, squires, and men-at-arms are taking provisions from this castle to Kingstan and stocking it there. This way, we can overcome a siege if need be."

Richard paused, and let these words sink in before continuing.

"Our mission here men," Sir Richard said, pausing as Alicia cleared her throat loudly, "And Alicia, is to reinforce Kingstan long enough and hurt the Morrs hard enough to make conquering the Waylin Islands nearly impossible. I received word this morning that the King is hurriedly calling together our army to invade Morrigan. That way the Morrs can make a decision of priority: what is more important—their home, or conquering that of another?"

Captain Richard sat down after his speech. His voice had recovered some of its commanding tone, but it wasn't complete yet, the drain of losing some of his comrades still apparent in his posture and in the confidence of his voice.

Leif walked to Captain Richard and asked, "Captain? I have a question."

Sir Richard nodded and Leif pressed on. "You didn't mention anything involving rescuing Xurxo or Lord Ive, but I'm assuming we're going to at least try, right?"

Richard's strong face, which had moments ago seemed so sure and confident, now fell. "I sent ten messengers this morning with news to the king. The message I sent contains statistics and other vital information about waging a war that would bore you to death. In addition though, there is a little part in the letter I prepared asking for permission to rescue Lord Ive and Xurxo. Egon begged me all morning to make it his mission to rescue the two men."

Leif nodded and stood on his toes, trying to see Egon. He spotted him right away, and walked over.

Egon's usually happy and energetic face was clouded with worry and showed the signs of a sleepless night. He looked down at Leif and managed as much of a smile as he could muster.

"What's up?" he asked.

Leif looked up at the man, and suddenly he wasn't so sure he could ask exactly what he wanted to.

"Um—well. I know you miss Lord Ive as much as me, and that he is probably captured and in jail, but well—uh—I was wondering . . ." Leif broke off. He wasn't sure how to say what he wanted to say.

Egon looked at him expectantly, a small smile playing across his lips. Apparently, he thought that Leif being at a loss of words was amusing. At this notion, Leif thought, *so would Lord Ive. He would think it's funny that I have no clue what to say.*

This thought made Leif concentrate and say what he really wanted too. "DoyouthinkthatweshouldgoandsaveLordIveinsteadoffight?" tumbled out of Leif's mouth, all in one breath.

"Whoa! Hold it pal. Say that again, just a lot slower." Egon said, laughing.

"Do—you—think—that—we—should—go—and—save—Lord—Ive—instead—of—fight?" Leif said, forcing himself to take a breath between every word.

Egon looked at Leif. His face showed no expression. Leif had not expected this. He had expected Egon to either go crazy with anger at the fact that Leif would drop his duty, or to say, "Sure, why not! I'll go pack!"

"So, you want us to desert for Lord Ive?" Egon asked.

"Well—yeah." Leif stuttered, grimacing at the sound of his own suggestion's cowardice.

Egon shook his head. "Lord Ive would want us to fight. To complete our mission, and not neglect our duties."

This is what Leif had been afraid of. He didn't want Egon to pull Lord Ive into this, and make him feel guilty. He knew Lord Ive wouldn't approve of deserting, no matter what. Leif just wanted Lord Ive back. He wanted him there to guide him, because he was scared of what could happen without him. Leif wanted to rescue Lord Ive for his sake as much as his own. It just made him feel better.

Leif accepted Egon's answer anyways. "Yeah," he said. "Sorry. Maybe we can get him after the battle."

Again Egon shook his head. "I highly doubt that. After we fight here, we will have to fight back home, since Richard wants the king to invade Morrigan. That attack will require our help. The King will show some sympathy on Lord Ive's part, but not too much. He'll say something like, 'Lord Ive is one life, right now we're working to save hundreds'." Egon added the last part in a high mimicking voice.

Leif laughed and Egon smiled at him.

"You know what? I'm really starting to like you." Egon said, rubbing Leif's head.

The Golden Arrow, along with an escort of knights, thundered towards Kingstan. They were riding beautifully white unicorns. Leif was riding bareback; no saddle was as comfortable as unicorn fur, which was soft and seemingly fluffy. Riding the unicorn was better than any form of transportation Leif had ever known; they were comfortable, fast, and amazingly graceful, making the ride smooth and with no rough parts like riding on a dragon.

As the land flew past Leif, he saw the signs of previous battles. Great big, black spots littered the earth; places where battles had happened and the victors had burned the battlefield and its dead occupants. Farms stood unoccupied at the side of paths and in the distance Leif saw smoke pouring into the sky. The group, which had been quietly conversing hushed as they passed through a deserted village. Doors hung on their hinges; furniture lay broken in the streets; a torn doll lay trampled on a broken wagon wheel. Leif turned his head away and fought back a wave of nausea as they shot past a dead elderly man, his eyes still opened in perpetual fear.

Finally the group left the town, returning to the open countryside where the boundless freedom of the unicorns caused Leif's heart to soar. Leif pushed his unicorn forward, urging it to a smiling Egon.

"How is it?" Egon yelled over the sound of the rushing wind.

"Beautiful," Leif yelled back, grinning from ear to ear as he felt the sensation of freedom lift his spirit. He had not felt this way since the day he had won the tryouts: his fears and worries seemed to evaporate in the rushing wind, his sadness seemed trivial to the world's contentment, and Leif could do nothing but smile.

The group entered a large forested and rode through it for several hours, using the dirt paths. The unicorns kicked up large clouds of dirt and dust, and soon their fur was more brown than white. Leif marveled at the fact that the stallions never lost energy, going twice the pace of a horse and never pausing. It would take Philip two days to cross this much land.

Finally the group burst through the trees and saw Kingstan. The land around it had been cleared, leaving no trees or land for two hundred yards in each direction from the town walls. It seemed that the people of Kingstan didn't farm.

The whole town was on a small hill and the walls of the city were at the base. These walls were about six yards high and about a yard thick. Leif knew these would not present much of an obstacle to highly determined attackers, yet they kept the houses behind it safe.

As Leif neared he saw the town more closely, watching in fascination as he saw men and women bustling through the streets, preparing for the inevitable battle and siege that was to come. Squires ran through the streets carrying weapons and armor, while peasants were laboring outside the castle, on the field, digging trenches and setting stakes in the earth. A group of stone masons were hurriedly giving stones round shapes to launch from the catapults. A group of woodcutters was feeding the fletchers wood and shaping trees into stakes that would protect ranks of spearmen, archers, and other warriors. Knights wearing simple mail armor or leather jerkins walked among the people, overseeing their work. Leif was awed at the efficiency of the town as it prepared for this oncoming horror—there was no panic, no harsh discipline, and no confusion.

As Leif was examining the different jobs of the people, another group of riders were coming out to intercept the Golden Arrow and its escort. This group consisted of about twenty heavily armored knights, complete with lances, swords, poleaxes, and maces. These were warriors, prepared to beat back any small force of Morrs that could be around and looked ready to kill. Leif knew they were on his side, yet he feared them.

Leif slowed his unicorn, which obediently shifted to a walk and then stopped. Leif's attention switched from the coming knights to the castle itself.

The stronghold was a massive, triangular stronghold, and Leif knew it existed to be defended. At each corner sat a large circular tower with waiting guards and a trebuchet. Between the large circular towers, were smaller square towers, and connecting these to the big towers at the corner were twelve-yard high walls.

When Leif got closer he saw that a much shorter, six-yard wall, went from the large circular towers to the massive keep in the center, dividing the castle into thirds. The keep was also triangular and huge in size with its topmost point being well above any of the towers.

Finally the interceptors reached the Golden Arrow and slowed. The leader of the knights, who had a purple ribbon tied to his lance, urged his warhorse forward. Sir Richard called a greeting and his unicorn also stepped a couple paces from the group, meeting the opposite leader in the middle. Leif waited anxiously as they talked and smiled at Egon. The assassin returned the smile, urging his unicorn over to stand beside Leif as Richard broke away from the Captain of the knights. Then the group proceeded, riding towards Kingstan as Leif and Egon chatted happily. Suddenly, as the Golden Arrow rode through the gatehouse, they hushed: they had reached Waylon's last stand.

Chapter 5

The sharp trill of a bugle cut through the air and woke up Leif. As Leif yawned and stretched, he thought he could hear the steady drone of drums in the distance. Again the bugle sounded, this time three ascending notes.

Leif jumped out of bed, now fully awake. He threw on some clothes and grabbed his bow, which was leaning against his bed. He strung the black-wood bow and pulled open one of his drawers. There he pulled out his quiver, which he pulled on, and filled it with arrows. Then he grabbed a leather bag and filled it with twelve bundles of arrows (each bundle contained 24 arrows). Leif washed in a rush, dumping a pitcher of water over his head and hurriedly drying himself. Finally Leif raced down the stairs to the balcony to look outside at what was happening.

What Leif saw caused both his bag and jaw to drop. Thousands of warriors in crisp, clean blood red uniforms were steadily marching towards Kingstan. The drumming sound came from the scattered drummers who were setting the beat for the march.

Leif couldn't identify the warriors from a distance; he couldn't see their weapons, or even if they were really humans. The one thing that Leif did see was the small group of black soldiers on the very left. There were perhaps fifty to a hundred of these superior looking soldiers. Leif swallowed, a sudden fear creeping into his body as he watched the masses of scarlet-robed warriors come, thousands upon thousands marching towards the castle. The army flowed down the road like blood; their red uniforms an unnatural shade, their weapons glinting in the sunlight, their ranks seemingly infinite.

Another bugle sounded, this one consisting of a short blast followed by a very long one. Leif looked down toward the source, and saw an official looking man dressed in green robes holding the bugle. Knights hurried past, reacting to the newest order.

A second bugle called its reply, and more knights thundered past. Leif looked at the castle. It seemed to reflect silver because of the many knights hurrying about in their shining steel armor. The place was covered in them, but it still seemed a small number compared to the amount marching towards them.

Another bugle sounded from the town, and Leif craned his neck to see what was happening there. Squires were herding families into the safety of the castle, while knights were loading ballistae and preparing to pepper the oncoming troops with flying projectiles.

The short walls of the town were covered in archers who were standing shoulder to shoulder with a bin of arrows in front of them. Knights and more archers were hurrying out of the castle to the field that covered the ground between Kingstan and the marching Morrs. This would be where they would make their first stand, and slowly retreat towards the safety of the walls. It was the killing place.

As Leif was evaluating their chances he heard someone pounding up the stairs and turned. Cuthbert was standing there, dressed in his light gray dragon armor with his sword hanging at his side. "You're supposed to wake up and report to the Main Hall where Sir Richard is handing out orders." He relayed, panting from the exahausting climb in the heavy armor.

Leif smiled and replied, "Well, I'm awake and ready so . . . Lead the way I guess."

Cuthbert nodded and spun on his heel, already heading down the stairs.

Leif picked up his bag and followed the apprentice whose silver cape was fluttering behind him as he hurried down the stairs.

Leif and Cuthbert entered the crowded Main Hall where Duke Cyril was standing beside Sir Richard who was addressing the Golden Arrow and a large group of warriors.

"—their forces are well equipped, and scouts tell us they're all human except for a group of Dark Elves with them. These are clad in Cursed, Blackskin armor, and are elite archers. Beware, their Cursed Blackbows have a range of 250 yards, and the Dark Elves are deadly accurate within 200 yards. That means that they will most likely be picking off leaders and other key men at will. Our plan is very risky, but we must get this group of troublemakers out of the way. The Duke and I have agreed to launch a cavalry charge right at them. This plan is a very basic whose goal is to kill all of the elves, and then rally and kill some more. When this charge goes forward, a group of archers will stand in the open and pepper the enemy with arrows, thus blinding the foe, and making the elves have to decide between the easy kill and the more pressing but harder kill."

Richard paused in his speech and a large group of archers and knights exited the hall. While the Captain waited, Ragnhild raised his hand, and Sir Richard acknowledged him with a nod.

"I've been thinking," he began.

"That's a first!" Egon smirked.

Sir Richard glared at him, but Ragnhild didn't take notice and continued on.

"Why don't we stay outside of the castle, and pepper the enemy with small attacks while they lay siege on the castle?"

Richard considered this for a second then answered, "Well, that is a good plan, but we need to help from the inside, until a relief force arrives. Also, it is too risky launching attacks on enemy territory, then withdrawing and camping on enemy territory. Chances are that if we are successful in annoying them, they'll send patrols out to get us, which wouldn't be good."

Ragnhild nodded, and Egon chuckled quietly.

By now everyone that had to leave had already exited, so Sir Richard continued.

"After we launch this attack, we will be sending a large group of mounted knights at the Morrs from the back. Cuthbert, you will join in this attack. You guys will ride through the forest and hide in the trees on the right flank of the enemy. Then you will plow into the enemy from there and get as far as possible in order to pave a way for Egon and Theron."

Now Captain Richard looked at these two men, who were already fully equipped for battle.

"Your job is to burn the supplies and baggage of the army, and then get out of there as fast as possible and stay alive."

Everybody left the room except the remainder of the Golden Arrow and the Duke.

Richard resumed speaking, "Leif," he addressed the nervous apprentice. "You will fight with the archers, and so will Myrddin." Myrddin picked up his staff and Leif followed him, standing beside the door as Sir Richard finished giving orders.

"Skinner, Gary, Ragnhild, Maccabee, and Hildebrand, you will be fighting in a group. Your job is to finish off any of the Dark Elves that are left. If none are left or you have accomplished the job, than you try taking down as many Morrs as possible without getting killed. Deacon will be sending messages from the Duke and me to you to tell you what targets to take down. Thank you and good luck."

The Golden Arrow exited the room, a strange calm existing between these seasoned warriors. As Leif turned to leave Maccabee pulled up beside him, holding a giant dwarf-stone hammer. The head of the hammer was about half the size of Leif, and the handle weapon was about as long as Lord Ive. Leif had no doubt whatsoever that if this massive weapon could be handled properly; it would splinter shields and put dents in armor. Leif whistled as Maccabee hurried to talk to Hildebrand, and the muscled warrior turned, smiling at Leif.

"It's a beauty isn't it?" he asked, gently stroking the hammer's massive head. Leif nodded and jogged in pursuit of Myrddin towards the battlefield.

Leif and Myrddin headed toward the archers. Leif wondered what Myrddin was doing with the archers. He was a magician, not a bowman. Leif pushed the thought out of his head, *If this is what Captain Richard says, than who am I to question it?* Leif thought as he walked towards the assembled bowmen.

Behind Leif the Duke, Sir Richard, and Deacon hurried into the stone tower that would serve as headquarters during the field battle, while Skinner, Gary, Hildebrand, and Maccabee hurried to a set position and waited. Leif looked but couldn't find Theron and Egon. He shrugged, deciding this to be a good thing.

Leif walked to the Master Archer and so did Myrddin.

"Ahh, so here is our legendary magician and our famous bowman apprentice!" the man said.

Leif didn't know about the famous part, but he was the bowman apprentice, so he didn't object.

"You're to go over there." The Master Archer said, pointing to two large wooden shields that were implanted in the ground. The shields were planted at a slant, so when arrows were coming, the archer could disappear behind the shield, safe from both direct shots and incoming volleys.

Leif nodded and hurried to the shields. They were about fifty yards apart, and perhaps 20 yards before the actual group of archers who were standing behind a line of stakes.

A bugle sounded, and the Master Archer yelled, "FORWARD!"

The line of archers walked past their stakes, and marched up to where Leif and Myrddin were hiding behind their shields. The archers pulled their bows to full draw, and the Master Archer told them their target.

"FIRE!" The Master Archer orderd and a cloud of arrows sped at the enemy.

Leif didn't participate in the first three volleys; he was busy setting up his hiding place. There was a little bin in front of him, which he filled with arrows. He unwrapped the bundles and placed the arrows in there.

After four bundles were in the bin, and it was filled, Leif put his back against the shield and peeked around it.

The attack on the Dark Elves was going badly. The Dark Elves were mercifully not to far inside enemy lines, so the attacking cavalry didn't have to cut through too many of the enemy, but Morrs on the knights' flanks fought fiercely and the Dark Elves seemed equally skilled in sword fighting as in archery.

The Dark Elves that were not busy fighting were firing at will, gently launching arrows over their comrades into the struggling mass of Waylin knights.

Leif was torn back to his position as the Master Archer called out yet another target. Leif set an arrow onto the string, pulled back to a full draw, and let one fly. Leif was close enough to get at the Dark Elves, and this arrow took down one of them. A minute later, five more were dead because of Leif's skill.

The emotion of killing was not one that appealed to Leif, yet it didn't disgust him either. *They are killers,* he thought. *They killed my father and stole Lord Ive.* As Leif's arrow claimed yet another life Leif conjured up the image of the dead man in the village through which they had ridden. "Killers!" Leif snarled at the Dark Elves, shooting with renewed strength and vigor at the Elves.

Minutes later the knights had engaged nearly all of the Dark Elves, so now scanned the battleground for a new target. Finding nothing, Leif drew an arrow and joined in the volleys, glancing sideways to see that Myrddin was doing the same. Leif watched Myrddin, his mouth spreading in a sly grin as he saw why Sir Richard had placed him with the archers.

As the Archer Master called out their next target, Myrddin began muttering words to his staff. Suddenly the blue sphere at its end glowed red, and began to expand. As it grew larger, it turned orange, and when the Archer Master yelled to release the arrows, Myrddin yelled a word to his staff, and the orange sphere exploded from it. The orange sphere turned out to be a flying fireball, which killed up to four people, igniting the whole area. Myrddin's blue sphere was still there though, and hadn't flown off as Leif had thought.

The archers continued to fire volley after volley, Leif shooting two arrows for every one that the archers shot. Meanwhile, the cavalry continued to plow into the Dark Elves, line after line of the enemy falling as arrows darkened the sky again and again.

Finally the Master Archer called, "RETREAT TO STAKES!"

The archers slowly walked backwards, still firing their volleys, while Myrddin and Leif picked off several enemy warriors that were giving the attacking cavalry a hard time.

Five minutes later, the leader of the knights called a retreat and the cavalry turned, fleeing the battlefield. The Morrs on the sides pressed inward, filling the gaps and then surging forward after the fleeing knights. As Leif watched in anticipation, shouts and cries echoed from the Morr leaders, commanding their men to stop their reckless charge, and the men reluctantly complied. Leif shook his head, realizing with a sudden clarity that they were fighting a well disciplined, superior force.

Leif finally cleared his head of the demoralizing thought and turned to see the outcome of the attack. The charge had been of about two hundred men, and Leif saw that about three hundred of the enemy had died.

The attack had definitely taken its toll on the enemy archers. Only about fifteen Dark Elves were left, and there was a definite gap in the opposing forces. As Leif evaluated the charge, he didn't realize that the second attack had begun; the second wave of cavalry had exited the castle and rode through the forest to the flank of the enemy.

Myrddin screamed at Leif and Leif looked up. Three arrows were arcing through the sky at him. Leif dove behind his shield, but one grazed his dragon hide armor into which he had changed. The armor turned black and melted there where it had been hit. Leif looked at the hole with fearful curiosity.

Myrddin saw what had happened and cursed loudly. "The arrows must be dipped in dragon's poison! It melts the armor or skin of a dragon!" He shouted to Leif. Leif nodded; his face white with fear: the dragon hide armor was now useless.

Leif quickly peeked around his shield again and saw that the knights had surprised the enemy and that many were routing, causing chaos, which made the attack many times easier for the Waylins. The knights charged forward, their lances couched, leaning forward in their stirrups, and then, with a resounding crash, smashed into the enemy lines. Even from where Leif stood, he could see the shapes of men flying through the air, limbs being torn from bodies, lances snapping as their victims folding in half over their points. Then the line of knights turned, galloping from the killing ground. As the line of Morrs regrouped, finding order once more, the second wave of knights crashed home, the chaos occurring once more as the flanks sunk in blood. Finally Leif tore his eyes away from the killing, focusing on his own mission.

Leif nocked an arrow onto his string and fired. He pulled another arrow, set it, pulled the cord past his ear and released. A Dark Elf fell, and Leif loosed another arrow, before diving behind his shield to avoid the arrow speeding towards him.

This continued, until the remaining Dark Elves, now about eight, retreated to a safe range. From there they picked off the men assailing them from the side.

The Morrs had stopped their march, or else they would be torn in two and defeated. This was good, because that way the Waylins would have a longer time to take wear them down before retreating to the safety of Kingstan.

Leif continued shooting until his quiver was empty and his arrow bin too. Then he unwrapped a couple more bundles before setting to work again.

Myrddin had to rest every twenty minutes in order for him to have his energy restored and for his staff to cool down, or else his staff would erupt in flame.

The archers behind Myrddin and Leif continued firing volley after volley at the enemy, and this was taking its toll. The archers didn't have to rest to get more arrows, because a steady line of squires were filling the archers arrow bins anytime they got to close to emptying.

Finally the Morrs couldn't stand it anymore; a long blood-curling shriek cut through the air, and suddenly the sky darkened with hundreds of dragons. The dragons bore down upon the archers, and some turned and fled. Leif dove behind his shield, retching upon himself as he witnessed a dragon swoop down and rip a man's head from his shoulders.

Three staccato notes were blown, echoing from the castle walls, and the ballistae and trebuchets released their missiles. The small boulders flew through the sky, and about twenty dragons fell to the ground, crushing many soldiers. The Master Archer ordered the archers to shoot at the dragons, telling them to fire at will, so their shootings would not be predictable.

Myrddin stopped shooting fireballs, because shooting fire at a dragon was like trying to kill fish by drowning them. Myrddin's new weapon was a basically a giant spear, which zoomed through the sky, and killed whatever dragon it hit. This weapon though was much harder to create, and Myrddin had to rest after every two spears.

The dragons now dove for the ground, burning and killing many of the assembled infantry. Before the infantry could do any damage, the dragons rose again. Then they sped at the archers, burning them and their stakes. Several tried to kill them with their spiked tails, but most of these dragons flew into the stakes and died. After this assault, the dragons ascended again, and flew back to their base, but not after flying low over the attacking knights on the flank, and lowering their number as well.

Leif reemerged from behind his shield to see the dragons leave. He guessed that about a hundred were left. That means they had killed about fifty of the horrible beasts, he thought.

Leif looked behind him and was stunned. About half of the archers were dead. Now only about a hundred remained. It would be a bloody battle.

Cuthbert cut and hacked at any warrior that got too close. He was leading the flank assault, and his silver cape marked him as the Golden Arrow's knight apprentice.

A Morr ran at him, his broadsword swinging in his hand. The man was coming at his shield side, and Cuthbert spun his horse. Then he galloped at the warrior, and swung at him. The warrior parried, and during that one-second pause, Cuthbert lifted his sword over the warrior and cleanly beheaded him from behind.

Cuthbert yelled in victory and pressed on.

The Morrs were now avoiding the young warrior, who had struck down at least twenty of them, and were attacking him only in groups of three or more, which Cuthbert had to skillfully defeat.

Suddenly an arrow flew through the air and struck him in the side. Usually dragon armor would easily protect someone from this, but for some reason the arrow burned a hole through the armor, and a warm rush of blood greeted the arrowhead.

Cuthbert screamed, and in his rage trampled over two Morr warriors. He looked for the source of the arrow and found the person. It was one of those wicked Dark Elves.

The Dark Elf had long pointed ears that stuck to his head, and long wispy black hair. The Elf's face stretched into a crooked smile, which pulled on his leathery brown face, and revealed many dirty teeth. He wore a black robe with yellow trimming, and a sword was buckled to his back.

In his rage, Cuthbert charged at the Elf, trampling dozens of enemy warriors. Suddenly his horse fell; it had been stabbed from behind. Cuthbert toppled from the steed, but immediately jumped to his feet, hacking and cutting at any warrior in range.

Cuthbert was surrounded and outnumbered. Slowly he began receiving wounds, and his guard dropped, as did the countless soldiers that faced him. The wall of dead soldiers around him grew, and blood flowed freely, making it hard for Cuthbert to get secure footing. Suddenly a blow hit him in the back of the head, and Cuthbert collapsed.

The warrior who had issued the blow roared a long and ear-splitting war cry before lifting his sword to finish off the apprentice.

"Stop!" the Dark Elf hissed. "He is worth more alive than dead!" he said, his voice coming out hoarse and strained.

The Morr warrior glared at the Elf. "Shut up! He my kill," he said in an emotionless voice. The warrior lifted his sword once more, but he never brought it down, for an arrow had cut clean through his throat.

The warrior opened his mouth and blood spewed from it. Then the man's eyes rolled into the back of his head and he collapsed: the man was dead.

"I said he's mine." The Dark Elf repeated and glared at each warrior in turn before walking to the apprentice. The Elf picked up the boy and dragged him with him to the prison carriage.

There the Elf locked the apprentice up, and relieved the guard. He smiled; he was going to make sure this boy didn't escape; he had plans for him.

The Elf climbed upon the wagon in which the prisoners were kept and his eyes scanned the battlefield. Everything was going as planned.

Leif popped out the right side of the shield this time. He loosed three arrows in rapid succession before the first shaft came arcing through the sky at him. Leif jumped back into the shelter of the shield. He was almost enjoying himself.

Leif nocked another arrow, refilled his quiver, and jumped into clear vision, about a yard to the left of his shield. He loosed two arrows, and then dove behind his shield, and popped out on the right side, another arrow at the ready.

The three Dark Elves that were trying to get at Leif were getting very annoyed. All three had their own private shield bearers, so that Leif couldn't get at them, but Leif had his own shield too.

Also, the three had figured out how to take down Myrddin's fireballs. If they sent an arrow through them, they would drop where they were.

Right now Myrddin was developing a new weapon; every couple of minutes or so, he would send some type of weapon at the enemy. He had sent nets, which tangled the enemy, thus making them easy targets, arrows (he took one of Leif's bundles and sent it flying at the enemy, although it was only good enough to kill one maybe two men, making it a waste of arrows), and even stones, which he had sent at the enemy. Every few minutes though, Myrddin would simply issue a wake-up call by sending another fireball.

As the men fought, another bugle sounded, this one playing three descending notes. Four men hurried out from behind a small shield, and immediately charged toward the enemy. Leif immediately recognized them as Skinner, Maccabee, Gary, and Ragnhild.

After the group had begun fighting, another bugle sounded, this one coming from the castle and blowing one long note. The bugle from the battlefield headquarters answered with three short notes. Leif smiled as he popped out again, this time two yards to the left. He loosed to arrows thinking, *Wow, Deacon really spent some time organizing the communication. He also did a really good job.* Leif dove back into the safety of his shield once again. He was trying to help Skinner, Gary, Ragnhild, and Maccabee, who had already paved a nice way to the three Dark Elves.

The four were fighting in a triangle, with Skinner in the middle. Skinner would lunge at any of the warriors, making all of them have to be on their guard double as much as when they fought a single person. Skinner was also disarming many of the warriors by skillfully wrapping his whip around one of their weapons and then yanking hard. The weapon would fly through the air and one of the three would kill the man.

As Leif continued popping out and taking down more and more enemy soldiers, he saw that the sky had once more darkened with dragons.

The dragons had giant stones and boulders clenched between their claws. As the dragons sped towards the Waylins, many people fled in terror, while others tried valiantly, but in vain, to bring down the dragons.

As the great beasts neared, a bugle sounded and the ballistae and trebuchets released their missiles, which flew through the air. Leif looked away as the projectiles slammed into the horrible beasts, crushing their heads, cutting through their necks, and ripping off whole wings. The creatures shrieked in pain, spiraling towards the earth like comets, a streak of fire pouring from their snouts as they thudded into the ground, dead.

Finally the dragons grew near enough for the archers to fire. They shot into the air, and many dragons dropped, along with the stones. Unfortunately, the dragons were now above the Waylin forces, so when one dropped, it crushed several warriors. The shrieks of the dragons combined with the screams and wails of the dying Waylin warriors, suffocating beneath the large bodies of the dragons, and Leif put his hands over his ears to block out the sound.

Finally Leif had had enough. Screaming in fury, he popped out of his hiding spot and started rapidly shooting at the flying enemy. He knew where to aim: the best place was the eye, it would blind the dragon and drive him or her mad, but this target was too difficult and small, so Leif aimed instead for the giant, pounding wings. The problem with this was that a dragon needed many holes through his wings in order not to be able to use them, but it was easy to hit them, so Leif aimed for the wings, pouring arrow after arrow into these thin membranes.

As the dragons flew over the assembled archers and Leif, their goal became clear. The massive beasts dropped their stones upon the castle, although many were killed doing this for archers were posted upon the towers and the ballistae were reloading fast.

One of the giant circular towers lost half of its top, when five dragons assailed it with boulders. Two of the small towers fell apart, and the walls broke down in several areas.

Leif cursed. This was bad. Their final safe haven was being destroyed. Shaking his head in frustration, Leif turned and grabbed another handful of arrows, sticking them in the soft ground to reload faster. Then he continued shooting. His beautiful bow worked perfectly, bending easily and gracefully contracting once more, spitting multitudes of arrows at the beasts. Leif was able to successfully bring down a whole dragon, the poor creature's wings having been punctured by so many arrows that it could no longer fly. The monster wailed and shrieked in agony as it tried in vain to fly, plummeting towards the ground. Leif watched in stunned horror as its rider jumped from his saddle, hoping to possibly land somewhere soft, but the man dropped towards the archers, embedding himself on one of the stakes. Leif turned away and threw up.

Finally the dragons had finished their attack, flying over the castle only to turn back once more, flying to the sides to avoid the castle and the wing-stabbing archers.

As the evil group of beasts flew away, some of them swooped down and killed some of the knights on the flank. Leif cursed, worried for his friend, Cuthbert.

Suddenly an angry roar rose from the Morrs.

Leif risked a quick look and peeked his head around the edge of his wooden shield.

What Leif saw made him smile, big. Smoke was steadily rising into the air from somewhere in the middle of the Morr army. Egon and Theron must have done their jobs well. The supply wagons were burning now.

Leif was still looking and smiling, when he realized that no arrows were rushing at him. Leif looked at where the Dark Elves had been, and smiled even bigger. There, still in their triangular formation was Ragnhild, Hildebrand, Gary, and Skinner, all of them fighting hard.

Suddenly a large man ran out of the headquarters, a golden cape trailing behind him, adding beautifully to his blonde hair.

The man, Leif realized it was Deacon, raised a bugle to his lips and blue five long notes and ten short ones: the signal for retreat.

Everyone continued fighting. The knights on the flank, who had already completed their job, had already begun retreating and slowly disengaged the enemy, fleeing into the forest. From there they circled around and entered through the back of the castle. The Golden Arrow triangle had also slowly begun their retreat. Now they earnestly fought their way back, and the Morrs were happy to see them go.

Then a line of spearmen exited the castle and stopped about fifty yards ahead of Leif and Myrddin. The men got into battle stance and crouched low, their spears in front of them. This gave the archers time and space to retreat.

Now the archers began to retreat: slowly walking backwards toward Kingstan. Once they got to the short town walls, they entered and hurried up to the walls, offering the spearmen time to get back as well. Leif was among them, having attached the remaining bundles of arrows to his quiver. These he now unfastened, leaning them against the wall. Leif nocked an arrow and waited.

The Morrs had resumed their march now, and had come into hand-to-hand combat with the spearmen. The archers shot volleys over these groups and into the third and fourth lines of the enemy. Finally, at the sound of a long bugle call, the spearmen turned and fled, acting as if they were routing in terror.

The effect was great; the Morrs, overjoyed at having finally forced their opponents into the castle charged forward.

Another bugle sounded and the sky darkened with flying projectiles. The missiles slammed home, and the first line of attackers fell. The second line of Morr warriors pounded forward at the spearmen, who were still seventy yards from the castle. The Master Archer called out to aim, and then roared, "FIRE!"

Leif released his arrows along with the other archers, and the sun was blocked momentarily as the arrows arced downward at the enemy. The second line fell, and not a single person had yet come even close to the "routing" spearmen.

Leif watched in fascination as the spearmen yelled in feigned fear, Leif being able to make out wry smiles on their faces. The pursuing Morrs were cheering as they hunted down these men, yet as Leif released his next arrow, along with the nearly two hundred archers lining the wall, the

Morrs faltered. The arrows tore through the ranks of running Morrs, men falling like dominoes as the shafts tore through their bodies. The men behind them tripped over their fallen friends, the next ranks slipping in the puddles of blood. Finally the spearmen stopped, turning and planting their the butts of their spears in the ground. Then they kneeled. The Morrs roared with a savage desire for Waylin blood, charging at the spearmen. The first line of Morrs attempted to knock the long shafts of the spears away, hoping to get within the warriors' defenses and kill them, yet the thousands of warriors behind them surged forward, eager to receive glory as well, literally pushing their comrades onto the Waylin spears. As the army struggled forward the spearmen were pushed back, hundreds of Morrs being brutally shoved onto their weapons.

Leif watched this gruesome scene unfold before him, constantly pouring arrows into the mass of Morrs along with the castle archers. The spearmen continued retreating slowly, walking backwards from the carnage they had left behind. The Morr army continued surging forward, yet less enthusiastically as more and more men were shoved onto the spears. Those that did not fight held their shields in the air, if they were fortunate enough to have shields. Leif and the archers were frenziedly working to darken the sky, the hundreds of shafts casting the crimson battleground into shadow.

Finally the last bugle sounded and the spearmen turned and fled, some dropping their weapons as they sprinted towards the town. The Morrs cheered, surging forward into the heavy teeth of archery. The archers were now shooting point blank, no longer lifting their bows to arc their arrows over the front lines, rather shooting straight at these men. Men fell chaotically, the arrows ripping through their chests and blood shooting into the air like fountains as the men struggled forward. Leif's face was a mask of steel as he rained arrows into the lines of Morr infantry, aware of the lives he was taking, yet for each life he took he knew he was avenging his father. Each Morr that died was coin of debt repaid. Finally the Morrs turned and ran as the spearmen poured into the town through the gate.

Then the Morrs began the laborious task of setting camp; the siege had begun.

Chapter 6

Leif was woken up at midnight to relieve guard. He took over for three of the guards and smiled, apparently he was worth three guards!

Leif had barely slept the couple of hours in which he was allowed to sleep. The continuous pounding of the stones flying at the castle just never ended. The enemy catapults were always firing, while the Waylins made sure only to fire when an easy opportunity arose, because they only had a certain amount of stones.

Anytime a tower fell, or the wall broke, the stones were used as missiles against the Morrs.

When Leif got to his position (he was stationed on the wall of the castle), his jaw dropped. Torches were everywhere, illuminating the scene, showing the hundreds of scarlet robed Morrs working tirelessly to set up camp. The torchlight lighted up the area well enough for Leif to see that countless Morrs were carrying timber to build siege equipment and create temporary bases. Other men were building small barracks and towers for the guards and officers of the army, but that wasn't what made Leif's jaw drop in astonishment.

Leif had expected the torches eerie glow to reveal the many dead soldiers left on the battlefield, but it was not so. The glow revealed a huge black spot where the ground was dead and burned, and the not a remainder of a human was left.

Leif shook his head, and suddenly he spotted a dragon. The dragon was flying towards one of the Morr camps, and Leif opened his mouth to shout when—

"Relax son, the dragons are coming every hour or so with more stones to pelt against us. They're nothing to worry about." A voice said from behind him.

A guard had walked up behind him, and Leif immediately took in every detail of the man's face. Leif judged the man to be in his forties. His black hair was entwined with gray hair, and his face wore a relaxed smile. The man's goatee hung just above his gleaming plate body, and his large metal helmet sat firmly upon his head. The man was leaning against his spear, and said, "My name is Altor. I'm one of our guard captains, and am supposed to guard this area along with you. May I?" Altor asked motioning to the unoccupied spot

Leif nodded, "Sure." Altor smiled his relaxed smile again and took his spot next to him.

"So what happened?" Leif asked, nodding to the great black spot.

"The Morrs torched the whole area, and killed all their prisoners in front of us. It was really horrible. The Duke got so mad that he broke his sword on one of the pillars and ordered a cavalry attack. Your captain, that Richard guy, stopped him from sending the knights on the suicide mission. He said we'd need all the men we got when it comes to the final battle."

Leif nodded, and looked down. He didn't want Altor to see his face. Tears had sprung into the corners of his eyes, and Leif was fighting furiously to keep them there. *Lord Ive is dead. He's either executed or on his way to Morrigan,* Leif thought. He wasn't sure which one was better, for he had heard some truly wicked stories about what happened to people who were imprisoned in Morrigan.

"Has everyone from my Golden Arrow group come back safely?" Leif asked, hoping for Altor to tell him that everyone was fine.

"I think everyone got back, but I'm not positive. The only thing I know is that Sir Richard's apprentice was supposedly captured. I heard Richard telling the Duke how much he wanted to out there and fight, but was holding back." Altor replied looking at Leif for feedback to this news.

The tears that he had successfully confined to the corners of his eyes now broke loose and rolled down his face. Leif made no move to stop them. Everyone had been taken from him; first Lord Ive, now Cuthbert.

Leif looked at Altor and said, "Can you cover for me, I need some time."

Altor nodded, and without saying a word, Leif ran toward his captain's quarters.

Leif threw the ornately carved door open and burst into Captain Richard's quarters.

A plush purple bed sat in the far right corner, with four expertly carved willow bedposts. In the opposite corner a large oak wardrobe took up the space, and a pack sat before it, apparently Sir Richard had not found the time to unpack yet. In the front left corner was a rack that held the Captain's armor, and on this leaned a gleaming, perfectly polished sword. In the center lay a bear rug, and to complete the room was an oak desk in the corner closest to Leif.

Here sat a bewildered looking Captain Richard, whose face was sunken and deep with sadness. Leif frowned at this, but didn't have time to dwell upon the fact. Sir Richard had been holding a red and black quill in his hand, and the desk was covered in papers. He had obviously been writing some kind of official report.

Captain Richard dropped his pen in surprise, but hastily recovered, "Leif! What on Earth are you doing, crashing into rooms like this?!"

Leif mumbled a quick apology, but could not bear to keep quiet a moment more. "Is Egon alright?" He burst out.

Captain Richard raised a hand and calmed the panting boy.

"Okay, let me explain what you've missed," He said, and began to fill Leif in on all that had happened.

"Theron got back fine, and reported to me. He told me that once they had started the fire, that they were attacked on all sides. He also said that he saw the Dark Elves running away with the prison cart. Anyways, they fought bravely, and were able to get out of the tangle. Then they hurried back over here to report for their next mission. While Theron was high-tailing it over here, Egon seemed to have slipped away or something. A loose arrow could have struck him, or something else, we don't know. Theron didn't realize because of the huge chaos going on around them: cavalry attacks, burning carriages, crazed horses, and panicking warriors. When he got back, we saw that Egon wasn't with him, so Theron, Alicia, and I decided to go out and find him. Theron was to retrace the path; I was to hold attackers at bay, and Alicia to help him if he were injured. Theron found the path, but unfortunately, he wasn't anywhere to be seen, and no sign of a struggle or of death was seen, although a faint path was found that led into the woods. Because of this, and the fact that Egon would have surely cried out had he been hit, we are almost certain he escaped on his own in order to rescue his good friend, Lord Ive. I'm guessing he saw the Dark Elves escaping with the prisoners and so decided that his true duty was to save them and get rid of these vile creatures. For him it was the ideal situation to rescue his friend in an honorable way. I guess you could say he hit two birds with one stone."

Now Sir Richard paused, and the sorrow that Leif had noticed earlier seemed to deepen and become more accented.

"What happened then was that we retreated and the siege started, as you know. Theron and Egon did a marvelous job. They bought us at least a week's worth of time for their whole baggage is gone. Hundreds of Morrs are hunting right now, replenishing their food, while others are raiding nearby villages for blankets, water, food, and anything else necessary for a siege. Other Morrs are on their way to Drayton to get supplies, so we should be unharmed for at least a week."

Sir Richard smiled as he relayed this good news, yet this smile now disappeared. "As I said earlier, the Dark Elves had run away with the prison carriage during the battle. In frustration, the Morrs murdered all the remaining prisoners in front of our eyes, it was horrible."

Leif nodded, he had heard this from Altor. As he looked up, he saw that the Captain's eyes were slowly growing moist. For a second Leif was scared that the man might cry, but then the burly knight pulled himself together and continued.

"I couldn't spot Lord Ive, Cuthbert, or Egon among the killed men, but then again they were held out of distance, so we couldn't shoot the executioners. Anyways, I believe, and so does the rest of the Golden Arrow, that the prison cart included Cuthbert, and maybe Lord Ive, and that the Dark Elves are taking them with them to Ashtoreth to sell for a ransom. Dark Elves are like that, they'll double cross anyone in order not to risk their lives, or for money. What they are doing now is actually what they would consider honorable, fighting and then taking your winnings. So, what I think is that Cuthbert and possibly Lord Ive are under their captivity, and that the Dark Elves are being tailed by Egon."

Leif nodded, it was a lot of guesswork, but he decided that it sounded fairly accurate to what he would imagine of Egon.

"I need to help him." Leif said. He wanted to go out there and rescue his mentor, because he owed Lord Ive for all the kind works that he had shown him. Lord Ive had been like the father Leif never had, and losing your Dad twice is harder than your Dad losing you once, Leif thought.

Sir Richard shook his head. "I want to go out there and save Cuthbert. He is like a son to me. Never has he failed me, and right now I feel it is my duty to save him, but I am refraining, because I know my true duty lies in protecting this castle and its members."

Leif nodded, defeated.

Then he turned and left, his head hanging, thinking of all the horrible things that could be happening to his mentor and friends.

Chapter 7

Dim sunlight filtered through the iron bars of the carriage. Cuthbert stirred and awoke, yawning loudly.

His body was one great expanse of pain; he had a throbbing wound in his side and an excruciating headache. Cuthbert moaned as he moved into a more comfortable position, and was thrown to the side as the wagon on which he was lurched to the side.

Now was the first time that Cuthbert got an appropriate look at his surroundings. His carriage had a dank, musty smell to it, and Cuthbert saw that what he had been sleeping on was straw. On both sides were holes, which had vertical iron bars in them. Although it was probably midday, it was not bright within his portable cell, for the 12-inch by 12-inch windows let in almost no sunlight.

Cuthbert also saw that two other people were in the cart with him. The first man was wearing a torn and blackened dragon hide suit. Cuthbert guessed that the suit had once been red, and after he had painfully shifted his position for a better view he saw that it was clotted with blood. Although for the blood, the face looked strangely familiar, but Cuthbert could not place the thought, so he let it go. Besides, thinking hurt with his pounding headache so Cuthbert simply held his head and moaned.

The second man had had most of his clothes ripped from him, and only his white undergarments remained. Had Cuthbert not taken a closer look, he would have thought they were red, for this man was covered from head to foot in blood, and was mumbling and moaning loudly.

Cuthbert felt the man's forehead and yelped in surprise. His companion's head felt as if on fire!

Cuthbert's small outburst had attracted a face, for a small head popped up on the other side of the bars. The young man immediately knew who this cursed creature was. It was the Dark Elf who had tried to murder him back at Kingstan.

The Elf saw that all was fine and left again, but Cuthbert's small discovery made him wonder.

Where was he? Was he captive, and if yes, where was he going? Who were these strange men? Were they alive or dead?

These thoughts clouded the boy's mind, but he could not answer any of them, so he fell into a restless sleep, filled with nightmares of the future, and flashes of his unfortunate past.

Hushed voices awoke Cuthbert from his troubled sleep, and he sat up with a start. This caused him considerable pain, and he groaned loudly, clutching his throbbing side, and holding his head.

The bloody men on the other side of the cart acknowledged him with a nod, the second one moaning as he moved his head.

"Aren't you Cuthbert, the apprentice of Sir Richard?" The man with the blackened dragon hide suit asked.

Cuthbert's mouth fell open in surprise. "Uh—yes—how did you know—who are you?" He stuttered.

The man smiled. Apparently he wasn't in as bad as a shape as he looked, because he changed positions and pulled out something from within his suit without moaning.

The item he pulled out was a golden pendant, with an arrowhead at the end. The arrowhead had a bow and a quiver of arrows etched on it Cuthbert saw.

"I'm Lord Ive of the Golden Arrow. You might remember me from the brief meeting we had. The bloody heap next to me is our Rider, Xurxo. He was shot multiple times before he was captured."

Cuthbert nodded, it made sense.

"Will he live?" he ventured.

Lord Ive considered the question honestly. After a short time he answered, "I think that they know we're worth a lot of money, so they will probably keep him alive, if just on the brink of death."

Cuthbert raised his eyebrows in astonishment to how cruel these men sounded. Then he looked Lord Ive straight in the eye and said, "We have to escape."

Lord Ive looked at Cuthbert and answered, "Impossible, I have already tried." Then he pulled up his dragon hide suit, wincing as he did so and showed Cuthbert his back.

It was covered in loose, dead skin, and flayed to bits. Blood still ran freely from his wounds, layering over the dried blood. A feeble attempt to stop the flow had been made, but the rag was a deathly red. Cuthbert's hand shot to his mouth to contain the bile that shot towards his mouth.

"That's what happens if you so much as attempt to escape. Think of what they would do if you happened to succeed."

Egon slowly crept toward the small camp of soldiers, making sure to stay concealed behind the bushes that crowded around them.

Fifteen Morr soldiers were crowded in a clearing, laughing and drinking in front around a fire. Two sentries were posted, one was high in a tree with a bow, and the other was standing on a rock on the other side. Another man guarded their horses with a spear.

Egon smiled and drew his saber, circling farther around toward the horses, making sure to stay out of the archer's line of vision. The man in the tree was not really paying attention, searching the area lazily.

Egon gripped his saber tightly and picked up a rock. The rock was a smooth stone and easy to throw. Egon peeked over the bushes again and waited for the perfect opportunity.

It came five minutes later. The sentry with the spear turned to say something to his friends, who roared with laughter.

Now that the sentry wasn't looking, and the horse guard was busy crooning to one of the battle-horses, Egon popped up and hurled his stone over the clearing and into the bushes on the other side.

The stone flew in a perfect arc, attracting no attention, and plopped into the bushes on the other side. The rustling immediately caught the sentry's attention, and everyone stopped joking and turned to find the source of the sound.

Right at this moment, Egon hurdled the hibiscus bush behind which he had been hiding, and ran into the camp.

The sentry didn't hear Egon until he was about a yard away. Egon had remembered one of the assassin's main teachings, "Save the surprise as long as possible."

The sentry turned, but before he could react, Egon slammed his sword into the man's helmet, which dented and the man crumpled to the ground, issuing a small yelp.

The outburst caught everyone's attention, and Egon jumped the sentry's rock and pelted towards the horses. Suddenly the camp exploded into action, every man but one, who oddly held back, drawing his weapon and charging towards Egon.

An arrow whizzed by Egon's ear and he turned to fight the horse guard.

Egon parried the forward thrust, and spun a backhanded cut at the man's side. The man moved to parry, but Egon's saber was already over the man's head and crashing into the side of his helmet.

Just like before, the man fell to the ground. Egon was about to run forward when an arrow cut through the air and grazed his sword arm.

Egon roared with anger and cut the horses' line. Five horses started milling about, stampeding in random directions because of the commotion. The horse closest to Egon reared and fell—it seemed that the archer's accuracy wasn't good enough for chaos.

Egon looked around and jumped upon a tall golden-brown Palomino. The horse neighed and shook his head, but Egon didn't care.

He reached down and pulled a random saddle on the horse, not caring to check if it fit. He didn't tighten it, because the warriors had now collected their weapons, and the archer was climbing down for a better shot.

A man with a flail was coming at him, and Egon knew better than to fight a flail with a saber, so he dug his heels into the Palomino's side and slapped its rump.

The majestic horse reared once, and all Egon could do was hold on to the horse's mane and pray that they would safely hit the ground.

The stallion's hooves were already churning in the air, keeping the man with the flail at bay, and when he hit the ground, they were off in a shower dust, dirt, and small pebbles.

A final arrow hit the saddle next to Egon's leg, and the horse reared again, but this time Egon was prepared and held on tight.

Then the two were off, pelting through the forest at break-neck speed. Egon made sure they were going in the right direction, but he had no idea where the exact path lay which the Dark Elves were using.

After hightailing it for about two hours, he stopped and dismounted, sweeping in wide arcs to find the trail that the Dark Elves were moving along. The map that he had with him was outdated and some of the paths that Egon found were not shown upon it, so he put it away after a while.

Finally Egon came upon a small dirt road, covered in fresh tracks. The trail had definite ruts in them from the prison wagon, and the two horses that Egon knew they possessed had their own, less defined hoof-prints.

Egon saddled the Palomino properly this time, and saw that he had actually picked the right saddle. This saddle was a beautiful and expensive one, decorated with fancy designs, but also in top quality. Egon whistled at his good fortune, and suddenly noticed a strange pocket attached to the saddle. This pocket was made of different leather than the rest of the saddle, which had been fashioned mostly for comfort and to serve as a mount from which to easily fight. The material of this pouch was a dull white and much harder than the soft leather of the saddle, and Egon's eyebrows drew together as he saw it had been sewn shut. Intrigued by this strange pocket, Egon drew his saber and attempted to cut it from the saddle yet he only succeeded in scratching the white fabric. Egon shook his head, deciding he would have to attempt to break open this pocket and get its contents later, for the pocket definitely held something, as could be seen by the bulge in its surface.

Finally Egon shook his head to clear it of the distracting thoughts, instead mounting the stallion and starting his pursuit of the Dark Elves. For four hours Egon rode the horse, going at a steady trot, until he finally found a good camping spot. Egon dismounted and examined the tracks. He was probably about two hours away from the group—no fire tonight.

The camping spot Egon had chosen had a large oak, which covered a small alcove of stones, and was away from the path. Egon was pretty sure that the warriors would try and follow him, after all—he had taken their most valuable possession.

Palominos were rare, and this one was exceptionally beautiful. The horse would most likely belong to the commander of the siege at Kingstan, as could be told by the beautiful saddle and the stunning strength of the warhorse.

He also knew that he could sell this horse for a small fortune. A skilled auctioneer could fetch perhaps a two thousand gold pieces for this striking mount. Egon whistled, his horse back home was considered expensive, but next to this one it would be considered cheap.

Finally Egon fell asleep; listening to the Palomino's munching next to him, and dearly wished for food.

Chapter 8

"We have got to get back that letter. It shows everything—even the secret passages in and out of the castle. What'll you think will happen if the Morr General gets it? We'll be bloody dead!"

Duke Cyril paced back in forth in front of Sir Richard. The Duke was wearing a simple chain mail and a red cape. A laurel wreath sat on his head, showing that he was the Lord of Kingstan and the senior lord of Arran. Richard sat at his desk, shaking his head and repeating over and over, "no, no, no!"

The knight finally popped up and shouted, "He's a boy! I can't send him into this kind of danger! He might not even get out of the castle!"

Duke Cyril looked skeptically at his friend. "Yeah right—a Golden Arrow member not even getting out of a castle? Besides, have you seen the boy? When he is not faking to be alright, he is in his room sobbing or remember his master. Now he has a chance to leave honorably and get something done for us."

Sir Richard shook his head again. "Your source told you that this letter is on the General's horse, 'a large and beautiful stallion,'" Richard quoted from the spy's report. "And you expect a simple peasant to leave our besieged castle, make it through the enemy lines, travel through enemy territory, and then defeat a group of trained warriors and steal their most prized possession?"

Now the Duke sat down, cradling his head in his hands. "We have to get that letter though," he said, "and the apprentice is the only one I know that both wants to leave this castle and actually has a chance of success." The Duke looked at Richard hopefully, "We could give him a partner," he suggested.

Captain Richard snorted. "He is peasant born and set to becoming the bowman of the most prestigious military group in all of Siddian. In other words, I wager he works best alone."

The Duke nodded, putting his head in his hands once more in frustration.

Finally Sir Richard sighed. He had sworn allegiance to the king and thus to this man because the king had ordered his obedience to the Duke.

"Very well, I'll tell him—but mind you, if this boy is killed or fails, it is your fault and you will pay dearly." With that the Captain left the room, slamming the oak door behind him.

Leif walked up to Altor, who turned and looked at him. Seeing the dragon hide armor, he whistled and asked, "So what are you doing tonight superstar?"

Leif couldn't help smiling and said, "Captain Richard sent me on a mission—top secret."

Altor whistled and Leif couldn't help but laugh.

Finally the apprentice gave in. "I'm supposed to intercept a group of Morrs who are bringing in the enemy General's horse and some important information. I have to get rid of the information or else everyone is doomed."

Altor smiled at the apprentice. "Whatever you say, good luck and go save the world!"

Leif laughed and hurried down the steps, aware of Altor's eyes burning into his back. The old man shook his head. He had grown quite fond of the apprentice.

Leif walked towards the main gate and immediately was stopped by a guard.

The man had unruly brown hair, coming out from beneath his helmet in all directions. The man's stubby little beard was in desperate need of a trimming, and his pike was blunt and unused.

"What'd you think yer' doin' sonny?" he asked.

"Um—I was sent for a mission. Top secret and outside castle and town walls." Leif replied.

"Sure ye wer'. And who may ye be to be so bloody special as to have top secret missions?" the guard asked, a small smile creeping upon his face.

"Bowman apprentice Leif." He said, and now it was his turn to smile as the guard stumbled over an apology, smiling to reveal chipped and yellowed teeth.

The gate was immediately opened, and the same was done for him at the town gate. Once out of the town, he unclipped his silver cape and bundled it up. It would have been like a torch in this blackness.

Leif stuck the cape into a small hole in the ground and nocked an arrow onto his string. Then he silently moved forward.

There were six checkpoints situated around the castle. Each had two catapults, three ballistae, and one trebuchet. Each checkpoint had about a hundred warriors with the headquarters having double that number. Three patrols of five knights rode from checkpoint to checkpoint, making escape very difficult.

Leif ran, ducking, towards the giant black spot. There he hit the ground, waiting for the next patrol. He scooped up some of the ashes and quickly rubbed it on his dragon hide armor. It would help camouflage him as he moved across the burned and blackened area.

The patrol came and went, going at a steady trot and the second they were out of sight, Leif picked himself up and sprinted towards the forest, which was about a bowshot away from where he had been hiding.

Suddenly a shout cut through the air, coming from the side where the closest checkpoint was. Torches illuminated the camp, and Leif saw everything that was happening there because of that. Tents were strung around in a circle, with a wooden tower in the middle, and four torches blazed upon this tower where lookouts with crossbows were watching for escaping people.

It had been one of these men who had issued the outburst. His weapon was raised and pointed at Leif. Seconds later, an iron bolt thudded into the ground in front of him. Two more followed the first, and Leif was only able to stay untouched by diving randomly from one spot to the next.

As Leif hit the ground, he looked up and drew his bowstring to a full draw. Then he loosed the arrow, diving again to avoid the next bolt. A scream of pain erupted from the tower, and seconds later, two bolts instead of three arced through the air toward Leif.

Twenty seconds later all the crossbowmen were dead, but an alarm had been raised, and the original patrol was thundering towards Leif.

In the camp on the opposite side, a new set of men were climbing up the tower, while warriors got out of their tents, weapons in hand, and began saddling their horses.

Leif drew and nocked another arrow, crouched low, and unseated the first rider. He did the same to the next, and the initial charge faltered. The men withdrew, shields above their heads, and Leif sprinted towards the woods.

Bolts began raining down upon him, and it was only by luck that he escaped without a wound. He was about thirty yards from the woods when the second charge came. The three knights were going at a full gallop with their visors down, shields raised and lances couched.

The arrows stopped falling around Leif, which was a temporary relief, but just then the knights came bearing down upon him.

Leif had no time to think, and the whole reaction was by instinct. Leif, who had drawn and nocked another arrow, dove out of the way of the horses' hooves and loosed the arrow.

The knight gave a short cry and fell from the horse, his foot getting caught in the stirrups. The horse stopped because of the weight of his dead master, and the other knights thundered past.

The crossbowmen in the camp didn't shoot for fear of hitting the horse, but Leif didn't care. He ran toward the horse, with his dagger drawn, cut the stirrup in half in order to release the dead man, and jumped onto the horse. Before anyone could react, Leif and his newly acquired stallion shot into the woods.

Leif had successfully escaped.

Chapter 9

Egon dug his heels into the Palomino's sides once more, and the horse gave another burst of speed, galloping towards the Dark Elves and their prisoners.

Egon had started early and wanted to close the gap between himself and the Dark Elves and widen the one between him and the Morr warriors. He knew that they were probably following him, and he was right.

About a mile off, the Morrs had fanned out and were trotting towards where they thought their quarry had gone. The men spanned across about 200 yards, each man barely seeing the ones right and left of him.

The Colonel was going from one end to the next, examining different "tracks" that the men thought may have been made by the beautiful Palomino.

An hour later, the Colonel, who was very angry now, trotted towards one of his men who thought they had found the track. It was on an old road and there were two sets. One was clearly new and one was old, probably from the night before.

"Do you think that might be the one?" the Colonel questioned his man, speaking in the accented dialect of the Morr nobility.

"Positive", the man answered, "These tracks be deep and new," the man continued, pointing to the fresh ones, "while these 'ere are probably from yesterday. I would bet with ya' that the blasted horse thief probably camped in the area 'ere." The man said pointing towards an oak that overshadowed a little alcove where a small stream trickled by.

The Colonel nodded and dismounted, handing his reins to the guard. He walked over to the area and looked behind the tree. A horse had definitely been there. The grass was closely cropped, and a pile of horse manure had been unsuccessfully concealed.

The Colonel nodded. "We have the man," he confirmed. Then he remounted and called in his troops. They were going to pursue this man, for no soldier would ever come before the Commander at Kingstan and tell him of such a mistake, for it would be death to do so.

Egon paused again, studying the track very carefully. The ruts and the hoof-prints were very new, and Egon thought he heard an occasional whip lash. He smiled; it wouldn't be long now.

Egon decided to slow his horse to a steady trot and every few seconds he paused to check for sounds of getting closer to the Elves.

It took him two more hours until he saw them for the first time. As Egon rounded a curve, he glimpsed the back of the cart and nodded. Then he stopped and matched their pace in order to stay at this distance. Tomorrow he would strike.

Leif thundered through the woods for three more hours, barely ducking branches and weaving through trees faster than he had ever done before. As he urged on his horse, relentlessly forcing it to continue the tough pace he was setting, he thought about his mission.

"A sympathetic Morr soldier has told us about a letter that could lead to the fall of Kingstan. This letter is from a leading Morr officer to the General of the troops besieging Kingstan. According to our spy, this letter contains all the maps to the castle of Kingstan. Not only do these maps show every last room safe place in the castle, they also contain its secret passages, and different records telling of the walls' weaknesses. This letter should be found with the General's horse, a large and beautiful stallion, and we expect it to be possibly in the saddlebags of this horse or possibly attached to the saddle itself. The problem however is that the horse is being escorted to Kingstan by a troop of armed soldiers, whose only job it is to bring this horse and its letter to the General. The letter is your priority, but you have my permission to try and rescue Lord Ive and/or Cuthbert if you are to see or hear of them along the way. Don't get your hopes up though, for we don't even know if they are alive. Your deadline is one month from today. If the mission is not completed by then, return to Kingstan immediately to await further orders. Good Luck."

That had been Sir Richard's mission briefing. Leif had almost hugged his captain after finding out that he had been given an opportunity to rescue his master. And Cuthbert! Leif had simply said, "Yes sir," but his heart had raced and his happy thoughts had already spun out of control, imaging the heroic rescue and the praise from Lord Ive. Leif's heart still beat at an incredible pace, but that was probably more of an aftereffect from his earlier near-death experience.

Night came on, yet he didn't stop nor slow. He continued on, galloping, until he reached a small road that had been highlighted on his map. This he followed for several hours until he stopped to rest for a little, praising his steed. The stallion had white foam dripping from its mouth, and its sides heaved in exhaustion. Leif felt sorry for it, even saying this out loud, but he knew it was necessary and promised to repay the horse with bountiful amounts of food if he ever got the chance.

After continuing for another two hours, now in a steady trot, Leif found a camping spot to his liking. It was a small clearing with a large oak tree that gave off a nice shadow, thrown before it from the glittery moon above. Next to it a stream flowed, and here Leif drank his fill.

As Leif prepared to sleep, a sudden pang of homesickness hit him. He imagined his Mom, receiving the news that her only son had been sent off to war. She would be devastated! The thought was almost too much to bear, and Leif began silently sobbing, remembering his mother and his comfortable straw bed in their hovel. He remembered the nighttime adventures which he had shared with his mother under the shadow of Keldon, with a blanket of stars as his only barrier to the dreams beyond. He remembered dreaming of becoming a knight, a great warrior that would go to battles like these and leave a hero. And as he remembered this, he thought of his deceased father, stolen from him and his mother by the greedy nobles who wanted only more, more, more. And suddenly the homesickness left, replaced by a fierce desire to see his mother again, to save Lord Ive, and most of all, to punish those who had wronged him and all of those he loved.

Egon woke up extra early—he had been trained to be able to wake up whenever he wanted, at what time, no matter how tired. The sun was slowly creeping over the horizon, and thin dew covered the ground. Egon saddled the Palomino and led it through the trees, always keeping an eye on the road. After about half an hour worth of slowly picking his way through the forest, he got to where the Elves were camped.

The elves were sleeping in the tent, the prisoners in their cart, and one Elf held watch on top of the cart. He was sitting cross-legged with his bow held over his legs and strung. Egon smiled, this was what he wanted.

The Colonel roused his men, while the last watchman saddled the horses and handed out a quick breakfast of *cram*, grains that had been cemented together with honey and offered a quick and fulfilling breakfast. Each man mounted their horse and ate the rest of their food, while the Colonel and the horse guard examined the tracks and planned their journey.

Minutes later, the pack of Morr warriors were galloping down the road in pursuit of Egon the horse thief.

The Elf was surprisingly alert considering that this was the end of his watch. Egon brushed aside this worry and mounted the Palomino who didn't make a sound.

The second that the Dark Elf turned and examined the woods on the other side, Egon stormed into the clearing, the Palomino horse charging at the cart on which the Dark Elf sat.

Egon's heels dug into the stallion's sides, the warhorse charging forward at an impressive speed. The wary Elf turned immediately, an arrow already set on his bowstring, and loosed his first shaft at Egon. Egon expected the early shot and swerved, the arrow instead grazing the rump of his horse. The Palomino reared, and Egon nearly dropped his saber as he clutched the horse's mane.

As the horse's legs hit the ground once more, the Elf screamed something in a low guttural voice, and Egon spat, the Elf should have been dead by now. Ignoring this, he roared his battle cry and the dug his spurs in again, the horse moving forward at the Elf who stood upon the prison cart.

This time the Elf was prepared. The creature drew back past his ear, sighted slowly and properly, and finally loosed. The arrow flew true, shooting at its target in a straight line, but Egon had also anticipated this shot and swerved again, but the arrow buried itself deep in the horse's shoulder. Egon cursed, a sudden fear gripping him. He had expected the Elf to hurry his shots and panic, rather than be calm and precise.

Egon urged the injured horse forward once more, the injured stallion lurching into a broken gallop to finishing the remaining yards, but the Elf smiled as he aimed a final time, the point blank range permitting a perfect shot. Yet by now the horse had learned its lesson, and before the final arrow could finish what the first had started, the enraged Palomino reared, its teeth bared and hooves churning, throwing Egon high into the air. Egon sailed backwards several yards, landing in a heap on the ground.

The final arrow sped over the horse's saddle, losing itself in the woods. The angry warhorse charged at the prison cart, ignoring the fiery pain within its shoulder and the bleeding gash on its rump.

At this moment, the other Dark Elves scrambled out of the tent, wearing undergarments, but nonetheless armed with bows and a quiver. They quickly nocked an arrow, but not quickly enough.

Egon, who was now one aching mass of bruises, picked himself up with a grunt and cut down the first Elf, and that lucky Elf received his comrades' arrows in the back. Egon now advanced upon the other two Elves, who dove back into the tent.

Egon roared in agony and frustration and rushed into the tent, cutting and hacking at anything and at anyone. In seconds the other two Elves had exited the tent, and so had a third who it seemed had been putting on his armor.

In the background, Egon heard a scream and the prison cart crash. More screams came, and suddenly battle cries filled the air. Ten armed Morr warriors charged into the clearing, and Egon had barely enough time to dive out of the way. Once he got up, an arrow pierced his shoulder and an excruciating pain swept through his body. Seconds later, another arrow dug itself into the assassin's leg, and more pain rocked through his body, but worse than the physical pain was the fact that he knew he had let down his friends; he had failed them, and that knowledge was worse than anything else.

Once Egon had fallen, chaos followed in the clearing, and two Morr warriors were hit with arrows while one of the Elves was jumped from behind and taken prisoner. In the midst of this confusion, Leif thundered into the clearing and jumped off his horse.

Moving as silently as he could, the young man ran toward the prison cart, while fights broke out around him. Some were physical and bloody fights while others were simply verbal fights. One of the Morr warriors charged Leif, but he was unseated in a matter of seconds.

Finally Leif got to the wagon, hiding behind it as he searched the clearing for the horse that supposedly contained the precious plans. Leif couldn't find it and spat, looking instead at the cart. The carriage had been tipped over in the fight, the small window and some of the surrounding wood breaking in the fall. Two of the people inside were unconscious or dead, and lay in a bloody mess, while another struggled to get out.

Leif ducked as an arrow whizzed over his head, and he pulled the young man out. The man looked into Leif's eyes, and together the two gasped. It was Cuthbert! Cuthbert hurried to explain, "That one is Xurxo and that is your master, Lord Ive. Both are unconscious and Xurxo may be dead." The words came out in a rush while Cuthbert jerked his fingers at the men.

Leif forgot the letter, his whole energy now devoted to pulling out his mentor, but his foot was trapped under a wooden beam, and his master just groaned and complained. At that moment, three arrows thudded into the wood next to Leif and Cuthbert, and shouts echoed through the clearing; the fights had broken up and the warriors were charging the duo. Leif yelled something to Cuthbert that sounded like, "Go! Go! I'll stay!" but Cuthbert pulled his friend from the wrecked cart and the two sprinted into the woods.

The warriors decided not to pursue them, and so Leif stole back into the clearing to get to his master, but arrows cut through the air toward him, and a line of warriors charged at him. Leif turned quickly, but managed to jump onto a horse quickly as he left.

The knights chased him a little after this, but they still had to settle their own fights in the clearing, and so gave up.

Leif pulled Cuthbert onto his horse and together they charged away from the fights, the wreckage, and Leif's master. Several hours later, they were resting under the oak tree, drinking from the stream, and exchanging stories.

Chapter 10

The Morrs settled everything with the Elves after two hours of intense debating. The Morrs believed that the Elves were transporting these prisoners to the headquarters in Rhona. The Morrs told their story; they were bringing the horse of the general along with an important message to Kingstan, but it was stolen so they had to get it back.

Once everything had been decided the Morr warriors moved from the clearing, permitting the Dark Elves to use it as they repaired the cart, and decided to search the surrounding forest for the precious Palomino. The men fanned out, following tracks of blood from the horse's wounds, yet they didn't find the warhorse until three hours later, when one of the soldiers spotted it caught in a thorn bush. It took ten men, armed with ropes, to subdue the still raging horse and bring it to their camp. Here the horse guard cared for it, nursing its wounds and putting different poultices on them. The Colonel decided to keep the saddle on the horse, something the horse guard disagreed with, because the officer didn't trust the important message attached to it to fall into any other hands than the Commander's. And finally, once the sun had disappeared below the horizon and darkness ruled the earth, the camp quieted and slept.

The next morning the Colonel ordered his men up early, the soldiers finding their way to the path as the sunlight crept over the horizon. The Colonel used a roundabout way to find the trail, spending an extra half hour to avoid the uncanny Dark Elves, who, unbeknownst to the Morrs, had spies following their every move.

It was these spies that reported back to the Elvin camp. The Elvin leader knew that he had to get rid of the Morrs. If the group reported that they had come across some Elves with a prison cart than the Commander would surely send a group of men-at-arms or knights to hunt them down and retrieve their prisoners. But the Dark Elves were selfish. The leader decided he must kill the Morrs so that the prisoners and their ransoms remained his. He also wanted the precious warhorse, for it could be sold for a fortune in Ashtoreth, where war beasts were considered the most prized of all creatures.

The Elvin leader ordered four of the Elves to stay behind, rebuilding their prison cart and desperately keeping alive the Rider. They expected a large ransom for their prisoners, and he was on the brink of death. A dead prisoner was a worthless prisoner. The other Elves, including the leader decided to ride ahead to intercept and attack the Morrs.

The Elves chose a different road than the Morrs, traveling parallel to them on this path. After pushing their horses hard until past noon, they cut through the forest, tied their horses to a tree, and set up and ambush.

The Morrs approached at a walk, two soldiers thirty yards ahead of the group. The group itself contained eight men, including the colonel and the Commander's horse. Thirty yards behind this group another two soldiers rode, their eyes warily scanning the trees. In one of the trees, high up to provide a long range, sat one elf, an arrow on his bowstring. In the bushes below was the leader, his naked sword lying at his feet and an arrow at the ready as well. Twenty yards ahead of them was the final Elf, hiding behind a large oak.

The leader of the Elves raised his hand slowly, making sure to keep concealed behind his bush as he did so. The man let the first two men pass him; then counting their steps until the central group was exactly ten yards from him: point blank range. Finally he brought his hand down.

The first arrow sped from the tree, throwing the colonel from his horse as it ripped through his shoulder towards his heart. At the same time the leader loosed his shaft, the metal-tipped point ripping through one of the soldiers' throats, a spray of blood misting the air. The final arrow came from the foremost Elf, whose shaft ripped through the eye of one of the two front riders.

The soldiers reacted immediately, the first rider galloping straight down the path. The Elf in front jumped out from behind his tree and sent an arrow into the man's back. Meanwhile the other riders milled in confusion, one man charging his horse into the forest towards the source of the second arrow. The leader of the Elves was ready, his sword in hand. As the man's horse jumped the bushes the Elf sidestepped, bringing down his sword on the Morr's shield arm. The shield broke, and the man fell from his mount, scrambling to his feet. At the same time the Elf in the tree loosed his second arrow, killing yet another Morr soldier. One of the men-at-arms dismounted hurriedly, attempting to save the colonel whose mouth emitted a gush of blood. This man received an arrow in the back from the foremost Elf who now walked forward slowly, arrows pouring from his bow.

Meanwhile the leader of the Elves faced the Morr soldier. The man charged at the Elf, who lazily flicked away the downward cut from the soldier. Then the Elf spun, his sword slicing at the man's back, yet the mail armor protected the Morr, who instead fell forward. In a second the Dark Elf was on him, lifting his head and cutting his throat.

As the Morr man-at-arms died, the Elf in the tree released another arrow, letting it thud into the chest of one of the soldiers. The two Morrs that had been behind the main group turned, fleeing in the direction they had come, while the remaining men, now numbering only three, galloped behind them, leaving the scene of the killing. It was one of these men that received the arrows of the Elf in the tree and the foremost Elf in the back. Finally the Morrs disappeared behind a bend in the road.

The Elvin leader smiled, complimenting his fellow warriors in their deep, guttural language. The Elves nodded to their leader, acknowledging his well picked position and timing, and then proceeded to drag the bodies into the woods. If a group of Morrs saw them then they would be suspicious, something that never led to anything good.

Finally the Elves retrieved their horses and galloped in pursuit of the Morrs. As they did this they carefully watched the edges of the woods for signs of places where the Morrs may have taken their stallions into the woods to find a different path or set up an ambush of their own.

They didn't find such evidence, and so after about half-an-hour of intense riding they stopped, led their horses deep into the woods, where they tied them to a tree, and set up another ambush. This time the leader placed the two other Elves into the trees, both high up in a large oak. The leader then crouched deep in the woods behind a rock, watching for the glint of armor that would betray the Morrs' presence.

The Morrs didn't come until late in the evening, riding together in a large group, the Palomino in their center. All had their swords drawn and their helmets on, prepared for combat. The group came at a walk, the men's heads spinning around as they searched the woods. The Elvin leader raised his hand once more.

The leader waited until the group was twenty yards from the location of the ambush. Then he dropped his hand.

The three arrows sped towards the group at the same time, one smacking into the foremost rider, throwing him backwards into the group.

Another arrow ripped through one of the side men's necks, the man sliding from his horse in a shower of red. The final arrow cut through one of the soldier's chests, the man swaying in his saddle before he fell.

The Palomino bolted, ripping through the rope that restrained it and galloping down the path. The three remaining Morrs thundered after it, fleeing the disaster. The Elvin leader smiled, jumping onto his rock and loosing an arrow into one of the men's arms. The man fell from his horse, miraculously managing to get free from his stirrups. The two Elves in the tree shot another of the Morrs, their arrows tearing through the man's back and throwing him over his horse's head.

The Elvin leader spat a gob of brown spit from his mouth, running onto the path and decapitating the fallen rider. Then he lifted his bow, pulled back past his ear, and released. The arrow flew in a slight arc, yet it missed. The shaft dug itself into the horse's rump, the horse faltering as it was shot, yet the stallion did not stop, the remaining man's relentless spurs urging it onward and its fear pressing it to insanity. Then the last man disappeared around a turn, escaping from the Elves.

The two Elves climbed down from the tree, one running to fetch the horses, yet the Elvin leader shook his head. They wouldn't be able to catch this one. He would undoubtedly take to the woods and slowly make his way to Kingstan, and so there was no use in following him. The leader's head hung; they had failed. The Morr would go to the Commander and tell him of the Elves, and the General would send a troop of men to find and kill the Elves, so all they could do was find the horse and make haste.

The Elvin leader knew this and mounted his horse, the three Elves thundering down the road in pursuit of the Palomino. Half an hour later they saw where the Morr had entered the trees. One of the Elves quickly dismounted, following the path, but it only led to the injured horse, which had wounds on its rump and sides, where the rider had spurred it on so hard that he had drawn blood. At the horse's feet lay a mail coat, a sword, and a shield. The clever soldier had abandoned the things that would slow him down or make him noticeable and had decided to continue on foot towards Kingstan. He could be followed, but by the time they reached him he would undoubtedly be in Kingstan. The Elf sighed and killed the horse, laughing as its eyes rolled backwards and the blood sprayed him.

Then they were on the move once more, overtaking the tired Palomino, which was peacefully grazing on a patch of flowers, an hour later. They easily subdued it, tying the rope with which they did so to their horses, and turned, heading back to their camp. Behind them the sun touched the horizon, signaling the end of the day.

Chapter 11

Leif woke up at the crack of dawn, and he roused Cuthbert. The young man got up and stretched, while Leif strung his bow and nocked an arrow. He was going hunting.

Leif left to get food, while Cuthbert scouted the area on the Morr horse. The horse was a stout Marwari that weighed probably 900 pounds, had a shining black pelt, and pointy ears. Cuthbert liked the horse, although it couldn't go very fast.

After scouting quickly down the road, Cuthbert went back to their "camp" and made a fire. Half an hour later, Leif returned with two rabbits hanging from a branch. They cooked and them and drank their fill from the stream. Then they sat down and discussed their next move.

Cuthbert had already made up his mind while away on the Marwari and immediately launched into a debate.

"I think we should go back to the castle. It is our duty and the right thing to do."

Leif didn't even consider this option, shaking his head and saying, "No. It's pointless. Not only are our chances of getting into the castle slim, but two extra warriors won't tip the scale in Kingstan. Anyways, how do you expect to get back in? Let's assume we can pass the siege lines. We still won't be able to get into the castle without being shot by the defenders. Arrows reach farther than vision, and so does fear. They'll shoot us before we can show our faces."

Cuthbert sighed, admitting that Leif had a point, so Leif pressed his advantage. "The best we can do is get the Golden Arrow members and get out of here. Our best advantage is stealth and secrecy. I vote we follow the Dark Elves and rescue Xurxo, Lord Ive, and Egon. That way we have more men to decide what to do next. And besides, we need their help. There's no better team than a Rider, an Assassin that can steal a dragon for a Rider, two bowmen who can pick off men at will, and an expert swordsman who can defend the bowmen." Leif smiled at Cuthbert and Cuthbert laughed.

Leif also had another reason. His mission hadn't been fulfilled yet. Leif had spied on the Elvin camp the day before, and had seen that the Palomino had been stolen from the Morrs, the saddle and its precious letter still on its back. Leif also knew that if the Elves discovered the letter they would sell it to the Morrs for a large sum of money, effectively letting Leif fail in his mission and grant the Morrs what they needed.

Cuthbert considered for a moment, finally shrugging and saying, "Fine! We'll rescue our superiors, and then I vote we let them decide our next move. Once they're saved they can make the decision. If we fail however, I think we should return to the siege, and instead of joining the garrison in the castle, we should just make a nuisance of ourselves. We could launch little raids, breaking siege equipment, shooting groups of warriors who are foraging for food, and burning their tents." Cuthbert smiled; a glint of adventure in his eyes. Suddenly the glint disappeared as he thought of something. "Leif?" he asked. "How do you suppose we rescue the Golden Arrow men, considering they're being guarded by several armed and trained men?"

Leif shrugged, and Cuthbert laughed. "I guess we'll just make it up as we go along."

Leif dismounted and hurried towards the clearing, while Cuthbert stayed on the Marwari.

Leif hid behind a large elm and looked into the clearing. The prison cart was standing there and the prisoners were tied to it. One of the Elves was cooking something while another guarded the prisoners by holding a knife to Egon's throat.

A tent was pitched in one corner, and the Palomino stood next to it. The majestic horse had four ropes tied from its bridle: one to the prison cart, two to stakes in the ground, and one long one to a nearby tree. The horse's saddle sat a couple yards from the stallion, one of the Elves resting his head on the soft material. Suddenly a metallic blow sound and Leif flinched, looking at the prison cart. One of the Elves there was busy repairing the cart, hammering two strong boards over the broken wood. As he did this the Elf muttered silently, and Leif gasped as he realized the Elf was enchanting the wood. Rescuing his friends would be tougher than he had thought.

Leif spat and backed away into the shadow of the forest. Then he turned and ran to Cuthbert, reporting what he had seen.

Captain Richard scanned the area slowly, taking in all the details.

The small wall that had surrounded the town of Kingstan was in ruins, and a chain of men were bringing the stones up to the castle to use for the trebuchets and the catapults. Enemy catapults were launching stones at the castle every hour, and the only thing that kept the enemy at bay were the archers and the constant patrols. Above him, another group of dragons rose up and left, evacuating the women and children to the nearby island of Islay. The dragons could hold only about six people, because they were already weighted down with six more warriors who protected the small pack. The castle of Kingstan was packed with people, and rations were at half. Warriors were digging trenches in front of and behind the walls of the town. These would be used to fire from and later would be filled with pitch. Then fire arrows would be released into them and the first line of the enemy would be burned to death. War was a cruel place.

Richard sighed, he had been hoping for news about his apprentice or the bowman apprentice. Sir Richard worried deeply for both. His instinct had told him that they were both okay, yet he was still unsure. He knew that Cuthbert was an able fighter and a rational boy. He trusted that the young warrior would know what to do in a difficult situation. He trusted Leif equally, yet he was scared that Leif would kill himself in his quest to rescue his master. He was equally scared that Leif would fail in his near impossible mission. That would mean the destruction of Kingstan and the conquering of the Waylin Islands.

Sir Richard now climbed down one of the stair cases and hurried over to the barracks where a troop of knights were saddling their horses next to some horse archers who were doing the same. A small surprise attack would be launched against one of the checkpoints. First, the horse archers would ride in and pepper the camp with arrows. Before any counter attack could be made though, the troop of knights would rush in and take down warriors and siege equipment. Then the two troops would retreat, regroup, and leave. These attacks were held at random times, sometimes during the day and sometimes at night, in order to make life hard for the Morr warriors camped outside. The sallies were composed of about fifty men, enough to be successful in destruction, yet not too many to result in a disaster should something go wrong.

These attacks were fairly simple and all had been successful so far. The enemy, having had to focus on getting supplies for the siege because Egon and Theron had burned their baggage, had had not time to construct earthworks, pits, or stakes to stop such sallies, leaving their camps vulnerable to any quick sortie.

Richard gave the Captain of the knights a nod and the man yelled orders to his companions. A roar of approval went up from the knights and they mounted their horses. A minute later, the portcullis was raised and they were thundering out into the town and then into the battlefield.

Leif hurriedly dismounted. "They're leaving," he hissed to Cuthbert.

The knight apprentice yawned looked at Leif, "What?" he asked.

"They're leaving," Leif repeated. "The Elves packed up this morning and are slowly moving down the road. Let's go!"

All the sleep vanished from Cuthbert's eyes as he pulled on his clothes. The two had decided to hold four hour shifts of spying on the Dark Elves. They would tie the Marwari to a tree some two hundred yards from the camp and watch the Elves. After the time was up, which they judged using the sun, they would mount the Morr horse, ride back to their makeshift camp and wake whoever was sleeping.

A couple minutes later the two boys were following the Elves, the Marwari walking perhaps two hundred yards behind the Elves, Leif and Cuthbert walking beside their horse and following the Dark Elves' evident tracks that told the boys of the creatures' path. The winding road allowed them to stay hidden from the Elves yet close enough to be able to follow their move and transition. Yet the two had no idea of the final Elf, riding two hundred paces behind them, sweeping their tracks with a pine bough.

Chapter 12

The Commander was a man to be reckoned with. He was short in size, but his lean muscle and battle-hardened face more than made up for that. The man's face was always an unreadable mask of steel and his eyes were enough to petrify a person. These piercing gray eyes locked onto a person and his steely gaze would make anyone nervous, making it impossible for a man to truly lie to him. No one knew where he came from or what his name was; he was simply "the Commander". Some said he was a demon from hell, while others believed he was Satan himself.

Now this man exited his tent, wearing full battle armor. He wouldn't actually fight, but it made him look superior and it motivated his troops. Today he would need all the rank and status he could get to pull off what he had planned.

Technically it was a little early to storm the town, for the troops had spent most of the time acquiring new supplies rather than creating breaches in the wall. As the Commander considered this he spat, angry that the two men with their golden capes had been able to burn his supplies. Even though the town was not properly damaged and the defenses broken, an assault was necessary because a dragon had recently brought in a letter from the Emperor. Siddian's armies were amassing, pulling together and slowly marching towards Morrigan. War was close, and the Commander had many of the troops with him here. In addition to the fact that Morrigan needed its army, the Commander was the best military leader in the army and had the respect of Morrigan's troops. Basically, the letter asked for the Commander to hurry up, secure the Waylin Islands and get back home.

Now the man moved toward his troops, who were already prepared for battle: a bugle had notified them two hours earlier. It was also this bugle that had called together the Council of War, which was made up of five men, all of them with a reputation as bloody and horrid as the Commander's.

The Commander now mounted a horse, a fierce white Lipizzaner that he was using while his own mount was being transported to the siege. The General's steely gaze swept across his gathered army and he nodded. There were enough men. Reinforcements had arrived that morning. He had perhaps a thousand men while the enemy had perhaps 400.

The Commander split the army into three groups. He would lead the largest and two of his most trusted men led the other two. These two other battalions consisted of infantry, while the Commander's men were all on horseback, mainly knights and scattered squires.

Captain Richard emerged from his quarters. It was the middle of the night, a full moon adorning the heavens. The sun wouldn't be up for another four hours, and Captain Richard was tired. He yawned, the exhaustion of the last weeks catching up with him.

Captain Richard paced back and forth in front of his room, thinking of everything that had happened and how he could put off the capture of Kingstan until reinforcements came. He knew that the key was the town—once the enemy was in the town than the castle and its keep would follow in only days. Richard sighed, fatigue causing him to sit as he contemplated the rule he and the Duke had agreed on—that one of the five officials had to be awake at all times in case a disaster happened. Today he had the second part of the night shift.

Suddenly a lookout ran up to him. The guard saluted and immediately hurried into a string of information.

"Sir! The enemy has been spotted amassing in three locations. They'll probably be attackin' soon. I'd say that there ain't more than about 1000 of 'em."

The man's heavy accent revealed this guard to be from some northern fief of Waylon and was probably sent here to help defend the Islands.

Richard furrowed his brow, thinking of what the best plan was. He squinted into the distance, seeing the glow of fire where the enemy camps were set up. He thought he could make out large groups bobbing lights moving in different locations. A particularly large one was in front of him.

"Rouse the troops, prepare the pitch, wake the Duke, and sound the alarm." The Duke said, already dressing himself for battle.

The attack started half an hour later; while the bugles were still sounding the alarm and confused troops were running all over the place. Peasants were pouring the remaining oil into prepared trenches and the archers preparing their positions at the town wall while phalanxes of spearmen moved to occupy the holes in the area.

The sun would rise in another three hours, and the night was cloudy. It was a full moon, but it was rarely seen. Richard could barely make out two groups of infantry, each with about 300 men, were at the southeast and southwest sides of the castle. A large group of mounted knights and men-at-arms were slowly advancing toward the north side. Here the enemy catapults and trebuchets had been doing their best work. The town wall barely existed anymore and here a temporary wood wall had been erected.

The advancing cavalry had stopped now, just out of range of the tensed archers. The alarm had stopped and the men running around were now simply reporting to their stations, ready or not while the able-bodied peasants ushered the women and children into the castle, grabbing all their leftover belongings.

Captain Richard hurried to the post that he and his men had selected. They would be leading the phalanx of spearmen on the north side. Gary was already there, issuing out orders and preparing the men. Myrddin was reinforcing the wooden wall, while Hildebrand sat and sharpened his sword with his whetstone. The fierce double-bladed warrior seemed relaxed and calm. The spearmen around him watched him in awe, feeding off of his peace. One of them even lay down, resting his spear against the wooden wall. Richard stopped and managed to breathe in and out, calming himself so that he could offer a good example. His face became peaceful and he walked towards the spearmen slowly, as if the rush of the castle had never existed.

"Everything is alright," Richard told himself. He had to laugh at that. His heart was thumping loudly and sweat was running down his face. The massive knight dried his hands on his weapon skirt and unsheathed his sword, taking his position at the front of the group.

Minutes later Ragnhild and Maccabee jogged up next to him, and Skinner slowly took his position between the two men. Deacon was busy sounding the alarm and rousing the people, while Theron was overseeing the construction of the various traps that had been devised for the day of retreat. Myrddin came a couple seconds later, having finally reinforced the wall with a set of spells and charms. He joined Skinner in the middle and sat down to rest. Hildebrand casually put away his tools and slowly walked towards Richard and his men, all of them tensed.

Captain Richard made brief eye contact with Hildebrand and saw that the double-bladed knight was just acting. Sweat was pouring down his face and his eyes nervously flickered across the wall.

Suddenly a long, drawn-out shriek cut through the air. The spearmen behind the Golden Arrow covered their ears and moaned while the trained warriors flinched at the sound. Cries of fear echoed around the castle and suddenly fifty giant beasts tore through the silver clouds in the sky and came hurtling at the castle.

The ballistae and archers were not prepared for this, so they suffered the consequence. The dragons sped toward the ground, burning the town destroying the wooden walls that had been put in place.

Myrddin's spell was not prepared for fire and the wall burst into flame. The archers near it jumped from the wooden palisade, and several spearmen turned and ran. The archers that had the sense to shoot at the dragons were picked off with the mighty tails of the flying beasts.

These tails had a spiked end and were as hard as metal, killing the men and destroying the wall, causing rocks to fly all over the place.

Captain Richard hit the ground, commanding the spearmen and his fellow warriors to do the same. The men did it just in time for a dragon sped over them, swinging his massive spiked tail. One of the spearmen hadn't dropped in time and this tail sliced his body in two. Some of the spearmen cried out and several jumped up and ran.

It was a stupid thing to do. Now that the dragons had put the whole town on fire, some of the burning wood had fallen in the stream of pitch that had been prepared. A wall of fire rose into the air, and some of the men that had been foolish enough to attempt escape were burned in the process.

They screamed in pain and Richard dropped his sword to cover his ears. He hated the sound of death.

Now that the ballistae had been given some time to prepare, they loaded and shot. Several dragons dropped, crushing the unsuspecting victims. The other riders realized that they had overstayed their welcome and immediately disappeared into the sky, the darkness swallowing them up quickly. Minutes later the shrieking and squealing of the dragons was gone.

Richard picked up his sword and stood. Suddenly the ground shook and he heard the pounding of hooves. He realized what was happening and grabbed his shield, kneeling behind it and swinging his sword.

Beside him Myrddin had developed a shield as well, and this blue wall wavered and flickered in the moonlight. Gary had rallied some of the spearmen and they had all kneeled together in a battle stance, their spears upraised.

Ragnhild and Hildebrand had decided to hide behind Myrddin's shield, and now Hildebrand wasn't even trying to hide his fear. Richard quickly scanned the ground for Skinner but he couldn't see the man.

Suddenly the wall before the Golden Arrow and the assembled spearmen broke in half, the blackened pieces falling to the ground, invisible as a cloud slid in front of the moon.

The Morr knights thundered into the town, some carrying torches, others spears and lances. They burned and wrecked everything, trampling and killing anyone. The men screamed and hollered as they circled the castle, wreaking havoc everywhere.

The moon didn't reappear for a while, which seemed merciful, for what was happening to any of the survivors was worse than most of them could have imagined.

Fire erupted into the sky in several areas, and screams of anguish and terror floated through the night. The silver starlight shone eerily upon the dead victims who were sprawled on the ground in unrecognizable shapes.

The enemy cavalry continued to ride through and destroy the town, showing no mercy and taking no prisoners. Everything was on fire and if a man was not burned or struck down with a sword; the horses running around in terror trampled him.

The archers on the castle walls had gotten over the initial shock of the dragons and were not picking off any man that came to close.

The groups of infantry on the southeast and southwest sides of the castle had charged and were screaming their battle cries as well, adding to the terror and horror of the night.

As the Morrs charged, their blood red uniforms shining dully in the moonlight, they slowly fanned out, and once they got to the town walls, they scaled them using ladders, other men's shoulders, dead bodies, or by simply scrabbling over the jumbled pieces of rocks.

Any archer left on the town walls was mercilessly slain and the remaining spearmen were engaged in hand-to-hand combat. Man after man fell, and soon not a single soul was still living in the town that was not wearing a Morr uniform.

Blood ran over the ground in small streams, and the fires that had recently illuminated the horror of battle now burned down or were put out.

Richard and his men had slowly started retreating after the cavalry charge. They stayed together in a circle, with Myrddin and Skinner in the middle. The whip master had been found on the ground, beneath the bloody bodies of two of the spearmen. He had a nasty gash on his forehead but nothing more.

The infantry that were raging around them tried to fight them but none succeeded in killing even a single one of the Waylins. Finally some enemy knights rallied together and charged the group. Richard ordered for battle stance, and the group stopped. Richard hid behind his shield and Myrddin started muttering the spell for a fireball. The spearmen dropped to one knee and held their spears forward, the bottom of it against the ground. This offered good support against the momentum of a cavalry charge, and the deadly spearhead would make sure that that particular horse never tried again.

The horses thundered forward as Myrddin released his fireball. The orange sphere of flame crashed into the first rider, lighting him up like a candle. The man didn't have time to scream and he fell from his horse, which stopped and stood dumbly.

Then the knights crashed into Richard and his spearmen. The men were pushed backwards, some of the spearmen falling and being crushed by the churning hooves. Ragnhild was behind Richard and Hildebrand behind Gary. The two men pushed forward and the horses that had smashed into the two warriors lost momentum and stopped. The stunned stallions stood there for a second, which sealed their rider's fates. Richard popped out from behind his shield and cut down the man on the horse while Ragnhild sliced another knight in half. Hildebrand's opponent was ready, swinging his sword in a large over cut strike. The double-bladed knight proved his skill by countering with a strike, thus slamming into the sword and jarring the knight's hand. Before the Morr could react, Hildebrand pushed his other sword forward, sticking it into the opening in the armor between the arm and side. The sword plunged into the skin and Hildebrand pushed it in deep, twisting it to kill the man quickly and spare him the pain.

The knight had no chance to yell and his eyes bulged, blood spurting from the wound. Slowly, as if in a trance, the enemy warrior slid from his saddle and fell to the ground, dead.

Although the cavalry charge had taken its toll, the spearmen had kept their formation and their lines had not broken. Two spearmen had been killed and another was bleeding from a head wound. About ten spearmen were left and the remaining cavalry had reacted to a bugle call and retreated.

The infantry remained, destroying the town and killing the few left over survivors. One of these groups, a small one of about twenty men, moved toward the circle of Waylin defenders. They fanned out, creating a large circle around the Waylins and their Sid leaders.

Richard immediately knew what he had to do and called out the formation immediately. "Golden Arrow! Spearmen, close in!"

The Golden Arrow members lined up behind Sir Richard in an arrowhead formation and the spearmen closed in behind them. Then Captain Richard charged.

The man cut right through the Morr in front of him and the wedge simply sliced through the shield wall that the men were trying to arrange.

After cutting through the men, they didn't stop, but continued charging recklessly, savagely cutting and hacking at anyone that came to close. They were now using basic survival instinct and no longer cared for anything else.

Ragnhild slid into his berserker mode and swung his massive battleaxe in wide arcs, maiming and killing men right and left.

Many foot soldiers had pulled together to resist this wedge, but they were routed and killed. The Waylins lost not a single man, but killed at least twenty. Soon the Morrs simply fled in terror, and once the group had reached the wall there were no more Morrs left to challenge them.

The archers on the castle walls had recognized the men by their yellow capes, and now opened a small side gate. This gate was a yard thick and reinforced by iron bars. It had been cleverly painted to look like the rest of the wall and only the top officials knew of it. Captain Richard was such a man.

Finally the spearmen and the Golden Arrow pushed into the bailey. The sun began to rise and slowly the Waylins counted their losses.

Eighty Morrs had been killed and a hundred injured. About two hundred Waylins lay dead on the battlefield. There were no real injuries—after all, no one had been spared.

Chapter 13

Richard stood on the balcony, his cape flying in the wind behind him, and his eyes drooping with tiredness. He looked at his fellow soldiers, now about two hundred defenders, and saw the restlessness and sleepless nights evident in their faces.

It had been two and a half days since the Morrs had taken over the town. Richard estimated about two hundred defenders to be left, each one of them tired and weakened from the past sleepless nights.

The enemy had been pounding their walls with stones all day and night. Their supply was unlimited and now they were close enough to fire at the castle walls. Richard was helpless as he watched each stone slam into the wall. The two-yard-thick walls were strong enough to resist the flying missiles but each hit shook the walls and echoed across the courtyard making sleep impossible.

The enemy was just as tired as the defenders, but the Commander had an abundant supply of troops and was more concerned for speed then the welfare of his men. He himself was disciplined and trained enough to sleep; his body was accustomed to getting all the sleep it could.

Richard was as tired as everyone else. He had gotten perhaps four hours of sleep for the past two days, and those hours were restless and he jerked awake at every explosion. The man had tried everything. He had slept in the cellar, covered his head with a pillow, and even stuck bread dough in his ears! Nothing worked, and slowly his nerves and the nerves of his fellow defenders began to deteriorate. Arguments were more frequent, and fights broke out daily. An officer had to be at each station at every time of the day, and getting back at the Morrs was useless.

The enemy had camped just outside the town, out of range of the ballistae and archers, but the catapults and trebuchets had been set up inside the town so that they could hit the castle walls.

These small targets could be hit by the mounted trebuchets, but so far all of the attempts had failed so Captain Richard and the Duke had decided not to waste the stone.

The day before, while the Morr men-at-arms, slaves, squires, and peasant warriors set up their camps and siege equipment, the Morr archers and crossbowmen had ventured forward, hiding behind hovels and charred debris that had been left over from the battle for the town. From behind these obstacles the men had shot bolts and arrows, the majority of the missiles thumping harmlessly into the castle walls, but two had hit Waylin guards posted on the walls, seriously wounding one and killing the other.

Because of this Sir Richard and the Duke had devised a quick sally, which they had undertaken the night before. The Duke had led the sortie, him and fifty lightly-armored men sneaking out of the castle with pitch and torches. The men had hidden behind the houses, the same ones that the archers the day before had hid behind as they assailed Kingstan's defenders with hails of arrows and bolts. Then the Waylin warriors had poured the oil over the wood, thatch roofs, and in the trenches that were left. After this they set fire to the pitch and threw the torches onto the thatch roofs, the fires climbing high into the night sky. The Duke and his men had then retreated, reentering the castle unscathed. In the mean time the conflagration roared on, the fire hungrily eating at the houses and the smoke spiraling into the air, eerily illuminated by the moonlight. The fire had spread quickly, the sparks and flames moving from hovel to hovel, setting everything that could burn alight. Finally, an hour later, the fires had burned down, leaving nothing but ashes and small piles of charred wood. Because of this small successful sally the Morrs could no longer deploy their archers against the defenders, and the success of the mission had strongly boosted morale. However, the joy did not last long. After another sleepless night, filled with the sounds of a siege, the happiness had worn off and now the men were tired and sore once more.

Now Richard rubbed his eyes and hurried down the stairs to meet one of his closer comrades. He stopped once he got to the central guard post on the Northern wall. His sword clanked against his armored legs and Sir Richard scanned the enemy camp.

There were no clouds in the sky, so the sun beat down on the Waylin defenders relentlessly, burning their exposed skin and causing those that were wearing armor to heat up. This didn't help the morale, and several weak soldiers fainted.

Richard could see the enemy camp, which was busy receiving reinforcements and preparing to storm the castle. The knight could also see mounds of dirt that had been piled up in various places, revealing the areas where the tunnelers were at work. These men, most of them Morr slaves, would dig tunnels to the walls and then collapse the tunnels inward on themselves, causing the wall to fall. Each day these mounds neared the castle, and Richard knew that soon he would have to order the catapults to fire stones on them, hopefully causing the tunnels to collapse.

Richard hated doing this, because he knew that the tunnelers didn't want to be doing this job—that they had been forced to this undesirable tasks. Some of them were probably Sid prisoners. Captain Richard spat, hate boiling inside of him as he saw another display of the Morrs' disregard for human life.

Richard shook his head to clear the painful images from his mind and nodded his head at the guard next to him, acknowledging his presence.

This guard had become one of Richard's closest friends, and his name was Altor. The captain guard saluted Sir Richard, who waved it off—in these difficult times Richard wanted friends with whom he could share the troubles of the siege. He believed that formality was wasted in sieges, where everyone was cramped together. Richard ate the same rations, used the same latrines, and was forced to endure the same hardships as Altor so for this time he saw the older guard as an equal.

The Golden Arrow Captain looked at his unshaven friend and asked, "Any news?"

Altor shook his head. It had become a habit for Sir Richard to ask the man each day for news on his apprentice or Cuthbert's friends. The old guard pointed towards the ruins of the town wall though, and said, "They stationed their camps just on the other side of the town wall, making it impossible for us to hit them with our long range weapons. A large force arrived last night; I would estimate perhaps a thousand men. Now the enemy has well over seventeen hundred men and we have about two hundred. I'll be honest," the guard said, looking at Sir Richard. "I'm pretty worried. We're outnumbered, extremely tired, and isolated. The chance of success is close to zero."

Richard nodded. "We have no choice," he finally said. "We must endure. And besides, the sound of the siege engines keeps them awake too."

Altor nodded, "True," he admitted, "But it's not as loud, and they've received a thousand fresh men, who are eager to fight and ready to also."

Sir Richard shrugged, "We must endure," he repeated as he nodded his goodbye and hurried towards the Duke's chambers. Once there he roused the veteran warrior and said, "Get all of the men, women, and children into the bailey, no matter what they're doing or what shift they have. Tell them to hurry."

Leif and Cuthbert had been tailing the Dark Elves for three days now and had noticed the outrider behind them. They had decided to follow this Elf, slowly riding down the road that was wiped clean of tracks. However, using a trained eye Cuthbert was able to notice the patterns left by the pine bough and he also noticed the pine needles that were sometimes present in the dirt.

The Dark Elves seemed to suspect that someone could be following them. They were traveling very roundabout ways, sometimes splitting up and creating obvious tracks down a path, only to double back and take a different route and clean up their tracks again. Cuthbert assumed that the Elves thought that a group of Morrs who had been given the duty of killing those who had stolen the prisoners, and they now wanted to confuse them. However, the tricks did not fool Leif and Cuthbert, for the latter was properly educated in tracking.

Cuthbert desperately wanted a sword. Leif told Cuthbert to be patient—the Elves would doubtlessly pass through a village soon to restock their food supplies—they couldn't last on berries forever. When this happened, Cuthbert could steal a sword.

The dirt path which Leif and Cuthbert were trailing the Dark Elves on did lead to a village on the fourth day. The trees through which they had been monotonously traveling through abruptly stopped, and grass countryside began. The road which the group was using morphed into a cobblestone street, and so the two young men had to double their distance from the Elves to avoid detection.

For three hours the Elves and their pursuers clopped along through the grassy land until the first signs of a village began to show. Fields and farms could now be seen, and as the Elves and the two Golden Arrow apprentices hurried on, these signs became more numerous. More fields were seen, but all of the fields were barren and empty. Some fields had been burned, and not a single farmhouse was not in any way unharmed. The different stores and farms had been looted and burned, while others had been smashed to pieces for reasons the two apprentices did not know.

Suddenly the two young men, both walking in order to spare the Marwari the extra weight, saw a horrible sight which made both gasp.

A farm and its fields had been burned to the ground, and all of the livestock had been slaughtered, but this is not what made the men gasp. The farmer and his family had all been shot with arrows, and the whole group had been thrown onto a pile with animal blood poured over the family.

Leif hurried to a tree and retched, while Cuthbert simply shook his head and swore loudly. Then the two hurried on, until they came to the village itself.

The village was made up of straw huts and a couple brick buildings. It had the central cobblestone street running through it, and dirt paths that had been beaten into walkways with years of use. In the center was a large house, which was made completely of stone. That was probably the keep. The whole area around the village was burned and blackened, and just about all of the straw huts and adobe houses were wrecked. The marketplace had been ransacked, and random things were lying on the ground; a doll sat untouched against a curb, two snapped wooden swords lay in the center of the street, and everywhere the two looked, were arrows.

Arrows were stuck in the mud of the huts and houses, and more littered the ground. Blood could be seen in several areas, but no people were to be seen. Leif and Cuthbert guessed that the little town was probably abandoned.

The Dark Elves were about ten yards away from the entrance the wooden palisade that marked the perimeter of the lord's property, and Leif and Cuthbert did not dare approach it closer, but hid in the wreckage of a toll booth. Here they tied up the Marwari and edged closer to get a better look.

The Dark Elves now rode into the town, the cart making lots of noise on the paved street. Suddenly, out of the shadows of the houses and huts, and on top of the keep, Elves materialized, and walked towards the group. The other elves gathered together behind one figure, who was wearing a red robe instead of the usual black. This man also had long, radiant blonde hair instead of black, and his face was pale instead of the leathery brown of the normal Dark Elf. The man also held a long red shield and a massive sword. The man spoke to the incoming Elves, and then the cart and riders clattered into the town. Minutes later, the town was quiet again, and appeared to be deserted; the Elves had receded to their posts in the darkness of the village.

An hour later, everyone was crowded into the central courtyard; women, children, peasants, soldiers, even some mules that managed to break free of their pen. Only a couple guards were left at their posts and Richard had already spoken with them.

Now these people in front of the Captain looked at him, expecting for him to say something. Richard breathed in deeply and began.

"Kingstan will fall. There is no longer any doubt about that. We are the last hope for the Waylin Islands and we will be destroyed sooner or later. Staying here is certain death. The reason we are defending Kingstan is because the army of Arganon needs time to assemble and prepare Waylon to withstand this conquest. We are Arran's last stand. I am telling you this to warn you. I have arranged for a small fleet of thirty dragons to land here in about an hour. All women and children will leave with them and any soldiers that want to. You will bring no personal baggage besides yourselves and what can fit into your pockets. This fleet of dragons will be the last chance that any of you men get to leave this place. If you choose to stay then you choose to die for Waylon."

Then Sir Richard unsheathed his sword. He stuck it into the ground and slowly walked across the courtyard, drawing a line in the dead grass and dirt that lay in the bailey.

"If you choose to stay then step across the line. And remember, there is no shame in leaving. You have already served Waylon in being here and helping prepare for the inevitable. Many of you have families and relatives. Cross only if you accept death and the inevitable."

At first no one moved. Then the Duke stepped forward, crossing the line and standing beside Sir Richard. Next came a small group of apprentices. As if in answer to this, the rest of the soldiers crossed the line, leaving behind only the women, children, some peasants, and a single soldier. The soldier had tears in his eyes, and he was extremely young, probably seventeen or eighteen. The young man had a whole life ahead of him and he wasn't prepared to sacrifice it all for some honor and glory.

"I am sorry. But 'tis not my fight." The man said, his accent telling Sir Richard that he had probably come from a northern province in Arganon.

Richard nodded, "Very well, I understand completely."

Then, as if on cue, a shout was yelled from nearby lookout and the courtyard was covered by a giant shadow. Some of the women and children screamed, but were immediately calmed when the Duke and his men cheered at the sight of the darkening shadows.

"Get out of the way! Move!" Richard screamed, hurrying out of the way of the rapidly descending dragons. Everyone quickly retreated towards the walls as the massive beasts landed in the bailey. Only six at a time could land, while the others remained airborne.

The soldiers quickly helped load those who had not crossed the line onto the dragons, putting two women and a child per dragon. Once each dragon was set to go and everyone that wanted to leave was on one, the final six took off, pushing into the air.

Minutes later the small fleet was gone, swallowed up by the sky.

Chapter 14

He was clad in white, his royal garments flowing to the polished marble floor. At his side dangled the most majestic and beautiful sword he had ever seen. The scabbard showed the scenes of hunts, jousts, and battles. Before him stood a man with short, brown hair, and with a crown upon his head. The man seemed to be glowing with royalty and righteousness.

Suddenly he was jerked onto the ground. As his knee touched the immaculately white surface below him, it seemed to tremble and flow outwards. As this ripple continued outwards from him, it touched everything. And everything it touched became . . . ugly.

The floor grew weeds and became brown and dead. His sword lost its scabbard and began dripping blood. He was sure it was the blood of innocent men, yet he did not know how or why he knew this. The majestic hall that had been spun around him suddenly rewove itself into a web, seeming to trap the boy rather than protect him.

The only thing that did not change was the man before him. He held his royal presence and continued to emanate justice. Then this man reached out with his sword, one made of shining white steel and forged upon the anvils of peace, not war. This he gently placed upon the boy's shoulders and then his head, speaking strange words.

Suddenly it all made sense. The blood of his sword was the price of his knighthood. The ugliness around him was the result of the blood. And as he stood, the net transformed into the world, showing everything that was, is, and will be. Images danced across it and the ground beneath his feet turned vibrant colors, flowers shooting in all directions. And suddenly the boy knew that this is would be the result of his knighthood. He would try everything to make it so. He would dedicate his life to the cause of redeeming the blood upon his sword.

And as the boy made these amends, he looked up into the eyes of his lord. All of a sudden the images dancing around the walls, which he had defined as fate and the floor beneath him which he called destiny, stretched out its long, slippery fingers and coiled them around the man's body. Before the boy could react, his king was ripped out of the room, and into the walls, disappearing in a single image. Through this image he fled, hurtling right into the deepest depths of Leif's heart . . .

"Wake up!" Cuthbert ordered, shaking his friend.

Leif's eyes shot open, his hands scrabbling at his chest, wanting to yank the "lord" back out of his heart.

Finally he calmed himself and breathed in deeply, pushing Cuthbert away. The young knight apprentice backed off, understanding the fact that Leif would have to deal with his nightmare personally.

Leif hurried to a secluded spot and sat down. This time the dream had felt so real. Yet he also felt distant in another way. It was almost as if the dream wasn't intended for him, as if he was simply substituting for the real person of the dream. The only part that seemed real and that seemed like it actually belonged to him was the end. His heart still ached from this transfusion. The "king" had gone *into* him! Leif could still feel the presence, like a dull throbbing in the corners of his chest.

Forget it! He thought. *It's just a dream that carried a little too far into reality. Get over it, silly!*

Finally Leif shook away the last tendrils of his dream. He rubbed his chest one more time and got up to return to their makeshift camp.

Cuthbert opened his mouth to ask something, but Leif simply shook his head. "It's over," he said. "Forget that it ever happened. It was nothing." Leif added, indicating with his head where he had slept, hoping to get the point across to Cuthbert that he meant the dream.

"Umm," Cuthbert tentatively said. "I just wanted to ask if I could watch you hunt today. I'd like to see a true bowman apprentice at work."

Leif laughed, and Cuthbert joined in, Leif nodding the yes to his friend. "Let's get ready," he suggested, the two preparing for a hopefully very successful hunt.

For three days Leif and Cuthbert had camped in the toll booth, while nothing moved in the town. The guard changed four times a day, and four times at night. These were the only times when the Dark Elves could be seen, and by now Leif and Cuthbert had memorized the guard positions closest to them.

Leif went hunting every day, and then Cuthbert would ride the Marwari away and make a fire. Then he would cook the meat and come back.

It was nearly midday when they left. The two rode the Marwari a fair distance away, into a nearby wood, and Leif dismounted while his friend tailed him, leading their horse. After thirty minutes of slow stealthy walking, Leif saw a rabbit dart through the underbrush. The rabbit hopped quickly, and sped along. It was already seventy yards away, and Cuthbert didn't even notice it, except that he had seen where Leif was aiming.

Leif waited for the right moment, and then in one fluid motion, he pulled back, drawing the bow to full draw and released. The arrow cut through the air and killed its target immediately, the rabbit flipping over twice as it was hurled through the underbrush. Leif's bowstring slapped his left arm, but that area was padded by the large leather glove that Leif wore for protection.

Quickly Leif and Cuthbert got the animal. Then the two went back to the road where Cuthbert made a small fire. He did this using Leif's tinderbox, which Leif had clipped to his double-quiver. Cuthbert was far more experienced than Leif in fire-making and got one going on his second try. Then the two roasted the rabbit, which Leif had already skinned and gutted, and decided to eat on the spot because they thought it physically impossible to see that wondrous meat; its fat dripping from its body, go to waste.

Once the two had eaten the whole thing, they journeyed to a nearby stream and drank, while the Marwari did the same. Then they filled a clay jar that they had found and went back to the road. A few seconds later they were walking down it, joking and talking merrily.

Suddenly, five men burst out of the woods on their left. Leif had unstrung his bow, and it was lying on their horse, so he had no time to react. Cuthbert grabbed his dagger, it was the one that Leif had given him, and rushed forward, while the Marwari bolted into the trees on the other side.

The men were clearly Morr soldiers, but in poor shape. Their red coats were torn and tattered, making them barely recognizable, and the men had taken on a wild look. They were all unshaven and wielding hatchets and spears. They screamed loudly as they charged the surprised duo.

The first man that got to Cuthbert was wielding a simple hatchet, and totally underestimating his opponent, tried slaying his adversary with a simple overhead stroke. Cuthbert flicked away the attack, and immediately thrust forward, catching the man under the shoulder. The man cried out and sank to the ground. The next two approached Cuthbert, and both wielded spears. They circled warily, while the remaining two charged Leif.

Leif had no weapon on him, and the second his first attacker came near enough, the apprentice dove forward and tackled the man by the knees. The man wasn't expecting this and fell to the ground. Immediately Leif was on him. The boy punched the man in the face and grabbing an arrow, slit the man's wrist in which he held his blunted dagger. The man cried out and rolled away, fleeing into the bushes.

The next man that attacked Leif kicked Leif's hand hard, and the apprentice's arrow flew to the ground several yards away. Then the man kicked Leif again, hitting him right in the stomach. Leif doubled over and sank to the ground, gasping for breath. The man walked forward, closing in for the kill when—splat! The man's face exploded with blood and he fell to the ground; dead.

Cuthbert had successfully disarmed his first opponent, who had retreated out of range, before stealing the first man's hatchet. This swung around and around as he closed in on the boy. Cuthbert kept lunging forward, keeping the spearman at bay. Once the not-so-intelligent Morr realized that his weapon was longer than Cuthbert's, Cuthbert would be dead, and so the apprentice had to act like he was in control of the fight and dominating it.

Suddenly the hatchet, which the other man had picked up, was spinning through the air at him, and the knight apprentice had barely enough time to duck. Immediately the thrower of the weapon was upon him, and punched Cuthbert in the gut. Cuthbert doubled over, cursing and spluttering with fury, but he didn't forget his essential teaching: never take your eyes off of your opponent. The young man kept his face up and aware, and now the man closed and punched Cuthbert in the face. Blood erupted from the apprentice's nose, and splattered the boy's face. Cuthbert fell to the ground, and the man picked up his hatchet again. The spearman was still a safe distance away, for he wasn't completely sure of what was happening. The spearman's companion had gotten his hatchet again, and closed in on Cuthbert in order to slit the boy's throat.

Cuthbert, in one last desperate attempt to stay alive, jumped forward and pushed his dagger home, sticking it between the Morr warrior's ribs and into his heart. The dagger got stuck, but the warrior fell down dead.

Now Cuthbert fell back, and the spearman decided to finish what his friend had started and moved forward for the kill.

Suddenly, as before with Leif, a disgusting "splat!" was heard and the man's face erupted with blood. The warrior fell to the ground, moaning and clutching his face, until a second splat was heard and more blood burst forth, issuing into the sky like a fountain. Then the man lay still, never to move again.

Leif had managed to stand again and hobbled over to his injured friend. Cuthbert lay on the ground moaning, and Leif examined him.

The boy had received two mighty blows. Cuthbert's stomach area was one huge bruise, which was already turning purple, and once Leif had stopped his friend's nosebleed, he saw that his nosed was crooked and definitely broken. The boy held his friend's head in hand and gripped the nose. The other boy screamed in pain, but Leif didn't let go. The boy popped the nose back in place and Cuthbert screamed again, louder than before.

Finally, five minutes later, after Leif had cleaned his companion's face and given him water that he found in a puddle close by, the boy was able to stand up. The young man hobbled toward his fallen opponent, and pulled out his dagger. This he wiped clean on the ground and then he and his friend moved over to the two men who had died with the "splat!"

After careful examination, Leif found two perfectly round stones embedded in the men's bloody faces. The men had evidently been hit by a rock, but by whom?

Suddenly, as if in answer to this question, the Marwari walked into the clearing. Leading it was a small creature. The animal, if it could be called that, was about a yard and a quarter tall, and was furry. It was like a monkey that could walk upright and function like a human. The furry creature had arms that reached its knees and a belt around its waist. The belt held a small sword, a dagger really, but compared to the size of the little creature, it was a sword. The animal-human was made of light brown fur, much like a monkey, but his eyes seemed more intelligent and in control than any ape's eyes could ever be. On the top of the creature's head lay a small mass of curly black hair.

Now the animal smiled at Leif and Cuthbert, but all this meant was that the creature showed its teeth. They were yellow and brownish looking, and all of them were at least partly chipped except for one long one in the center.

"'Ello!" He shouted to the two in greeting. A sling was slung over the monkey-like animal and a small pouch of stones hung at the monkey's belt.

"Umm—hello," Leif ventured, stepping forward. Cuthbert held back and said nothing, studying the animal.

The creature showed its teeth again and then said—equally as loudly as before—, "Caesar rescue you and horse. Caesar save you! Caesar want to follow and help you! But first Caesar want food!" The last part the little creature screamed, and then it showed its teeth again.

Leif smiled back awkwardly and said, "And you are?"

"Caesar!" The animal hollered at the two.

"And what is Caesar exactly?!" Cuthbert yelled at the animal, getting annoyed while Leif chuckled.

"Caesar be monkey-man! Caesar is smarter and better than animals, but humans and elves and dwarves not like him! Caesar like and help them but they not like and help him back! Caesar be exiled from monkey-man forest because he want to help humans beat mean people! Caesar want to help you and Caesar want food!" Again the monkey-man ended in shouting.

Leif nodded and walked forward, taking the Marwari from the little monkey-man, and whispering a quiet "thank you". Caesar looked at Leif and yelled loudly, "WHAT?!" shutting his eyes as he yelled at Leif. Leif winced and repeated his thank you, now saying it louder, while Caesar yelled back at him, "No problem! Now Caesar want food and to go with you!" As usual, Caesar screamed this and then he held out his hand. Leif took the horse's reins and gave Caesar the rest of their meat. Then he left to consult with Cuthbert.

Cuthbert was for letting the monkey-man stay with them, for so far he hadn't done anything wrong, and he had proven himself worthy. Leif agreed under one condition, which was that Caesar would no longer scream at them, for they would like to remain secret.

These terms were discussed with Caesar, who replied by yelling, "OKAY!" and showing his crooked teeth.

The two apprentices laughed and told him that being quiet started here and now, so Caesar agreed and would not raise his voice above a whisper. Then Leif and Cuthbert dragged the dead men to the side of the road and covered them with branches. Afterwards they mounted the Marwari and, leaving Caesar on the ground, staring at them, galloped away. The two needed to get back right away to see if the prison cart had left again, and they wanted to test Caesar's speed.

The two galloped onward, and Caesar ran away into the forest.

Leif and Cuthbert looked at each other and stopped. Cuthbert was about to turn the horse around when Caesar popped out of the trees twenty yards ahead of them.

"Coming?" he whispered. Leif and Cuthbert nodded, confused at how fast Caesar could travel through the trees to get ahead of a galloping horse.

Finally the two drew even with the monkey-man and they looked up, seeing that he swung from vine to vine, and grabbed tree branch after tree branch, swinging and jumping from one tree to the next. This was a lot faster than walking, and as fast as galloping on a horse. Furthermore, Caesar did this silently, so that he couldn't be noticed unless one knew he was above him.

"He'll be a good guard if we travel." Leif remarked pointing upward where Caesar swung from one vine to a branch and jumped to the next, soundlessly.

Cuthbert agreed, and fifteen minutes later, the trio arrived at their make-shift camp in the toll booth.

An hour later, they were all soundly sleeping.

Leif woke up and stifled a yawn. Then he stretched his cramped arms and prodded Cuthbert next to him. The young warrior grunted something and turned over. Sighing, Leif nudged his friend again, and Cuthbert yawned and got up. Then the two climbed out of their makeshift bed, which was a pile of straw with a piece of leather from the toll booth, and Leif rubbed his hands together. It was really cold during the night because they couldn't make a fire. Leif and Cuthbert had worried about this at first; scared that an animal could attack during the night, but apparently the animals were smart enough to know that the village was best avoided.

Cuthbert crawled out of their little shelter, and then the two dressed quickly, Leif donning his dragon hide suit and double quiver, while Cuthbert simply put on a cloak they had found. Then they walked to where the Marwari was peacefully grazing. They had tied it to an oak tree where Caesar could hold watch from above.

Leif got out the remains of their food, while Cuthbert went to wake up Caesar. A second later, Cuthbert reappeared next to Leif and said, "He's gone. I can't find him—Caesar has disappeared!"

Leif frowned and quickly climbed the oak. Cuthbert had been right; the little monkey-man was nowhere to be seen.

The two shrugged and decided to simply have breakfast—Caesar could come when he wished. As the two ate their meager breakfast of rabbit meat and berries, they decided their next move.

Leif popped one of the raspberries into his mouth and chewed slowly, savoring the taste. All of a sudden a brown animal jumped in front of them and whispered, "'Ello!"

Leif fell back with surprise, and Cuthbert burst out laughing. Then the monkey-man threw something into Cuthbert's lap, and a wrapped bundle into Leif's. With a quick, "Caesar be back soon!" the monkey-man was gone.

Cuthbert gasped, and Leif looked at his friend. In his hand was a beautiful sword! The two quickly clambered after their companion and hid behind a cracked and broken crate. There they saw Caesar.

The monkey-man was inching towards the village in a very peculiar manner. His arms were at right angles in front of him, brushing away rocks and other small obstacles, while his head was on the ground. His backside was raised into the air and his small legs pushed him forward towards the camp. Caesar must have picked some type of path, because he seemed to randomly change directions at certain points, but Leif saw no evident trail that their companion was following. Finally Leif saw what the monkey-man was doing and raised his eyebrows in surprise—their furry companion was smarter than they had thought.

"He's staying in the brown patches, so that it is impossible to see him when the sun is in your eyes like it is now—it's genius!" Leif told Cuthbert.

Cuthbert let out a low whistle, and Leif smiled. Then the two retreated to their camp and Cuthbert continued his breakfast. Leif unwrapped his bundle quickly, which was wrapped in goat hide. Inside were two dozen white arrows! The arrows had perfectly made black-wood shafts and beautiful white arrowheads. Leif whistled in amazement. White arrowheads were the rarest type of rock. They were razor sharp and could pierce any armor except matured dragon armor, but they could scratch and dent that pretty well. Dragon arrowheads on the other hand, could pierce iron and bronze armor, but not steel, which they could dent and scratch. They couldn't even make a mark on dragon armor.

Leif had also heard a lot about white arrows and about why they were so special. White could only be mined in certain areas of Ashtoreth and these areas were jealously guarded by evil creatures. The Dark Elves had an easier chance of getting at the White because they lived in Ashtoreth, whereas the only way to get it in Siddian was by speaking to a brave and bold merchant or dealing in the black market of weapons.

Leif put his arrows into one side of the double quiver, and crammed his remaining dragon arrowhead arrows into the other side. That way he could grab whatever arrow was necessary for the situation he found himself in.

Cuthbert gave Leif back his dagger, and the two left their breakfast to examine their new weapons. The White arrows had the same weight as the dragon arrows, so there was no difference, and Leif didn't need to practice. Cuthbert on the other hand had to accustom himself with the new sword which had a different size and weight. The beautiful sword was undoubtedly made by goblins and forged with great care and skill. Inscribed on the blade were words that neither Leif nor Cuthbert could read or understand, but besides that, the sword felt almost familiar. It was perfectly balanced, except for the fact that it was slightly longer than his original. Also, the scabbard was made for the back, so Cuthbert had to practice drawing the sword without getting it stuck. After a while Cuthbert realized that drawing from the back was quicker than from the side, and carrying it there was easier too.

Finally, half an hour later, Caesar crept back into their camp and hurried over to where Leif and Cuthbert were playing with what Caesar called their "toys." Caesar dumped a final load on the ground and fell over exhausted.

Cuthbert hurried over to see what the strange red thing was and yelped in surprise, at which he earned himself a swift kick by Leif, and a strange look from Caesar. The red object that Cuthbert had admired was chain-mail! Once Cuthbert had overcome his surprise he tried on the chain-link armor. The mail hung down to Cuthbert's knees and could be tightened using a strap around the waist.

Cuthbert smiled as he examined himself with his new weapon and armor. After the initial surprise his face formed into a frown. "Why red? Why not something less—" Cuthbert searched for the right word, "obvious," he finished.

Caesar looked at him as if the answer were three times as obvious as walking around wearing red chain-mail. "You supposed to be obvious! When enemy see you, they shoot you and not see bow-boy or Caesar. Then bow-boy and Caesar kill them while sword-man look obvious and charge enemy."

Leif cleared his throat loudly. "The bow-boy's name is Leif," he said.

"Okay bow-boy," Caesar whispered, for the monkey-man had not raised his voice above a whisper since Leif had threatened to make him leave if he did.

Leif cleared his throat again and said, "Then please call me Leif, *monkey-man*," Leif spat at Caesar while Cuthbert howled with laughter.

Caesar looked confused, and so he just nodded dumbly. Then he moved to where the remains of the breakfast lay and helped himself generously.

Chapter 15

Zoticus popped another blood berry into his mouth. The fruit stayed true to its name, exploding in his mouth and gushing red liquid everywhere. The young warrior struggled to keep it in his mouth, not that it would matter if the juice spilled on his uniform.

The uniform was already torn and tattered, covered in blood, dirt, and mud. It didn't matter anyways, it already was red. The Morrs had worn red in battle since the first emperor. The red was there in order not to discourage any one of the blood on his garments or those of his neighbor. In battle you were supposed to be brave and valiant, not scared and sickly.

Zoticus shook his head, causing some of the blood berry's juice to dribble out of his mouth. The Commander would be mad. The uniform was a soldier's pride and signal of rank. He had ruined his, but at least with good reason.

As Zoticus walked on, he heard the clang of weapons and cries of triumph, followed by wails of death. The young man's jaw dropped, spilling red juice everywhere, but Zoticus didn't even realize. He ran forward, sprinting easily without the weight of this sword, shield, and mail coat. Finally Zoticus reached the edge of the forest and hurdled the bushes there, landing on open and burned ground. He quickly drew his knife, the only weapon he had left.

Zoticus had arrived. Using only his natural sense of bearing and a compass, Zoticus had managed to get from nowhere to somewhere, and that somewhere was exactly where he needed to be.

In front of him raged chaos. A small group of Waylin knights had raided a camp. Zoticus cursed and thundered toward the small battle, but by the time he got there the knights had retreated and fled to the safety of their castle; the cowards.

The young warrior would have helped pick up the remains of the battle, after all, he was ranked lower than most of the men cleaning up, but Zoticus didn't have the time.

He turned and ran to another camp, 200 yards away from the wrecked sight of the battle. He needed to speak to the Commander.

Zoticus entered the camp, but no one took notice until he marched right up to the Commander's tent.

One of the guards on duty stuck out his pike, poking Zoticus in the ribs none too gently. "Yeah right! Like ya' really off to see the Commander, sonny?!" The guard barked at him.

Zoticus mumbled a reply, stumbling forward.

The guard prodded him again, this time harder. "What was that toothpick?" He shouted.

By now a small crowd had gathered and the guard was enjoying himself while Zoticus reddened and tried to explain.

"It's urgent. I've got to speak with him now! It's concerning his horse and some Dark Elves." The young man managed to get out before being viciously poked with the pike.

"Quit it!" Zoticus screamed. "Just stop poking me with the pike!"

The guard pulled his weapon away and raised his hands.

"Sorry peanut." He said, laughing at his own joke.

Suddenly the guard dropped his pike and his face turned red. The small guard was lifted off his feet and the man struggled to breath. Finally he was dropped, revealing the Commander, who had been choking him from behind. Gasping for breath, the guard took his pike and crawled away.

"You! Come in." The Commander barked, pointing at Zoticus.

Zoticus mumbled a reply and followed the man in.

The Commander's tent was huge. In one corner was a desk, covered in papers. Another corner held a bed and a small divider shielded it from view, but this was currently open, allowing Zoticus to see the perfectly made bed. A weapon stand stood in one corner, and in the middle of the room was a table that was an exact model of the area, complete with the castle, the broken town walls, the blackened battle grounds, and the Morr camps.

The Commander sat down in a chair and pulled one forward for Zoticus, but the little man was too nervous to speak, instead saluting and staying standing.

The Commander fixed Zoticus with an ice cold stare and muttered, "Sit down." Zoticus immediately plopped down into the chair.

"What do you need to tell me that is so important as to interrupt me while I am writing to the Emperor?" The Commander never raised his voice, but that didn't matter, it seemed to echo around Zoticus and the young warrior flinched for no apparent reason.

Zoticus stumbled over an apology and immediately hurried into his tale.

The Morr warrior reported everything. He started by telling about how the Commander's horse had been stolen, at which the man didn't even react to, and then continued on, telling about following the horse thief.

Zoticus didn't stop, telling about the encounter with the Dark Elves and how the horse had been lost. He told the Commander how they were never able to find the beautiful stallion and about how the Dark Elves had attacked them twice on the road. Then Zoticus took a deep breath, continuing with him escaping into the woods and slowly making his way towards Kingstan, willing and trying move in that direction, but never sure if he was going the correct way. Zoticus ended with describing his arrival.

After the young warrior had finished, the Commander was quiet for a moment, allowing Zoticus to study his face.

The famous general had dark brown eyes and short brown hair. His beard was perfectly trimmed and gray strings of hair were slowly working their way into it. The man was not as tall as Zoticus would have expected, but the Commander more than made up for that with lean and trained muscle. Right now the man was wearing a blood red battledress, and the man's steely gaze was fixed on Zoticus.

"So, you mean to tell me that my horse has been stolen, the Dark Elves that have deserted us have more captives than we thought, they are fleeing towards the port, and that once you found out about this you didn't go back and right your wrongs?"

Zoticus shifted uncomfortably in his chair. "Someone had to be told." He finally said.

The Commander nodded. "I agree. You did the right thing."

Zoticus smiled, it was rare to receive such praise from this hardened man.

"Now, tell me about these prisoners." The Commander said.

Zoticus briefly described each man; the speedy assassin, the two bloody men in the carriage and the escaped boy. He also described the young archer. Zoticus asked for the knight to elaborate on the two younger boys, and Zoticus told him everything he knew. They were probably still following the elves. One uses a sword and the other a bow. They stole a horse and seem to know how to handle one.

The Commander nodded. "Round up a hundred troops. Go to Krun; tell him that he is in charge of the army until I get back, and not to do any major moves. Then get all the men onto horses, make sure they are all knights, and tell them that we will leave in an hour, from headquarters. Also, hand this to Krun. You will be one of the troops leaving with me."

Zoticus mumbled a quick "yes sir" and stumbled out of the tent, frowning. Why would the Commander want to leave now, when everything was set for storming the castle? The young warrior didn't have the authority to question his leader's orders so he simply cleared his head of the thoughts, obediently jogging to Krun's camp.

An hour later the Commander and his hundred knights and Zoticus thundered into the forest, their horses laden with armor and weapons.

Captain Richard saw this and hurried to the Duke.

Chapter 16

Egon was jolted awake as the prison cart was opened. The assassin groaned and moved his back away from the wall. Egon had been mercilessly flogged once the group had arrived in the village. Now Egon's back was torn up and bloody. The man had shown some fight, cursing and making fun of the Elves, but it simply wasn't worth it. Egon had decided one thing though, which was that they would never get him to Ashtoreth alive. He would escape or die trying.

Now the door to the cart opened, and a face poked in. It was the leathery tan face of a Dark Elf, and the Elf hopped into the cart. The creature, Egon had ceased to think of them as anything but vicious and barbaric animals, dragged out Xurxo and Lord Ive, and then he came back and got Egon.

Xurxo was taken to a wooden hovel, and laid onto a table. Minutes later an elf hurried in and started bandaging the prisoner and applying different poultices to his wounds and sores. It took two hours to properly bandage Xurxo and make him a recognizable human being. The elf-doctor estimated that in about two weeks Xurxo would be fine again. Then they could leave.

Then an elf came and took Lord Ive, shackling him and throwing him into a cage. Then the Dark Elf grabbed Egon, fixing iron bolts around his legs and arms, which were attached to a cage. Egon was thrown into this cage and landed on his back, causing him to roar in agony.

The Dark Elf smirked and cursed at him. Egon looked at the Elf and smiled.

"Twenty Elves can't even take on three nearly dead, unarmed, starved humans? I've changed my mind about you. Now you're not just barbaric and vile animals, but barbaric and vile cowards," Egon said, vehemently spitting the final word.

The Dark Elf drew his whip and slashed Egon across his face, and the assassin screamed. "Look whose laughing now!" The Elf hissed, a sharp accent causing him to sound hoarse and raspy. Then the Elf smiled, a savage glint in his eyes and he spat Egon in the face.

Egon wiped his face, laughing out loud. The Elf got insanely mad, pulling Egon from his cage and whipping him mercilessly, while blood, flesh, and skin flew through the air, amidst screams of agony and pain.

Finally the Elf was torn from his bleeding victim by his white-haired leader. The Elves conversed quickly in their throaty language and they finally tossed Egon back into his cage.

Egon moaned, wiping blood out of his eyes, and spitting it out of his mouth. The reason that Egon had laughed though, was not because of the Dark Elf, but because a small furry creature had just stole the keys to Egon's cage, without the Dark Elf noticing.

Alicia stirred the potion carefully before giving it to the injured soldier. Then she put the green liquid away and left the tent.

The Waylins had built a makeshift healing house, which was really no more than a huge collection of wood, stone, and cloth, all worked together with no apparent architecture.

As Alicia walked towards the keep she saw a group of apprentices training with bows and arrows and Alicia had to wipe her eyes. She dearly missed Lord Ive. He was funny and kind, and also very dedicated to his work. His best friend, Egon, on the other hand, was a jokester and a prankster. Egon could be a little obnoxious at times, but when the man was with Lord Ive, he seemed to shine just as much as his friend.

Now Alicia was hurrying toward Captain Richard's quarters in the north tower. She wanted to ask for permission to go out and help find more of the wounded, although she was pretty sure he would say no.

The knights had been coming and going; raiding the enemy camp which was now easier to attack than before. Alicia shook her head. Sometimes she hated being the only woman. It seemed like everyone always was so protective of her. That was another thing she liked about Lord Ive. He treated her like an equal and respected her like one too.

Finally Alicia got to the room and what she heard was not what she had expected. She thought that Richard would have been writing an official report, but instead she heard what she thought was crying.

Alicia tip-toed further and slowly opened the perfectly oiled door. Inside, Captain Richard sat at his desk, tears running down his face, and sobbing at a picture. The little portrait was of Cuthbert, and the painting was fairly old, but clearly recognizable.

Alicia stared. She had never seen the captain break down like this. It seemed that the big man really loved his apprentice. Alicia turned to go, when—"Stay. It's all right. I don't know what's gotten into me."

Alicia turned and muttered an apology, but Captain Richard just waved it off. Then Alicia asked the captain if she could go and help find more wounded, but as she had feared, the big knight shook his head and told her that they needed her here.

Alicia was about to leave for a second time when Sir Richard said, "He was like a son to me."

Alicia turned and listened.

"I loved him more than I have loved anyone else. The little boy was my greatest treasure. I would give anything for him." Richard shook his head and continued sobbing.

Alicia left while Richard continued crying behind her.

Chapter 17

"I vote we get in, unlock Egon's, Lord Ive's, and Xurxo's cages, and then get out." Leif said looking at Caesar and Cuthbert. Cuthbert nodded slowly, his mind churning. Caesar just stared dumbly back at Leif, and Leif felt had a strong urge to clap his hands in front of the monkey-man's face.

"I disagree." Cuthbert finally said. It seemed his mind had finally worked things out. "I think we should unlock everybody from their cage and then start a fire and a riot. That way we can get out easier and we give the Waylins a fighting chance."

Suddenly Caesar jumped up and yelled, "Fighter is fool!" Cuthbert and Leif jumped at the furry creature and tackled him, Cuthbert covering his mouth with his hand.

"Idiot!" Leif hissed. "Do you want us to get killed?"

The two apprentices finally released Caesar and the monkey-man looked at them as he quietly and slowly whispered, "Most of men hurt. If men get out then Elves shoot and men die. Not good! Best leave men in cage."

Caesar shook his head and crawled over to the horse, busying himself with some berries that the trio had picked the day before. Cuthbert looked at Leif and the apprentices nodded at each other. Caesar made sense.

"Fine," Cuthbert said. "But wouldn't it be easier to just let Caesar go in and unlock their cages? I mean, he's done it before."

Leif shook his head. "But they haven't." He objected. "They won't know how to get out, where to go, when to go, or where all the guards are located. We know that, and besides, don't you think those grown men will trust themselves rather than Caesar?"

Caesar seemed not to have heard the last statement, and Cuthbert finally conceded, his friend had a point.

Leif thought for a second and then said, "Okay. I know what we'll do. We'll get in there and Caesar will have the keys. He'll open their cages while we sneak into Xurxo's little hovel. Then we'll hand Xurxo a paper that tells him where to go and then we'll leave. He seems to have gotten much better the past week, and I believe he is the most able-bodied of them according to Caesar because they've been attempting to fix him up—a dead man is a lost ransom. He says that Lord Ive and Egon have been just about whipped daily. Especially Egon. We'll help them out and meet up with Xurxo. How about that?"

Cuthbert considered Leif's plan for a moment and then reluctantly agreed.

"What about the paper, though?" He asked.

Leif smiled at his friend and moved over to where the actual toll booth had stood. The trio was currently camping in the man's hut which was attached to the toll booth, so Leif had to be extra careful not to be seen as the crawled toward the booth. Once there he unsheathed his dagger and cut off a decent size sheet of canvas. Then he crawled back.

Five minutes later Leif was ready, the piece of canvas in front of him and a coal in hand. Leif had sharpened the coal to a delicate point in order to write legibly. Then, in his best handwriting, Leif wrote,

Xurxo,

> **Get out of the town by means of the front gate. Stick to the shadows and move very slowly for there are guards on a hovel there, two hiding in the shadows of the wall, and another one on the wall. Once you are out, get safely to cover. Then continue along the road until you get to a burned out farm. Stop there and wait for us. If we don't come in the next two days, leave without us and get to Kingstan.**

—Leif and Cuthbert (bowman and knight apprentices)

Then Leif gingerly rolled the canvas together and stuck it into his pocket.

The Commander drove his troops hard, and the hundred knights thundered down the paths kicking up large dust clouds. The forests on the right and left blurred as the men pushed their horses to the limit. The Commander had specifically said that he wanted to attack tonight.

Zoticus was riding up front, right next to the Commander. He was leading the way and sitting on a brand new warhorse. His old one was too tired and too slow. The young man smiled, his career in the army was getting better than ever. All he wanted to do now was fight.

Finally the group thundered into the clearing where the small battle between the Morr, Elves, and "rescuers" had occurred. The Commander got out a map and spent the next ten minutes going over it with a small council of men in which Zoticus was not included. Finally the men urged on their horses and galloped on.

They rode for several hours without stopping. While they spurred on their horses the sun sank below the horizon and night began to fall. Finally they left the cover of the forest and continued onward on a village raod. Now the Commander slowed the troops and they trotted towards their goal. There was not a sound besides the horses' hooves on the ground. The Commander had ordered all the armor to be oiled and padded in order to make the men quieter. No food had been taken, and now the men ate what they had brought in their saddlebags quietly, sometimes stopping on the side of the road to go to the bathroom.

As they rode, they passed gruesome scenes of blood and gore. Many men shuddered, wondering what kind of evil would commit such terrible acts. The Commander didn't react to them, his face as set and determined as ever.

Suddenly the Commander raised his hand and the men stopped. Then the General slipped down from his horse, and his knights followed suit, buckling on the remaining pieces of their armor. The men now led their horses onward, quietly going along.

Leif and Cuthbert, both caked with mud and covered with pieces of grass crawled forward on their stomachs. They could see very little besides the large keep in the center of town, which was illuminated. Caesar inched forward ahead of them, showing the two apprentices the way. They had all agreed only to bring daggers, and knew everything about the village from Caesar's inspection trips.

Finally they got to the walls and Caesar rolled against them. Ten seconds later Cuthbert and Leif did the same. Then Caesar rolled around the corner and Leif and Cuthbert followed. The trio slowly advanced, hiding behind bushes, ruins of hovels, statues, and sometimes in large flowerbeds when a guard patrolled by.

After another half an hour of silent crawling, Caesar signaled, pointing at a run-down hovel and then quietly disappeared into the darkness.

Leif looked around and crawled forward. There was no one in sight. Suddenly a scuffling noise came from the top of the hovel. A second later a strange, guttural curse sounded and a rock thudded into the ground near Leif.

Leif backed off into the shadow of a tree. The Dark Elf walked on, patrolling the roof and constantly vigilant. Leif sat and thought of what to do. He needed a plan.

Suddenly Leif saw Cuthbert edging forward on the ground! Leif wanted to cry out or to move forward and grab Cuthbert, but he knew it would give both of them away.

Leif held his breath. Either Cuthbert didn't know about the guard, which Leif doubted, or the knight apprentice was going forward to get rid of the guard.

Leif cursed. With the knights it was always, "Act first then think."

Cuthbert was now next to the hovel. The young man slowly straightened up until he was standing. Then he took his dagger and set it between his teeth, slowly extending his hand upward until he was holding on to the top of the roof. He was going to pull himself up and fight the guard!

Leif needed to do something and fast. The Golden Arrow apprentice looked around. Finally the young man jumped up and climbed the tree he had been hiding behind. He got to the branches without making a sound and continued forward. He was now above the hovel. Cuthbert was already pulling himself up, very slowly, using every ounce of muscle power.

Leif grabbed his dagger, which he too had clamped between his teeth, and jumped off the branch.

Leif soared through the air in clear sight of every sentry, including the one on the hovel. Luckily the Elf on the hovel had been turned around. Leif heard the tree branch snap behind him, and in front of him the guard slowly turned. This, more than anything sealed his fate for him. Had the Elf stayed turned around he would have been struck in the back and lived. But the guard turned and Leif fell on top of him, the dagger plunging into the Dark Elf's chest, sliding between his ribs and puncturing his lungs. Then the tree branch crashed on top of both of them, knocking the air out of Leif and crushing him to the roof.

The Elf opened his mouth to scream a warning to his comrades, but no sound came out of it. His black robe turned a deathly red and the Elf slowly closed his eyes and died. Leif looked away, disgusted with what he had done. Then the young apprentice tried getting out from under the tree branch, but succeeded in only getting stuck more firmly.

Cuthbert quickly entered the hovel, waking Xurxo who had been sleeping. Xurxo had had a rope holding him to his cot and Cuthbert quickly cut this with his dagger. Then he shoved the rolled piece of canvas at the Rider and left the hovel as Xurxo sat up, slowly taking in what was happening.

Only now did Cuthbert realize that Leif hadn't gotten off the roof. The young apprentice hoisted himself up, but he slipped and fell, emitting an, "oof!"

Suddenly the young man cried out, a searing pain driving through Cuthbert's shoulder. The young knight looked at the wound where blood was now pouring to the ground. An arrow was lodged in his shoulder!

Above Cuthbert, trapped on the roof, Leif screamed, desperately clawing at the tree branch. He had to help his friend!

A small group of Dark Elves ran to the site of the sound and immediately grabbed Cuthbert. One Elf knocked him senseless with the end of his mace, while another pulled himself up onto the roof. The rest of the group carried Cuthbert away, while the Elf on the roof got his buddy.

Leif stopped moving immediately, not daring to even breathe. The Dark Elf lifted the limp form of his friend and gently lowered it down to a waiting Elf. Then the Elf scanned the roof and suddenly saw Leif.

The Elf spat at Leif, covering Leif's face with brown spittle.

"You!" The Elf rasped; his voice hoarse and scratchy. Leif flinched at the sound. The Elf's leathery brown face strained to get out the word. The large black robe that was rimmed with yellow fluttered in the wind, revealing the Elf's dagger. The Elf didn't reach for this though, but for its sword, which it had slung over his back with his bow. The Elf raised the blade and brought it down hard.

Leif screamed, terrified. The young man could imagine the feel of the cold metal cutting into him like a lance of pain, taking away his life forever. Tears of anger and frustration leapt to his eyes, as he thought, "All of this work, just to die now? All of these years ahead of me, but I die now? For nothing?" All of this happened in the split second where the blade was whistling through the air, and suddenly a Herculean strength coursed through Leif as such tremendous power and might pumped through his body as he had never before felt in his life. The young man cried out in pain and in sheer frustration as he thrust forward his body, rolling the branch away.

The sword that had been moments ago speeding towards Leif's throat lodged itself in the tree branch as the piece of wood moved into the Elf's line of attack.

The Elf tried to dislodge the sword but it was hopeless, and in this time Leif rolled off the roof.

The Elf cried out and unsheathed his dagger, springing after his quarry.

Leif landed in a flowerbed, falling forward to cushion the force of the landing. Then Leif popped up, and suddenly he was running faster than he had ever run in his life down the paved street in front of him, oblivious to the danger crowding in around him.

Leif sprinted for a few seconds until he allowed a look back, only to see that the Elf had stopped, drawn his bow, nocked an arrow, and was pulling back the string. Leif dove forward, but it was too late.

A searing pain shot up his leg and gripped Leif's body like an ice-cold dagger. The young man cried out in pain as the arrow clattered to the ground beside him. It had not actually gotten him, just glanced off his leg, but that was enough; a second later the Dark Elf towered above the crying apprentice.

The Elf's eyes blazed with hatred and the beast, which is what Leif now thought of this *thing*, picked up the boy and smashed his head against the hovel behind him. Leif just cried out again, his outburst lost in the sound of his sobbing.

A thunder sounded overhead, as if adding to the suspense, and sudden rain trickled down as the Elf took Leif's neck in his hands and began squeezing as hard as he could.

Leif choked and sputtered, as life slowly drained out of him. Pain was coming from everywhere now, as the blood from his leg washed down the road, and black spots appeared on his eyes.

Suddenly a cry cut through the air and hooves clattered down the road. Someone cried out from somewhere and a horse whinnied loudly.

The Elf loosened his grip for a second and Leif grabbed a quick breath until the Elf finally threw him on the ground and descended upon him, his dagger glinting in the lightning behind him.

Leif was barely conscious now, not caring or knowing what was happening to him. The Elf lifted his dagger for the last time, and brought it down at Leif's throat, when—an arrow cut through the wind and into the back of the Elf.

The Elf's back snapped forward, and he cried out as he fell forward, on top of his dagger—dead. The Elf lay on top of Leif, his dark red blood mingling with Leif's and the rain. Leif breathed in deeply and then passed into a world of darkness.

Zoticus's eyes blazed as he mounted his horse. His heart pounded and adrenaline coursed through his body. The young man breathed in deeply, drawing his sword and waiting for the command to attack. The village was in sight in front of him and the Commander had ordered for ten scouts to skirt the outsides to find two boys, but more than this Zoticus did not know.

Finally the Commander gave the signal by drawing his saber and pointing it at the village in front of them, about 250 yards away. Zoticus charged forward, digging his spurs into the sides of his warhorse as the hundred other knights did the same.

Zoticus waved his sword above his head, holding onto the reins with the other hand. He opened his mouth and roared, screaming with his hot-blooded companions.

Shouts echoed from the village and arrows arced through the sky at the group.

Zoticus brought his sword hand down and held onto the reins with it, while lifting his shield with the other hand in order to protect himself from the arrows. A single shaft thudded into the limewood, nearly throwing Zoticus from his mount.

A minute later Zoticus charged into the village as one of the first Morrs inside.

A paved street ran down the center of the village, and in front of him the young man saw an Elf strangling a boy. Whoever the boy was, Zoticus figured that the enemy of his enemy was his friend. Apparently his fellow knights agreed with him because one man brought forth a bow, and in one swift motion, he shot the Elf.

Suddenly the man next to Zoticus fell from his horse, a random arrow in his heart. The horse whinnied loudly, bolting down a side street and kicking up a cloud of dust.

Zoticus screamed. This time the scream was high-pitched and of terror, not excitement. War wasn't such a fun place after all. Zoticus had known that people died in war and that it was a cruel place, but he expected there to be more honor and glory. Not for a man to be randomly shot off the face of this earth. He had expected it to be a place where he would be famous and each kill just intensified his honor and status. But war wasn't like that. War was basically "kill or be killed", and no one truly knew why they were killing, or why death had to exist in this manner and pain anyways. It seemed so pointless.

But Zoticus couldn't think for long, because suddenly a line of Elves advanced towards him. The apprentice knight spurred on his horse, ducked low, and raised his sword, bringing it down as he thundered through the line, taking down two men; trampling one and smiting the other.

His horse reared and Zoticus shouted out in fear, dropping his sword and holding on to the reins. His horse didn't want to be here, and suddenly Zoticus didn't want to either.

The young man tried turning around, but the torrent of knights pressed him and his horse on, giving no rest. Zoticus's horse bolted forward and the apprentice held on just to survive; falling would mean being killed by the churning hooves below.

As the warhorse bolted around, kicking up dirt, mud, and slipping in the rainwater, Zoticus survived by pure instinct. He didn't think, he just held on and prayed that a stray arrow wouldn't catch him. The battle raged around him while Zoticus was at the mercy of his horse, which was at the mercy of the fight around him.

The young warrior had no clue how long the battle lasted and who died. He didn't know who ended it and how, just that when everything calmed down, he was dripping wet and covered in blood. The blood was not his own, and fires raged around him, crackling and hissing as the water poured down upon them. The keep in front of him had been ransacked and blown open. Cages filled with starved and beaten people had been stacked near the keep and a young man, very muscular and seemingly unhurt except for a bloody wound on his head was held in shackles there.

Supposedly a group of about twenty Elves had escaped with the most valuable prisoners, and a small group of knights were deployed after them.

The dead were heaped in the square, where the dead Elves were burned and the dead knights loaded onto carts and attached to the horses left in the stables. Injured or captured Elves were swiftly beheaded, and thrown into the fire, their hair exploding into flames. Zoticus looked away, dismounting and throwing up onto a tree.

He didn't like war. He wanted to leave. This was horrible.

The bonfire in the center of town rose high into the sky, and the shackled, young prisoner was brought to the front. Here he was tied to four stakes which had been hammered into the ground. The Commander slowly walked to the boy, asking him something. The prisoner simply whimpered in reply, and the Commander ordered a heated iron to be brought. A knight quickly fetched an iron from the nearby stables, the tip a burning white. Once the man had returned the crowd of ninety knights had circled around the Commander and his captive, Zoticus among them.

The Commander asked the boy again, yet he only received a sob in return again, some of the knights jeering at him and laughing. An icy glare from the Commander silenced them.

Shaking his head in sick amusement, the Commander ordered the knight to hand him the heated iron. Again the General asked the boy his question, this time placing the burning iron onto his chest.

The iron burned through the boy's shirt, searing his skin. The young prisoner cried out in agony as the gathered knights howled in laughter, Zoticus turning away and covering his ears. The Commander kept the iron on the boy's skin a moment longer, the captive screaming in agony, yelling, "Yes! Yes! I am!"

The Commander removed the torture device, handing it to the waiting knight. Then the General ordered a group of jeering knights to find some proper clothes for the prisoner and treat his burn, head wound, and bleeding shoulder where the arrow's stump was still poking out. The knights grudgingly obeyed, dragging the boy from the circle of onlookers.

Finally, once the Commander had congratulated his knights and told them that the keep was off limits for everyone except him and his right hand men, the Commander let his troops loose. Some knights had the decency to bring their horses to the stables, such as Zoticus, but most tied them to a nearby tree or pole and set about looting the town. The men ran through the streets like wild animals, throwing open hovel doors and taking anything of worth.

Zoticus cleaned and fed his horse alone in the stables while outside the shouts of drunken men scared the tired horses. Finally Zoticus finished and made himself a bed on a bale of hay. He fell asleep a couple seconds later, and was haunted by a night of torturous dreams of death, blood, and the cruelty of war.

Most of the knights were hung over and half asleep as they swayed in the saddle. Their horses were loaded down with little objects of value. Nearly half of the men hadn't even slept during the night, having been busy celebrating.

Zoticus shook his head. How could they celebrate death? The young warrior urged his horse away from the group and toward the front where the Commander and his men were. He knew that they wouldn't be drunk nor would they have pillaged the town. After all, they had more than enough anyways.

Zoticus approached them and saw that the cart with the boy prisoner was right next to the Commander. Zoticus wondered what could be so special about a single boy. The young warrior shook his head and looked through the bars.

The boy had on good silk clothes, which were black and red and had probably once belonged to a Dark Elf. The boy's hair was messy and his face was bruised and dirty. A bandage had been put on a wound on his head, and a sling held his arm. As Zoticus examined him, the young man opened his eyes.

Zoticus looked curiously at the boy. The boy glared back, his eyes blazing with hatred. Zoticus wanted to shout out and say, "Wait! I don't know what's happening! Why are you mad at me?" Instead the warrior shook his head and slowed his horse, letting the cart move on ahead.

Zoticus wondered about why the boy was mad at him. What had he done? And then the young warrior realized why. It was because he was a Morr and this boy was a Waylin. They were simply born on opposite teams, but at heart they were probably the same. Zoticus wondered how many other innocent, nice people had been murdered. "How many good people's lives have I taken?" He wondered. "Just because I wear a different uniform and have different leaders, I must kill them and they me. Why can't the good stay with the good and live in peace, while the evil simply quarrel alone?"

Zoticus finally sighed and pushed the philosophical thoughts out of his mind. All he wanted to do now was survive the war and go home where he would retire from the military. It was just too cruel for him.

The Commander kept his troops moving at a steady, even pace. They set their horses at a walk, and stopped for lunch at an apple farm where they ate apples and drank from a nearby well. Here the Commander counted his remaining troops and saw that he had just below ninety men left.

The prisoner was given food and water, and a chance to stretch his legs, and then they were off again. They didn't stop until dusk, where they camped at a clearing that Zoticus had shown the Commander in the beginning.

Guards were assigned to the trees, horses, and certain other positions, and then shifts were distributed. There was no dinner, and while the horses grazed, most of the men fell into a deep sleep.

Zoticus barely slept. He had been given the last shift, and once again his dreams tormented him with images of battle. The warrior tossed and turned in his grass bed, sometimes crying out, but no one noticed because all of the tired, drunk knights were busy catching up on their sleep.

Finally Zoticus was woken for the last shift. He sat in a tree for three hours before waking the camp as the sun slowly rose into the sky.

Then the men saddled up, cleaned up camp, and an hour later they were off, this time trotting down the dirt path.

The Commander, his seventy-five men, and the treasured prisoner entered camp late that evening, once the sun had already set. They were greeted with ale, celebration, and good food. A sturdy cell was immediately built for the prisoner, and five guards were set to watch it at all times, one of them crouched on the roof.

Zoticus grabbed some food and went to his tent, where the other apprentice knights were already sleeping soundly. The warrior looked at them and a tear trickled down his face. They were all so young and innocent. They had no clue what was in store for them or what lay ahead of them. Zoticus wept for his fate and his friends' fate, until at last he fell into a troubled sleep.

Leif woke up as sunlight filtered through the trees above him. A furry face looked down at him and yelped with delight.

"Bow-boy!" Caesar shouted with glee. The little monkey-man hurried over to a dented helmet, which contained a mixture of herbs, water, and plants.

Leif sat up, wincing as he felt a sharp pain in his leg. He looked down and saw that it had been wrapped in a green plant. Suddenly the images of the night before flooded into his mind: crawling into the village, the Elf trying to kill him, the Elf being shot, Cuthbert being kidnapped—"Cuthbert!" Leif screamed.

His eyes wide opened, he forced himself to his feet, ignoring the sharp pain in his foot. Caesar jumped up and ran to the apprentice bowman.

"Sit!" the monkey-man commanded, dabbing his wound with a strange ointment.

"But Cuthbert—he was captured. We need to get him—Cuthbert!" Leif hurriedly explained, screaming his friend's name as he ended.

Caesar shook his head and said, "Fighter gone."

Leif stared dumbly at the furry creature, slowly shaking his head in disbelief. "No. It can't be. We need to save him. What are we waiting for?" He said.

Caesar looked at Leif and finally made him calm down. Then he stood over him and explained slowly what had happened.

"Okay. Caesar go to bow-boy's friends when Caesar hear loud crack from where bow-boy was. Caesar turn and go to bow-boy, and see Elves carry away Fighter. Then Caesar see bow-boy run and a Elf chase. Caesar run too, but then attack! Caesar hide. Then Caesar get bow-boy and run. At night Caesar see evil Elves leave. Elves have cart and pretty horse. Caesar also know where Elves hide with bow-boy's friends today. Caesar and bow-boy close to Elves and friends. Knight attackers gone with Fighter."

Leif shook his head, mumbling a low, inaudible "no". Caesar looked at Leif and said, "Yes". Leif shook his head again, and this time Caesar nodded.

"So let me get this straight," Leif said, attempting to understand what had happened. "Cuthbert was captured by the Dark Elves, but then a group of knights—"

"Red," Caesar interrupted.

"What?"

"Attackers red."

"Oh," Leif finally understood. "Cuthbert was captured by the Dark Elves, but then a group Morrs attacked, which is why I didn't get killed. They must have been the ones that killed the one strangling me. The Morrs then captured the town, including Cuthbert. Then a couple of those Elvin cowards escaped with Xurxo, Lord Ive, and the Palomino. Finally, once the battle was over, you rescued me, and started following the Dark Elves that ran away."

Caesar nodded vigorously and, after a long time, he was able to talk Leif into leaving Cuthbert. The monkey-man told him that Cuthbert and his Morr capturers were heading towards Kingstan. Leif now grudgingly agreed with Caesar to follow his mentor and Egon. Caesar told Leif that Cuthbert was probably going back to the castle and would be ransomed. He also explained that he had already chosen to follow the Dark Elves, who were lodged in a nearby cave. Leif had even stolen a rickety cart that Leif could lie in until his arrow wound healed.

What finally convinced Leif was that his duty lay in following the Dark Elves, for they still had the papers that Leif had been ordered to take because Caesar had told them that they had the "pretty horse" with them. His responsibility was to get these and destroy them, and Leif knew that if he followed his orders and trusted in Sir Richard's ability as a leader, everything would be okay. Also, Lord Ive and Egon were still being held captive, and perhaps Leif could save them and then double back and quickly rescue Cuthbert! Besides, Caesar had even stolen a cart for Leif!

He now realized how important Caesar was. Without him, his whole mission and the whole adventure with Cuthbert would have been a complete failure. Caesar had supplied their weapons and armor. He had rescued him from the Dark Elves and stolen a cart for him. He had killed the Morrs that were attacking Leif and Cuthbert in the forest, and he had got all the necessary information that they had needed to free Xurxo and now to make the decision whether to follow Cuthbert or his duty. "Large blessings sometimes come in little packages." He said.

Caesar looked at Leif and smiled one of his toothy, show-my-teeth, smiles. Leif laughed, and an hour later they were clattering down the road after the Dark Elves who were supposedly holed up in a cave somewhere.

The apprentice was so worried about his friend that he completely forgot about Xurxo. Leif sincerely hoped that Cuthbert would be ransomed as Caesar had said. Little did he know how right he was.

Chapter 18

It was a huge building. Because it was in the middle of the night, everything was black except for the castle before Xurxo. The giant castle was alight with torches, emitting an eerie glow. The town of this castle did not have a wall and the fields reached all the way to where Xurxo stood. The large fortress five hundred meters away had impressive twenty yard high walls and its keep was a large square, different from the one in Kingstan. The castle may have once looked inviting, almost friendly, but this effect was completely destroyed by the red uniformed sentries patrolling along the walls.

Xurxo moved forward. He was not scared of being seen from this far away, but he still walked bent over. The Rider moved with a slight limp and could not go any faster than a walk because he had not completely recovered yet.

The large warrior now involuntarily thought of the apprentices who had freed him. Xurxo still carried the canvas that the apprentice knight had given him. He wondered what had happened to them, for Xurxo had waited three days in the field that the apprentices had described, even daring to light a fire to alert the apprentices of his presence. On the fourth day Xurxo had scouted around the town, searching for the two boys, but he had not found anybody. Then Xurxo decided to obey what Leif and Cuthbert had put on the canvas about going back to Kingstan. It made Xurxo laugh at how confidently these two handed out orders to a warrior of much higher rank. The Rider was not worried about the next generation of warriors if this was how they acted.

Xurxo had decided to obey the "order" with a twist, walking instead in the other direction, away from Kingstan to Drayton, the headquarters of the Morrs in the Waylin Islands and the area where they held their dragons.

Xurxo was now in sight of the sentries, crawling through a wheat field only a couple hundred yards from the nearby gatehouse. If they looked hard enough they could maybe see the small indentation in the wheat.

The farms close to Kingsburg seemed to still be functioning, for a farmer was steadily working his way through the field toward the area where Xurxo lay.

The Rider quickly rolled out of the man's path, flattening the wheat and completely exposing himself to the farmer. The wheat farmer frowned and walked mor quickly towards Xurxo.

The warrior had no choice. He lashed out with his foot, catching the farmer in the stomach. The man fell to the ground and in an instant Xurxo was on top of him. Xurxo found one of the man's pressure points and pushed hard, causing the farmer to lose consciousness. Then Xurxo quickly undressed the farmer and slipped into his clothes. The Rider cut his own clothes into strips and tied the farmer's legs, arms, and gagged him. He would eventually rip the fabric, but Xurxo only needed a few hours.

Then Xurxo stuck the silly looking farmer hat on his head and got up. He walked to the farmhouse and looked inside. Large bundles of flour were heaped against the wall and Xurxo went over to these, loading several into a small cart. This he attached to a mule he found in the stables and then the Rider left the farm, clattering down the paved road toward Kingsburg.

Although it was still several hours until daybreak, the gates were open and Xurxo was admitted inside without as much as a glance by the guard there. Xurxo guessed that the kitchen was already preparing for the morning meal so it wouldn't seem odd that a shipment of flour was coming in.

Xurxo led the mule to where he would expect the kitchens to be. He would act like he was delivering the flour to the cooks, which is what the farmer would have done sooner or later anyways, since he probably paid his taxes in products.

The courtyard was just about empty and from the inside Xurxo saw that there were not as many sentries as he had originally thought. Two large stone buildings stood before Xurxo now. One was about five times the size of the other and about ten yards tall and fifty wide. Grunts and growls were coming from inside.

The other one was probably the kitchen and closed for the night. Xurxo tied the mule to a post and, making sure no one was looking, rolled into the deep shadows by the larger building.

This building was obviously the stables and Xurxo peeked in through the door. A guard was walking up and down the central aisle. On the two sides were giant metal stalls that held the dragons. Xurxo was impressed. The Morr sure knew how to take care of dragons, and the Waylins knew how to build proper stables. The stalls were large enough to for the dragon to move around a little in, even a very large one. None of the dragons were wearing muzzles, which was a great sign of trust and training, because that meant that any of them could roast the sentry in the middle at any time. Large open barrels filled with water were in one corner for the dragons to drink, and the carcass of some animal lay in the other. New hay had been put into the stalls recently, which really amazed Xurxo since it was the middle of the night. The Rider also realized that each of the dragons had armor, so they were all very mature. As Xurxo carefully examined each dragon he saw that they were in excellent shape, with bulging muscles and trained wings. He wondered why they posted only one guard to guard such a treasure.

Probably because they think they've got Arran now. And it doesn't seem like any of the peasants have rebelled. The Morrs seem fair enough at first but . . .

Now Xurxo quietly slipped into the stables, opening the door a little wider and squeezing through when the sentry was at the other side of the stables and no one outside was looking. One of the dragons near him grumbled, but the sentry didn't see a thing.

Xurxo was lucky. He had entered near the whips and other necessary items. Quickly he selected a particularly long whip and waited for the guard to patrol into sight.

The guard finally walked forward, and Xurxo popped up, flicking the whip forward and slashing it across the young man's face. The guard didn't even have time to scream before Xurxo was upon him, punching him and knocking him out.

Some of the dragons roared and Xurxo pulled the unconscious soldier into the corner. Then Xurxo sat down and closed his eyes. He focused all of his power, might, and being into a central spot in his chest. A renewed sense of peace swept over Xurxo and the dragons noticed it, calming down again. The Rider coaxed this inner flame within him, and it burned to life. He almost forgot where he was and what he was doing as this power consumed him.

Now that Xurxo had found his inner being, his soul and spirit, he moved to the dragons, using it to calm them and speak to them not through words but intentions. Once he had finally calmed them, he got up and scanned the dragons until he saw the one he liked. It was the best one, huge and muscular with thick armor.

The Golden Arrow Rider reached out with his spirit. All of the energy he had focused into his chest he now let pour forward at the dragon, speaking to his consciousness through it properly now. Dragons were semi-intelligent beings and so they did not think as much as choose. They lived by instinct but lived consciously, choosing wisely and for a reason. They knew what they were doing and why, just not always how. They had all the abilities of a human, simply not the ever-present question of "why?" that made Xurxo's race excel.

Xurxo's spirit reached for the dragon.

Howdy Xurxo thought. *I am your new master. You will fly for me and obey me. You will not protest, understood?*

The dragon growled deeply but finally agreed, giving in to the powerful force coaxing it into obedience.

Then Xurxo got a saddle and whip and strapped the saddle to the dragon. He also changed into some leather chaps and a new wool vest. Then stroked the dragon's scaly neck and led it to the back; the front entrance wasn't large enough.

Xurxo opened the back entrance, slowly and only enough to see through a small crack. Then he got onto the dragon and spoke to it for a few seconds, telling it what to do. The dragon was old and wise and new immediately what its master wanted.

Xurxo then strapped his legs to the saddle and softly flicked the whip against the dragon's neck. The massive beast let a small gush of flames loose as a reply and charged forward.

The large back doors to the stable were about a foot thick and reinforced with iron. The enormous beast charged into them though, ripping them from their hinges and causing them to crash to the ground.

Shouts of surprise echoed in the courtyard and from the walls of the castle, but Xurxo took no notice, urging the dragon forward and then into the air.

The huge beast leapt upwards, its giant wings carrying it up into the air. The sentries on the walls didn't know what was happening, and many were reluctant to shoot the dragon but several did. None of the arrows struck the dragon's wings and Xurxo assumed they were aiming for him, for most of the arrows hit the color-changing armor of the dragon and glanced off.

Finally the dragon was up in the air. It glided even higher as more arrows chased after it, the archers now not caring who or what they hit. One arrow ripped through the dragon's wings and a bright gush of orange flames poured from the beast's mouth.

Xurxo was an experienced pilot though and cleverly maneuvered the dragon, keeping it out of the way of the majority of the arrows.

Finally Xurxo reached a safe altitude and glided away, disappearing into the darkness.

Chapter 19

Richard emerged from the room, tired and exhausted. Sleep was impossible with the enemy siege equipment continually pounding on the walls and even if they weren't, he would never be able to shut an eye knowing that his beloved apprentice was out there somewhere.

Richard knew he would sacrifice anyone and everything for him. He would go the ends of the Earth to get the boy back. Richard wiped a tear away and looked into the distance.

Suddenly he heard a trumpet call: two ascending notes and then three staccato notes at the same pitch—the sign for a parley.

Richard momentarily forgot his troubles as he squinted into the distance. A second later a horse galloped into view, its rider carrying a white flag. Richard shrugged and hurried to the bailey where a group of knights were preparing to intercept the rider.

Richard jumped onto a horse, the duke doing likewise beside him. The Lord of the castle said something to him and Richard ignored it. He blamed him for losing Leif. The bowman apprentice should have returned several days ago, and there was still no sign of him.

Finally the group was ready and the gate was opened. The small group of knights, about ten warriors, thundered out towards the flag bearer. Richard led the group, Duke Cyril at his right, and other officers around them.

Finally they met the Morr, a young man, probably twenty-five years old with a clean-shaven face. He had a large mass of brown hair that hung to his shoulders and kind, inviting eyes.

Richard could hardly believe that these were the type of men whom he was killing. They were scarcely men!

The Captain pushed the thought out of his head as the Morr said, "The Royal Commander of Morrigan and five star General wishes to have a private audience with Sir Richard, Captain of the Golden Arrow of Siddian."

Richard's eyes widened as he heard his name and all of the information about him. They knew his name, rank, and where he was from! He wondered how much they knew about the other Golden Arrow members.

The other officers behind him started mumbling and the Morr repeated the request but was interrupted by Sir Richard who said, "Yes?"

The knight stopped reading at looked at the Golden Arrow Captain. "Is that you?" he asked.

Richard nodded and the knight spun around his horse, slowly walking back to his camp. Richard looked around him and grabbed the Duke's white cape, tying it to his sword. The Duke started to protest but Richard just told him to shut up and then he followed the Morr knight, now protected by his own flag of truce.

Duke Cyril shook his head, yelling a final curse after the belligerent knight. Then he turned and rode back to the castle, his faithful knights following him closely.

An hour later Richard slowly rode back into Kingstan, his eyes glazed and his lower lip quivering as if in anger or sadness. His face was hardened and his knuckles were white from gripping his sword so tightly.

Duke Cyril tried to find out what the meeting had been about, even ordering the knight to tell him. Captain Richard just ignored the Lord of Kingstan and went to his room, locking his door. Once inside he began to cry, sobbing as he began writing the most cunning and evil plan he had ever thought of.

Was it worth it? He thought. After a while he decided that *yes, it was.*

Chapter 20

Leif lay in the cart as it clattered down the road. Caesar was up front, sitting on the Marwari and guiding it down the cobblestone street. The little monkey-man looked funny, sitting on the large horse. Leif did his best not to laugh.

The bowman apprentice's leg still hurt, and the road was not easing the pain for him either, but at least they were doing something.

It had been two days since the battle in the Dark Elf town and Leif and Caesar were still following the Dark Elves. The vile creatures had left their cave and were now hurrying towards the coast. Caesar and Leif were constantly riding to catch up with the fleeing Elves. Caesar rode during the day while Leif slept and massaged his leg and then they switched roles for the night.

Leif could walk now and the nausea was gone. He limped, but could at least move around without crying out in pain.

The Dark Elves traveled mainly at night so the duo had to be very cautious and quiet during the day. As Leif continued thinking these dull thoughts, sleep suddenly overcame him.

Leif was woken by a strange rushing sound. It seemed like a steady roar and somewhat familiar. Suddenly it hit him: the ocean! They had arrived!

Leif looked at the area around him. It was dark out now, and Caesar was still patiently guiding the horse down the cobblestone street.

"Bow-boy!" He hissed. "Caesar want to leave cart and go find bad guys, bow-boy like?" He asked.

Leif considered this for a minute and then nodded, "okay."

Together the two hid the cart in a nearby patch of trees, and Leif grabbed his bow and filled double-quiver.

The duo stayed in the bushes as they walked along the road. Leif nocked an arrow and Caesar drew his dagger. After walking for a couple minutes they entered what seemed to be a town.

The town was very clearly occupied by Morr soldiers, for a large red flag flew from the town hall and red uniformed guards were all over the place. It seemed that news hadn't reached this area yet for the Dark Elves were simply walking right down the center street, unscathed.

Leif and Caesar entered the town, telling the guard they were returning from an unsuccessful hunting trip. The guard accepted the explanation, strangely eying the monkey-man, yet not saying anything. Then the guard demanded for Leif to hand over his bow and arrows—weapons could only be handled by Morr soldiers within the town. Leif smiled as the guard confiscated his weapon—he had hid his dagger within in his shirt. Also, if the guard was charged with taking weapons from people, then that meant the Morrs were scared of rebellion. In the distance the sun slowly crept over the horizon.

Leif could see the cages of Lord Ive and Egon. They were next to each other, surrounded by a sea of crates and barrels. The beautiful Palomino stood there as well, tied to one of the cages. On a sudden impulse, and to satisfy the curiosity that had been eating away at him for days now, Leif jumped up and ran toward the cages.

The Elves were walking away, their backs turned. The sailors were busy rolling barrels up the gangway, and the street was deserted. *They should call me Lucky Leif,* Leif thought with a smile as he hid behind the nearest crate. A group of sailors came back and got more barrels, and Leif saw Caesar frantically motioning for him to get back. Gritting his teeth in determination, Leif shook his head and crawled from crate to crate, slowly inching towards his master.

Finally he was close enough to talk to Lord Ive. The large Palomino looked down at him, snorting once, but not minding him.

Leif gasped as he looked at the beautiful horse. On the expertly crafted saddle was a strange, discolored piece of leather. Leif quickly drew his dagger and popped up, not caring if anyone could see him. Then he began sawing away at the leather, cutting through the soft, brown seat to steal the lighter pouch. Meanwhile the Palomino quietly sniffed Leif, finally busying itself with chewing on Lord Ive's cage. Leif smiled and dropped behind his crate once more, expecting to hear accusing shouts from the nearby sailors. There were none.

Once Leif had opened the pouch and seen the treasured letter, which also included a map of Kingstan and its castle, including all the secret passage ways and weaknesses, and skimmed a list that told of Kingstan's construction history, he remembered the question he had wanted to ask Lord Ive since his master had been torn from him in the aerial fight. That question now burned in his mind. He *had* to ask it—in case there wouldn't be a chance later.

"Lord Ive, it's me, Leif." Leif said.

The cage clanged and scraped as Lord Ive turned, scanning the crates for his apprentice.

"I have one quick question," Leif said. "How did you know my father?"

Leif peeked around his crate, and Lord Ive's eyes rested upon him. Without asking how or why Leif had gotten there or even to this port, Lord Ive answered. "Your father volunteered to go instead of your younger brother. Because of him, I didn't have to go to war."

The world spun around Leif. He had no clue what was happening any more. Suddenly a shout echoed from the ship. A sailor had spotted Leif! The bowman apprentice jumped up and sprinted toward Caesar. An arrow whizzed by his ear, and more shouts sounded. Footsteps pounded behind him as the Dark Elves and sailors gave chase.

Caesar grunted something along the lines of, "Bowboy be idiot!" and removed the sling from his belt, quickly fitting a stone to the cup shaped end. In seconds the first of the Dark Elves was down.

Leif cursed his luck, wishing he still had his bow. He ducked his head, his mind still racing with what Lord Ive had said, as he hurried to his furry friend. Caesar loosed one last stone, smashing one Dark Elf in the face. None of the Elf's friends stopped to help, and the sailors eyed the downed soldier skeptically, unsure of what to do.

"Quick! Follow me," Leif hissed, pulling Caesar with him.

The two sprinted down the street and through an alleyway. Then Leif headed toward the center of the town. *If the market is crowded, then maybe I can lose the Elves,* he reasoned.

Leif was in luck. The marketplace was filled with people, haggling over prices, shouting their wares, or simply eyeing the different things on sale. Leif quickly pulled his short friend next to him and whispered, "Let's split up. We'll meet again in three hours somewhere near the front gate."

Caesar was gone before Leif finished, losing himself in the mass of shuffling feet. The monkey-man skillfully dodged around the legs, crawling in between and sliding by others. Most of the people didn't realize him, but those that did often yelped in surprise. Thankfully Caesar left the marketplace before a full-scale riot could start, and the monkey-man became lost among the buildings, jumping from one to the other.

Leif tried his best to blend in, but that was easier said than done for him. He was still wearing his now tattered and stained dragonhide suit, but had gotten rid of the coif. His hair was a mess, and he was in desperate need of a bath. The young apprentice hurried through the crowd though, hoping to lose the Elves as quickly as possible.

The Dark Elves had no regard for the humans before them. The vile creatures unsheathed their daggers and swords and pushed people aside, forcefully threatening them with their weapons if they didn't move fast enough. One Elf trampled over a young girl, and the father pushed away at the Elves to get to his daughter. The closest Elf spat at the man and lunged at him with his short sword, slicing open his chest. The man cried out and hit the ground, blood spewing from his wound and creating a red puddle around him.

Suddenly everyone began shouting and running out of the marketplace. People were shoved aside and trampled as everyone struggled to get away from the Dark Elves and their cruelty. Leif hurried out among the people, doing his best to get away from the Elves as well. Leif's unnaturally tall height for his age made him even with most of the adults, yet he was still pushed back and forth, jostled in the crowd.

The Elves ran after the crowds, in search of Leif, but because of this, the people grew more frightened, starting a full-fledge riot. The air filled with shouts, screams, and curses, as the people shoved each other out of the way, starting small fights as one man pushed another.

Leif quickly dodged into an alley, along with another family who had two young children. The smallest was crying and blood was running down her cheek, proof of the gash on her forehead. A sudden sadness overcame him of what he had done, his escape attempt having possibly killed someone, and injured many more. *Get on with it!* He thought. *If I do not make my getaway now, then I am dead for sure.*

Abandoning his feelings of pity and guilt, he sprinted down the alleyway and around a corner. Leif cursed as he saw that it was a dead end. Behind him he heard the family shriek and scream, and then he heard the running approach of footsteps. *Dark Elves!* Leif cursed. Panic arising in his throat, the young man looked around him for a way out.

The buildings were two stories high, the one on the left being the larger of the two. The other one had a large padlock and was definitely impossible to climb. The town wall in front of him was at least 20 feet high, and Leif knew he would never climb it in time. Shaking his head in frustration, Leif turned to the building on the left and yanked open the door.

The door slid open easily and Leif popped in, slamming it shut behind him. Quickly he slid the bar in place, locking it, and turned to examine his surroundings.

The building was a huge warehouse. Hundreds of crates were piled on top of each other and barrels lined the walls. Behind him, the door creaked and groaned as the Dark Elves rammed into it, trying to beat it down.

The only other door was on the other side, too far away for Leif to get there in time. Quickly, the apprentice ran over to the closest set of crates, all of them marked with an odd red stamp. He threw open the closest one and saw it was half empty, partially filled with daggers and swords, wrapped in expensive silk and linen. In one corner sat a small, perfectly circular rock, probably used for sharpening the blades. Leif picked this up and flung it into the far corner of warehouse. The stone bounced off of several of the crates, making quite some noise, and then rolled to a stop somewhere. Leif smiled and then disappeared into the crate, pulling top down over him.

Leif hadn't hid a moment too soon. The cheap wooden door burst open and a heavy Elf fell in, grunting something that sounded particularly vile as got up again. A flood of Elves ran in, sprinting towards the opposite door and towards the area where Leif had thrown the stone.

Leif watched through a crack in the wood as Elves beat down the door on the other side as well and rushed through, not even bothering to simply open it the proper way. The remaining Elves threw off the tops of the crates near where the stone had landed and used their blades to cut open the barrels. Wines, spices, and other things spilled over the floor, the Dark Elves not bothering to do their search in an orderly fashion. After ten minutes worth of searching, the last of the Elves cursed and left, hurrying out the exit way that their comrades had created.

Leif didn't dare leave the crate in the minutes that followed, and was happy he didn't. A guard entered the room, yelling at the top of his lungs and wielding a spear. His eyes wide in fear, he sprinted to the corner of the warehouse and began crazily ringing the bell there. When no one responded, he sagged to the floor and stopped. Then he climbed on top of a hill of crates and stood watch.

Suddenly, a tornado of brown fur hurled itself at him from the ceiling, whirling around in a frenzy of attacks. A second later, the guard was unconscious, lying on top of the crates. "Bow-boy!" Caesar cried.

Leif smiled and threw the lid of his crate to the side. "Caesar!" he exclaimed, his genuine happiness of seeing his friend again leaking into his voice.

Caesar quickly jumped to him, bounding off the crates and landing in front of Leif. The monkey-man gave an awkward bow and Leif laughed as Caesar immediately launched into an explanation. "Caesar be jumping from houses, when Caesar see bow-boy by small street. Elvies be running behind bow-boy! Caesar watch bow-boy go in big building. Then Caesar have climbed on roof and break hole. Caesar wait. Then Caesar rescue bow-boy!" The monkey-man ended by showing his teeth once again, and Leif smiled at his newfound friend. What had begun as an edgy relationship had now evolved into an everlasting bond of friendship.

Outside the sounds of rioting and chaos echoed into the large warehouse. Timed footsteps sounded, seeming to be marching in the direction of the building in which Caesar and Leif were hiding.

"Let's go!" Leif said to Caesar, already hurrying through the rows of crates toward the back door. They stepped over the beat down door and hurried down the alley.

The street was a disaster. People were trampling each other as they hurried into one direction. The town guard, angry sailors, and Dark Elves were heading in the opposite direction, some looking for Caesar and Leif, others simply hoping to end the chaos. A young pickpocket was using the opportunity to earn some money, deftly snatching people's purses and wallets from their very person. A particularly muscular fellow suddenly turned on him, grabbing his hand mid-steal. With a roar of anger the man slapped the boy who fell to the ground. Soon a fight was started and Leif and Caesar used the opportunity to slip into the crowd heading towards the harbor.

As they hurried through the streets, camouflaging themselves with the rioters the best they could, a Dark Elf spotted them and sent his knife whizzing past Leif's ear. Caesar turned and loosed a large rock at the Elf, but unfortunately missed. A troop of guardsmen had just turned the corner and witnessed the attempted murder. They sprinted in pursuit of Leif and Caesar who turned the corner and ran.

The duo sprinted through a complex set of alleys, streets, markets, and wharfs, hoping to lose their pursuers. Several times new groups of sailors and Elves would pick up the chase, yet Leif and Caesar never stopped running.

Two hours later the chaos had settled. The town guard now circled the village, having doubled their shift and placing men along the walls to prohibit Leif and Caesar from escaping. The Dark Elves had given up the chase after an hour and a half of running, and had instead contented themselves with taking over an inn, kicking out its guests and demanding ale, food, and rooms. The frightened innkeepers hurriedly agreed, rushing about to do the bidding of the Elves. The sailors had also retired for the night, the usual servants and low paid "lifters" carrying the cargo aboard the various ships.

Leif and Caesar were hiding behind a pile of rubbish in a dumpster. The dumpster was located on the actual pier and mostly filled with what smelled like dead fish. Leif wrinkled his nose as Caesar simply ignored the odor, focusing on what they had to do.

"We're trapped in the town." Leif reviewed the situation. "There's no way out, and staying any longer than tonight is suicide. What do we do?"

Caesar took a deep breath and answered slowly and thoughtfully. "Bow-boy," he began. "And Caesar be trapped. What bow-boy and Caesar must be doing, be hide in box and be put on ship. Or else be dead."

Leif nodded, appreciative of the fact that his friend recognized the circumstances and the most suitable option. He had been debating the question within his mind ever since he had hid in the warehouse.

I know what I want to do, he thought. *The question is if that is what* we *should be doing. Is it for our good? The good of Waylon and Siddian?* As Leif pondered these difficult questions, he examined their chances of hiding in a crate unseen.

There were six men out tonight, working on the pier. Two were on a ship loading the items into the hold, and the other four were carrying or rolling the crates and barrels to the gang plank. A single guard held watch from the mainmast of the tallest ship at the port, a large war galleon. If they were going to hide in a crate that night, he would estimate their survival chances at pretty high.

Finally Leif came up with a solution that had been forming in his mind for a long time. "I think we should go ahead and be stowaways on the ship that Lord Ive and Xurxo are on. We'll follow them wherever they go," Leif bit his lip in order not to say Ashtoreth, "and then work with Lord Ive and Egon to either take over the ship or to escape from wherever we land."

Leif didn't let his doubts seep into his words and Caesar finally nodded.

Quickly, the two jumped out of the dumpster and crawled over to the nearest box. It was a very large one and Leif removed his dagger and pried it open, making sure the guard was looking into the opposite direction and the sailors were busy with another ship. Leif was sure that this was the pile of crates for the Dark Elves ship, for they had a strange stamp on it, which looked like an arrow with rings around it. Leif actually thought the stamp looked pretty cool. *That'd be a good design for the Golden Arrow's coat of arms,* he thought. This was also where Lord Ive and Egon had been sitting before having been loaded onto the ship.

While none of the workers were watching, Leif quickly emptied the crate of its contents. Inside of the crate were a lot of Dark Elf robes, similar to those the Dark Elves wore. There was also a small bow and a bundle of arrows. These he emptied into the dumpster, leaving only a thin layer as padding for their journey, the bow, and the bundle of arrows. In the meantime, Caesar used Leif's dagger to make small, crack-like slits in the side of the box to provide the duo with air until they could get out of the crate. Finally they were done, having completed this without the notice of the sailors and the guard.

Five minutes later, when they had made completely certain that no one was watching, the two jumped into the nigh empty crate and closed the top. Now came the most risky part. Leif put an arrow on the bowstring and pulled back as far as he could in his cramped quarters. Then he released and the arrow thudded into the lid, burying itself in the soft wood.

The lid jumped up but didn't fly off. If anyone was watching then the two were goners. Thankfully no one was.

Leif grabbed hold of the arrow, and using it as a handle, he put the lid back on. Then he held onto the arrow, so if a worker tipped over the crate the lid wouldn't fall off and expose himself and Caesar.

Suddenly the crate was jerked forward and they were jostled around, but they didn't make a sound for the remaining clothes provided good padding. They continued to be thrown around as they were put onto a small cart and rolled up the gang plank.

A couple minutes later Caesar looked out of a crack in the wood and said, "On ship." Leif smiled, they were now officially stowaways. Several hours later the ship departed from the harbor; they were leaving for Ashtoreth!

Chapter 21

Water dripped onto the heads and shoulders of the Golden Arrow members as they walked single file down the tunnel. The tunnel was very small and wet so the members walked slowly in order not to slip.

Ragnhild, Richard, and Deacon had to duck so they wouldn't hit their heads against the ceiling and Gary had to walk in the very back so he would have room for his spear.

Richard had tried to get the members to leave their weapons but they had all said no. It was a time of war and they might need them, they said. Richard shook his head, wiping away a tear: they were right.

Alicia walked right behind Richard, who was up front. The woman had noticed something odd about her leader. He seemed less calm and was nervous and fidgety whenever he talked to the Golden Arrow. Now he kept breathing deeply as if to reassure himself. It was all very strange, she thought.

The Commander had seen the signal. The large boulder had raced across the sky, thudding harmlessly into the ground several hundred yards away from their camp. It could have been a setup or trap to lure the Commander into a bad position, but the man didn't care. He was going to attack no matter what. He knew a liar when he saw one and this

Richard could not lie. And anyways, his men outnumbered the Waylin defenders about five to one.

The Commander turned and surveyed his troops. They were ready. It had been many days since the siege had started and time was running out. All of them were eager to get this over with and they were all well equipped. Even the lowly apprentices had on chain mail and carried swords.

Now the Commander turned and looked at Kingstan falling apart before his eyes. The General had ordered all of his siege equipment forward and at high-speed, directing their fire at the north wall, the weakest area. The wall here was falling down slowly, and the gatehouse was dented and the wood splintered in several areas. Reinforcements had been ordered to the ramparts but that didn't matter, they would kill them all sooner or later.

Behind the Commander a large battering ram was being assembled. It would require fifty men to operate it, and the Commander had already assembled a large group of slaves to do the backbreaking work. Also, his tunnelers were busy weakening the wall. The whole group had been sent to work at midnight, slowly digging their way to the wall and probably their own death.

The Commander glanced at the sun. It was nearly time to storm the castle. With his face a mask of steel, the Commander nodded to an apprentice standing near him. The young boy picked up the blood red flag on the ground beside him and hoisted it up. It meant that no prisoners would be taken; each defender would be slain and not even the rich and valuable could hope for a ransom. The apprentice then ran to the lookout tower and climbed to the top. There he tied it to one of the posts, the flag waving wildly in the fierce wind. A large cheer went up from the gathered Morr warriors. They wanted blood and blood they would get.

Richard reached the end of the tunnel and stopped. He turned around, looking at his fellow Golden Arrow members and climbed the ladder in front of him. The tunnel was about two-and-a-half yards under the ground so Richard had to climb up to the very top where a trapdoor was. As he neared the top of the little tunnel the packed dirt and mud bricks turned to stone and Richard took a last deep breath. A tear slid down his cheek as he pushed open the door, flooding the tunnel with sunlight.

Richard stepped into the clearing, squinting in the harsh light. It was noon; he was right on time. Then the Captain moved to help Alicia out of the tunnel and turned his head away, avoiding her eyes.

"Sir?" Alicia asked, her voice conveying her worry. "Is everything all right?"

Richard nodded; he didn't think he could speak without his voice cracking.

The rest of the Golden Arrow emerged from the tunnel, dusting themselves off. They had entered a large circular clearing. There were trees around the clearing and bushes in front of these. Behind the warriors a small gap lay in the trees. Through here the enemy camp was visible, bustling with activity. Before the camps had moved forward they would have been about twenty yards from this area. Now only a small camp was left there, where blacksmiths were mending the final weapons before the large attack.

Maccabee had chosen his mace and he let it drop, the heavy, spiked ball of metal thudding into the ground. The bushes near him rustled suspiciously but he ignored it. Myrddin was panting, leaning on his staff for support. The man was getting old and this was not his type of work. Skinner was twirling his whips around, showing off to absolutely no one. Finally Hildebrand pushed him from behind and the whip master took a step forward, right into the path of his whip. Skinner cursed at Hildebrand who doubled over laughing.

Once everyone had settled down, they looked to Richard to tell them what to do. His eyes glistening with tears, the large warrior dropped his weapons which clattered to the ground in front of him. Then he took several paces back. The rest of the Golden Arrow looked at him as if he was insane. Maybe he was.

Suddenly the bushes in front of them erupted outward as warriors jumped out of them, crossbows at the ready. There must have been at least forty of them, all of their crossbows leveled at the Golden Arrow. A horse trotted in through the gap in the trees, the man on top sat smiling at his impressive catch.

"Well, well. What do we have here?" The man, probably a colonel in the Morr army, dismounted, handing the reins of his beautiful white battle horse to a nearby man who briefly lowered his crossbow.

Now the Colonel was circling the group of warriors. "Drop your weapons!" he commanded.

The Golden Arrow didn't move; all of them tensed except for Richard who was now sobbing loudly. "Do as he tells you," Richard said, the words coming out between sobs.

Still the Golden Arrow didn't move. The Colonel backed away and beckoned to one of the crossbowmen. "Hit the wizard's staff." He said.

The man kneeled leveled his crossbow and shot. The bolt cut through the air, slamming into Myrddin's staff. The treasured piece of wood flew from the magician's grasp and landed in the soil, the spell he had been preparing flying into the trees.

The shield Myrddin had been conjuring was still in its middle stages so it slammed into the tree, exploding and causing the oak to catch fire. The blue fire seemed to eat inward upon itself, not spreading to the rest of the forest as expected.

The Colonel spat at the Golden Arrow, narrowly missing Ragnhild who grunted something at the Morr. "Fine!" The Colonel shouted, his eyes blazing.

"You can keep your weapons with you for now. Try something foolish and you're all dead."

The Colonel nodded at one of the crossbowmen who ran in and grabbed Myrddin's staff and Richard's weapons. He put them into a small sack he had laying in the bushes.

His eyes still burning with fury, the Colonel ordered the crossbowmen to advance. The Golden Arrow finally started moving when the Morrs prodded them with their loaded crossbows.

Richard continued to cry and Alicia, her heart pounding didn't know what to do. The whole timing of the situation seemed so suspicious. In addition to the fact that the crossbowmen had been prepared, hiding in the bushes with their crossbows loaded, Richard seemed to obey without hesitation. She glanced at the crossbowmen near her. They couldn't really be called men, she thought. They were all boys, some of them probably weren't even shaving yet!

The Commander raised his sword high into the air, where it glinted in the sunlight. His men roared with anticipation. The horses pawed the ground and the young men-at-arms continued to sheath their swords and then pull them out again.

Now the Commander raised his eyes to the castle, the northern wall now weak and falling apart. He turned to his aide and gave the order for attack.

The Golden Arrow was marched into the small workers' camp, where the blacksmiths were settling down now that the final battle was starting. In the middle of the camp four rows of soldiers stood; half of them with loaded and leveled crossbows, the other half with pikes at the ready.

The Colonel ordered his men to move out of the way, ushering the Golden Arrow into the center of the Morr troops. The soldiers backed to the sides, revealing a cage in the middle.

Alicia's eyes opened in horror. Within the cage sat Cuthbert, the boy dressed in a Morr battledress. Cuthbert cried out when he saw the Golden Arrow and for the first time that day, Alicia saw Richard smile.

His eyes glinting with victory and his face barely keeping back a large grin, the Colonel said, "Here is your prize, soldier. Now hand over your dues."

Richard took a deep breath, wiped away his tears and said, "Drop your weapons and surrender."

Alicia gasped. Richard was a traitor! He had sold off the Golden Arrow for his apprentice!

An angry rage surged through the healer's body, possessing her and her emotions. Without knowing what she was doing, Alicia unsheathed her dagger and plunged it into Richard's back.

Once Richard was down, chaos raged in the small camp. The Golden Arrow exploded with activity, charging at the Morrs.

The crossbowmen cried out in surprise, firing their bows while the pike men stepped forward to engage the Golden Arrow.

The crossbow bolts shot across the clearing like silver hornets. Alicia was struck in the side and blood spurted from the wound. An unimaginable pain swept through her body, like a lance of agony. The healer cried out, clutching her side where the warm liquid was already flooding out. The woman tore off her cape and held it to her side to stem the flow.

The rest of the Golden Arrow had been trained in such combat and immediately had hit the ground, the bolts speeding over their heads and slamming into the crossbowmen on the other side. It had been a miracle that Alicia had been struck by only one.

Several pikemen had been hit and the Golden Arrow immediately moved forward, finishing them off and taking down as many crossbowmen as possible. The other pike men moved forward in unison, shoving their pikes at the Golden Arrow members.

The small battle seemed to have a kind of horror music; the sharp, grating sound of metal striking metal, the crash of a splintering shield, all pulled together by the wails of agony, echoing through the clearing.

Richard was not fighting. The dagger still protruded from his back, but luckily for him it had missed all his vital organs, yet it still caused excruciating pain. The knight howled in agony, writhing on the ground, clutching at his back. Blood was pouring from the wound, but the dagger had been lodged in it so firmly that most of the flow had been stemmed by the weapon. Myrddin hobbled over and yanked out the dagger, Sir Richard roared in agony, his arms flitting around to strike the creator of his pain. He connected with Myrddin who swore as blood erupted from his nose, splattering over Sir Richard's golden cape. The magician quickly put his hand over the now blood-gushing wound and muttered a hurried spell. The skin over the area connected and Myrddin slumped from the effort of such a demanding spell.

The magician now hurried to Alicia who had managed to wrap her cape around her injury, but was still whimpering in pain. Myrddin waited a second for his energy and magical substance to reenter his body from the nature around him, and then sent this magic into Alicia's wound, the supernatural matter healing and connecting her tissues and mending her broken body in that area.

Myrddin then slumped to the ground, exhausted, as Alicia rolled over and began to keep the old wizard conscious. She nearly laughed of the irony; Myrddin healed her and then fainted himself. She didn't laugh though, concentrating instead of saving this selfless Golden Arrow member.

Gary was at an advantage with his long spear, being able to take down both the pike men and the crossbowmen. He was already sweating, yet his body was only getting started, the adrenaline coursing through his veins and causing him to fight with such accuracy and strength as never before

Ragnhild had slid right into berserker mode at the beginning, charging into the soldiers. He swung his large battleaxe in large arcs, maiming and killing. Broken weapons, splintered shields, and bleeding human limbs flew through the air around the massive warrior. Ragnhild opened his mouth and roared with such strength and wildness that for a second he lost everything that made him human and became an animal, relying completely on instinct. He cared nothing for his own safety and life, just making sure that the others around him lost theirs. A crossbowman near Ragnhild retreated and finished loading his crossbow. He walked forward, kneeled, and shot.

The bolt struck Ragnhild in the left thigh, digging in as a fountain of blood erupted from the wound. Ragnhild's roar of attack slowly became a cry of pain and agony, as fury built up inside the human monster. With blood spraying from his wound and sweat dripping from his body, Ragnhild advanced, killing anyone in his way and maiming dozens of unfortunate men.

Skinner was at a complete disadvantage with his whips, not being able to strike the Morr soldiers for their long pikes kept the frustrated warrior at bay. All that Skinner could do was disarm the men, but it grew harder as the soldiers gripped their weapons tighter and fought harder, forcing Skinner to slowly give ground. The soldier knew that sooner or later he would be hit and die, yet this fear of death just moved to motivate him. The Golden Arrow warrior slowly began growing fearless, disarming and striking anyone who came too close. The man began gaining ground and with that a sense indestructibility, which spelled his end.

The crossbow bolt raced through the air, thudding into Skinner's chest. The whip-master had been wearing light dragon-armor, but the bolt cut through it, lodging itself in the poor man's chest. Skinner cursed as he fell to the ground where the pike men surrounded him, stabbing him repeatedly.

Theron and Deacon were working together, Deacon keeping the Morrs at bay with his short sword and Theron loosing an arrow every ten seconds into their midst. Although for their superb effort, Theron was soon distracted because he had to keep the Morrs from charging in where Skinner had fallen. Deacon was steadily giving ground, outnumbered and sometimes outclassed.

Hildebrand and Maccabee were properly defending half of the clearing, both of them unhurt and very aware of what was happening. Maccabee was swinging his mace wildly and using its long range to take down any man that got to close. Hildebrand was expertly wielding his swords to fend off attacks and land stunning blows on his opponents, his body count steadily rising.

The Golden Arrow had already drawn a tight circle because of their small number, but slowly, bit by bit, the men gave ground, the circle tightening.

In the middle Alicia lay, gritting her teeth and assisting Myrddin. A crossbow bolt had rammed into the elderly man's thigh, and Alicia was now working to lessen the pain and heal the horrible wound. Richard was sobbing and crying at Cuthbert's cage, trying to break open the lock with a crossbow bolt. A small trickle of blood still flowed down his back, where Myrddin had done his best to heal him, but could not force so much magic into his Captain's body as to completely get rid of the wound.

Inside the cage Cuthbert lay, moaning in pain. A crossbow bolt had glanced off the bars of the cage and slammed into his head, stunning him while another had grazed his side. The final bolt had lodged itself firmly in Cuthbert's leg, and the boy had kept it there in order to keep pressure on the area.

The crossbowmen had now abandoned their weapons, fighting instead with short-swords, daggers, pikes, and any other weapons they could find. Shooting crossbow bolts was too dangerous, for they could hit anyone, friend or foe.

The Morr Colonel had retreated, issuing orders from the sidelines and sending for reinforcements. Theron had aimed at shot at his horse and struck its rump, causing the large battle horse to rear and run away, leaving its master on the ground, winded and humiliated.

The battle was not going well. The Golden Arrow continued retreating, backing towards Cuthbert's cage. This fight would soon be over. Richard finally broke open the lock, shouting with glee. He threw open the door and grabbed Cuthbert. Cuthbert spit at his face and slapped him.

Chapter 22

The battering ram had shattered the door in the first half hour of trying. Immediately the cavalry rushed in, thundering into the open bailey and challenging the gathered men-at-arms there. The archers on the walls had turned, now firing into the castle, but soon Morr knights climbed the stairs and challenged them too, throwing them off the wall or simply impaling them with their razor sharp swords.

Twenty minutes after the gatehouse had been seized, the Commander ordered his infantry forward, the ladder men running ahead of them. Twenty-eight ladders had been readied and were now leaning on the wall, the Morr warriors pouring into the fortress like an endless stream of death.

The Duke and his bodyguards were prepared, manning the keep with the other lords. They had already vowed to fight until death, no matter what. The Waylin main army needed time to assemble and prepare, and their lives were buying this valuable time.

The small army of Waylins was not properly suited to man such a large castle, and so had already divided their guard sparingly. The men who were in position were tired and exhausted from the days of constant bombardment from the enemy siege equipment. Reinforcements were answering the loud alarm and running to the walls and into the bailey, some properly dressed for battle, others wielding swords and dressed in commoners' clothing.

The Waylins had nothing to lose. They were all going to die here; the question was how many they would take down with them. The three hundred or so Waylin warriors fought more bravely then any army before them, five Morrs dying for each Waylin that fell to the ground.

Screams cut through the air. Agony and suffering were evident everywhere, and the loud sounds of war seemed to echo off the walls and fill the very hearts of the warriors, filling each man there with such a despair that they all knew that death was coming, and their lives being measured by seconds. Boundaries that had separated Kingstan were knocked down and the enemy flooded into the castle, their blood red swords glinting in the sunlight.

The perfect weather seemed to mock the men dying below, the clear blue sky and brilliant sun beating down on the dead and dying.

The battlefield was littered with bodies, some still slowly moving and moaning, others still and dead. The ground was slick with blood and the smell of the dead hung heavy in the air.

The horror of battle raged around each man present as they fell to the ground, dead. Slowly the Waylins retreated toward their keep, archers taking down one man after another from the fortress. The Morrs surged forward, and it seemed like the army would never end, a steady flow of people pouring over the walls and flowing through the gatehouses.

Someone set fire to the stables, the straw and wood building immediately being consumed in flames. Frightened horses thundered into the battlefield, ramming into people and stepping on the dead. The smell of burning flesh filled the air as the fire spread, taking its toll on the two armies gathered below.

Slowly the ring of flames tightened around the keep, and the Morrs were unable to advance, turning and fleeing from the conflagration. The Commander cursed as he saw his army being burned alive. Horrible cries of anguish cut through the air and even the Commander turned away.

It took two hours for the fire to extinguish itself, and for those two hours the Morrs camped right outside the castle, some daring archers even mounting the walls and acting as lookouts. In the mean time the Waylins had all retreated into the keep and were preparing to hold out as long as possible. They knew they would die and small groups of men held silent vigils, while others wrote letters to their families. A small group of boys got together and prayed while others simply sat and stared out of the arrow slits, preparing for the final battle.

The Duke and the other lords walked around the keep, encouraging and their men and preparing the keep for battle. Finally the Duke reached the apprentices who were playing cards. Some acted cheerful, others seemed as if in a daze, while yet others were quietly sobbing.

The Duke pulled the young men, some of them still boys, to the side and told them to kneel. The confused apprentices did as they were told and the Duke walked by each one, knighting them for their courage, honor, and loyalty to the Crown of Waylon.

Finally the fire went out and the Commander signaled for the final attack. The Morr archers mounted the walls, firing at the windows and arrow slits, but most of their arrows simply hit the yard-thick stone walls and clattered to the ground. The Waylins did not return fire for they were saving their arrows until the enemy finally came into range.

The Commander signaled the engineers next, and they marched into the burned and blackened bailey, setting up their equipment. Minutes later large stones and burning spears were being launched at the keep, forcing the defenders to back away from their posts a little.

Next came the slaves. Together they carried a battering ram. It was slightly smaller than the original, and this time had to be carried for the engineers didn't have the time to attach wheels. About thirty slaves were manning it; each one only outfitted with a loincloth and told to break down the door into the keep.

The Door was about a foot thick and made of iron-wood, the strongest type in the Waylin Islands. It was reinforced by steel and backed up by all sorts of furniture, which had been packed against it by the defenders.

The red flag that meant no mercy was carried to the conquered gatehouse and mounted there, being escorted by a small band of Morrs. The band played a very cheerful tune, reminding the Morrs of home and what they were fighting for. Personally the Commander despised it, but he knew it was necessary for motivation so he just let them be.

Six hours after the start of the final battle, the slaves advanced toward the keep, arrows flying from the arrow slits to them. Several of the slaves fell, dying on the spot. Others pushed on; wounded while yet other slaves were not hurt at all. Their march quickened, the slaves pushing towards the keep.

Finally they arrived, now about twenty of them, and together the grunted a rhythm, slamming the battering ram into the door. It thudded against it repeatedly, slowly weakening and splintering. The Morrs milled about near their camp, eager to fight.

As the slaves continued thrusting the ram against the door, Waylin archers took aim, picking off the unarmored men. The Commander spat, ordering more slaves to be sent to break the heavy door. Any slave that refused to go was killed on the spot and soon nearly a hundred Morr slaves were busy with the ram, yet over a score of them died, spitted on Waylin arrows.

Meanwhile, the Duke was delivering his final speech, motivating his men to fight for freedom and honor, promising them everlasting glory as the final defenders of Arran.

Chapter 23

It took nearly an hour to break a hole into the door of the keep. In this time the Commander organized his troops. He ordered all the cavalry to dismount and then told them to charge once the gate broke. The charge would be led by one of his younger aides, who was up front encouraging the infantry.

When the hole was finally made, a cheer erupted from the Morr troops, and for once a smile lit up the iron face of the Commander. The cry died away when a black cloud of arrows sped out of the hole, killing all of the remaining slaves.

The Commander cursed. "Open fire!" he bellowed.

Immediately the waiting siege equipment erupted into action, hurling stones, spears, and flaming arrows at the door. In minutes the door was gone; burned and broken.

The Commander nodded at the young lord leading the charge and the man advanced slowly. The knights cheered as they charged forward, pouring into the keep. Arrows sped from the arrow slits, the archers within the keep picking off the Morrs at will. The charge did not falter though, and the first lines exploded into the keep.

Inside the keep the archers had been placed around the Great Hall, firing into it as the troops charged inward, engaging the waiting men-at-arms immediately.

At first it seemed that the Waylins were winning, slowly pushing the Morrs back out the door. Then more and more Morrs poured in, overwhelming the Waylins and breaking down all of the doors. They spread throughout the keep, fighting and killing everyone.

Finally a small group entered the Duke's chambers where the Duke and a small squad of twenty warriors were waiting. The second they got into the room, a small battle exploded.

The Duke charged forward, engaging the center in combat. He parried the first strike, then swung around and cut into the man's exposed side with a quick back-handed strike. The young Morr swung an overhead cut which the Duke sidestepped and then retaliated with a quick thrust into the boy's side. The Duke pulled out the sword and looked away as the young soldier died.

The Duke could not dwell on what had happened for long, because the next warriors burst into the room and once again the senior warrior was locked into mortal combat with the enemy.

Soon masses of Morrs exploded into the room and slowly the small squad of Waylins gave ground, retreating to the stone wall at the other end.

The rest of the castle had been conquered, and within half-an-hour the whole keep was a graveyard except for the Duke's chambers.

A brave charge had been led by the apprentices at the beginning, cutting through the Morr defenses and out into the bailey. It had reached as far as the destroyed gatehouse until it was mercilessly cut apart by several volleys of Morr arrows.

The Duke's chambers had become a sea of red Morr uniforms, with only the Duke and five other Waylins left, fighting for their lives in the back corner. They were surrounded and cared not for their own safety or lives, just taking those of the enemy around them. The Duke's eyes blazed red and sweat mixed with the blood around him. His face was covered in gore and his side was a deathly red. No one knew whether it was his own or someone else's, for the Duke fought fearlessly.

Slowly the Morrs pushed inward though, taking down two of the remaining Waylins. The other three slowly started receiving wounds, and soon they were not recognizable, spurting blood from at least twenty places. Finally they were taken out of their misery, being slain mercilessly.

The Duke fought for the final seconds of his life until he received a fatal blow to the head. With his eyes open and still burning with fury, the Duke hit the floor. Immediately the Morrs were on top of him, stabbing, punching, and maiming him.

Kingstan had fallen.

Chapter 24

Xurxo spied the castle from a distance. He was flying at an extremely high altitude to remain unspotted, and the fact that a couple low clouds had rolled in really helped.

Xurxo let his dragon cruise in order to make up for the thin air. He didn't want to waste its energy. The Golden Arrow warrior spotted the large fortress from nearly a mile away, and immediately he knew he was too late.

The gatehouse was broken and a steady stream of smoke spiraled into the air from inside the keep. Xurxo sighed and slowly descended.

The Rider knew something was up right away. His dragon growled deeply and Xurxo patted it softly at the neck. The dragon growled again and Xurxo looked around for the cause of the dragon's unhappiness.

Below him a small battle raged. A cube-shaped cage sat in the middle of a Morr camp and on top of this stood a man shooting arrows. Around the cage were several different warriors, fighting off the attacking Morrs. Xurxo judged there to be about forty Morrs and six defending warriors, not including those huddled in the cage.

On the right side of the cage was a knight fighting with two swords and effectively beating back his attackers. He was fighting very defensively. Next to him, at the back of the cage, were two men. One had a spear and was fighting offensively and the other a short sword and waging a perfectly defensive fight. On the left side was a giant. The man was huge and battle-scarred, a steady roar coming from him. His huge battleaxe swung in wide arcs, killing anyone within a two meter range. At the front of the cage was a man wielding a mace, which he too was swinging in large arcs. This man was receiving the most help from the archer on the cage and Xurxo knew that this battle wouldn't last long.

Xurxo also recognized the golden capes, fluttering in the slight breeze. The Rider laughed for the first time in weeks. Of course his comrades couldn't be beaten! Heck, they were the Golden Arrow!

The Rider quickly angled his dragon into a steep downward dive, his hands gripping the reins firmly.

Xurxo pulled on the reins right at the last minute, sticking his spurred shoes into the underbelly of the dragon as he did so. Orange flames burst from the mouth of the dragon and lit up half the clearing, burning several of the Morr warriors.

Before anyone could turn and see what was happening, Xurxo guided his dragon up and flipped, shouting with joy as he did so.

He yelled again, battle joy alive within him, as he dived once more, this time spinning his dragon by twisting with his heels as to force the dragon to swing his tail. The large, spiked weapon wiped out half of the Morr force, including their frightened Colonel.

This time some of the Morrs saw him and so did the archer on the cage who Xurxo recognized as Theron.

A couple Morrs threw their weapons at the dragon, but Xurxo had already led his dragon out of harm's way and into the sky.

"Hold on now!" Xurxo yelled to his Golden Arrow members, "This ain't gonna take long. I'll kill 'em quick!"

With that he dove at the ground again, once again sticking his heels into the underbelly of the dragon as he dove. As before, fire erupted from the mouth of the giant beast and lit up several of the Morr warriors like candles.

Xurxo kept the gush of flames going as he circled the clearing, burning half of the Morrs in the process.

Xurxo smiled savagely as he marveled at the sheer power and grace of the dragon.

The Morrs were now scared. Something bad was going to happen to them if they didn't figure out something quick.

The clever smiths in the nearby camp apparently though the same, for they had assembled a metal defense mechanism that shot large iron arrows, and Xurxo wasn't going to wait and see if it worked. The Rider pulled his dragon back into the air and dove at the smiths.

Just as the dragon got close enough to burn the men, they released their arrow. It raced at the dragon and only Xurxo's quick reflexes saved them. The Rider swung the reins to the left and leaned over, causing the dragon to roll over in midair.

The iron arrow grazed the dragon's strong side armor, scratching it and leaving a definite dent.

The dragon roared and a gush of blue flames spat from its mouth. It was mad.

Xurxo struggled for control of the enraged beast, finally gaining the upper hand. In the meantime the smiths had set the next arrow and were carefully aiming it. The Morrs closed in on the Golden Arrow below. Defeat was seconds away.

In that short moment Xurxo made the biggest decision of his life. He dove at the small battle, pulling the dragon into a spiral and causing it to roll over repeatedly in air. The clever move tricked the smiths and the metal arrow sped by, missing the dragon.

Xurxo dug his heels into the dragon's belly and a gush of flames started a human bonfire. The Xurxo pulled back on the reins as hard as he could, causing the massive beast to stop in midair.

The Rider hoped he had picked wisely and pulled the reins upward while digging his heels into the soft underbelly. The dragon grunted, but understood the command and hovered in midair.

"Get a move on!" He shouted at the Golden Arrow.

Theron didn't wait to be told twice, jumping onto the dragon and resuming shooting from there.

Next Alicia handed up Myrddin and clambered on herself. Then Deacon abandoned Gary and climbed the cage, jumping onto the dragon's back. The dragon grunted at the extra weight and Xurxo softly patted its neck.

At a shout from Maccabee, Gary and Hildebrand abandoned their posts as well, climbing the cage faster than they had climbed ever before, and jumped onto the dragon.

Ragnhild grunted something and without even climbing onto the cage, jumped up and grabbed the dragon's leg. Then he climbed onto its back. The dragon sank a foot lower with the extra weight, and only with Xurxo's coaxing did it rise a little again.

Some Morrs attempted striking the dragon's underbelly, but the beast's tail swatted them away like flies. The smiths were scared to shoot in the fear of hitting one of their own, and for the first time that day, the Golden Arrow felt kind of safe.

Maccabee then motioned for Richard to get Cuthbert onto the cage and the Captain obeyed unquestioningly. Xurxo frowned at this for usually it was Richard who gave the orders.

The Morrs quickly crowded in on Maccabee, but the warrior was too fast for them, leaping onto the cage and then onto the dragon. Richard heaved Cuthbert onto the beast and attempted to climb on himself, reaching for Cuthbert.

Xurxo forced the loaded down dragon into an ascent and the massive animal slowly rose.

Cuthbert opened his eyes and looked at his master. Without even saying good bye, he pushed Richard off the dragon and into the bloodthirsty Morrs below.

Epilogue

It had been a week since the fall of Kingstan.

Xurxo had expertly flown the dragon to Waylon, stopping only once on the way in a deserted field so that the poor beast could rest. They arrived late that evening, towards midnight, and immediately arranged for an escort to fly them home to Siddian.

The Council of Waylon had demanded the Golden Arrow members stay and tell their stories to them, so each member recounted his or her version. Finally the group of warriors was left alone and they fell into a deep sleep, only to be awakened a couple hours later for the flight home.

Cuthbert had been taken to a healer in Waylon and was properly bandaged and cared for that night, so the next morning he was ready to go. Hildebrand had sort of taken over the group and seemed to be their leader by an unspoken consensus. Richard had been the commander of the Golden Arrow and Lord Ive was second in command. Skinner had had the next highest ranking, but he had also died, leaving the Golden Arrow leaderless. Hildebrand quickly filled this role but not as completely or fully as Sir Richard had. The double-swordsman was not as confident as Captain Richard had been and not as speedy a decision maker. On the other hand, Hildebrand carefully weighed each option and his decisions were always for the good of the group.

It took two days to cross the Sea and land in Siddian. The Golden Arrow had been escorted by twenty dragons that were there to protect them and carry documents to the King of Siddian.

It seemed that news had somehow traveled ahead of the Golden Arrow, for their horses were waiting at the port where they landed. For the next three days the Golden Arrow rode through the land until they reached Siddian's southern most borders late at night.

The Golden Arrow fell from their horses, rubbing their backsides and imagining the warm, soothing waters of a nice hot bath. The warriors had been urging on their horses for the past days, riding for an hour at a steady trot, then walking their horses for half-an-hour and then riding for another hour. They did this all day, resting only twice, once for breakfast and once for lunch. They stopped at sundown and started at sunup. They got to a city or town twice and were immediately cared for at the inn, no matter who else had booked a room. On the last day they finally reached the Sid Army's camp.

The camp that the soldiers had set up was very organized. It had been set in proper grid formation, and the colorful tents seemed to radiate light even at that late hour. Flags fluttered in the wind, revealing the coat of arms of the noblemen of the large force.

In the middle of the large square of tents were the King's pavilion and the pavilions of his most trusted dukes and barons. About three hundred yards away from the city of tents stood the fort that protected Siddian from any possible Morr attack. The small stone fortress had been alight with torches and even at midnight guards patrolled along its walls. It had been reinforced with about a hundred men and Cuthbert had estimated that the Sid camp probably held about five to seven thousand soldiers, along with perhaps a thousand or so horses and mules which were grazing in a fenced and guarded area of land about a hundred yards from camp.

Cuthbert had not thought much about the camp, instead looking forward to a nice bath and good night's sleep in a warm, cozy bed. He got neither. Guards had alerted the King of the Golden Arrow's presence and the mighty monarch had immediately wanted to talk to them.

So, just after midnight, the Golden Arrow was forced to recount their story yet again. The King had first asked where Richard was and Cuthbert had bluntly replied, "He's dead."

The King had turned away, his head shaking. Finally the wise leader overcame his sorrow and took a deep breath, asking what had happened. Each member told his story separately while the others were treated to a small feast.

Cuthbert had been the first to tell his story and when he told the King about the betrayal the wise man turned away, tears rolling down his cheeks. Once the powerful ruler had gained control of himself again he listened to the rest of the story, not saying a word.

Now, two days later, Cuthbert knelt before the king, his head bent. The beautiful pavilion he was in was decorated in red, purple, and gold, symbolizing the King's military prowess, his royalty, and his just claim to the throne. The pavilion was made up of five rooms, two on each side and a large one in the middle. A chandelier of candles hung in the middle and small holes had been punched into the ceiling to let smoke escape. A plain red rug adorned the floor and the King's golden throne sat at the end of the room.

The King stood before Cuthbert, his bejeweled sword gripped tightly in his hands. The King had perfectly cut brown hair that reached his shoulders and a clean shave. He wore a long red cape with golden trimming and a purple battledress. The mighty monarch smiled at Cuthbert, yet the boy simply closed his eyes and bowed his head.

Now the King lowered his sword, briefly touching Cuthbert's left shoulder and then his right. Finally he lightly tapped his head.

"I knight you, Sir Cuthbert, a loyal warrior to Siddian and a faithful member of the Golden Arrow."

Cuthbert stood, his immaculately white battledress flowing to the floor and his scabbard swinging at his side. Then the young knight bowed to his King as the lords and barons behind him applauded the young warrior.

Sir Cuthbert turned and walked to his fellow Golden Arrow members as an equal. He was ready to save Leif.